FISH

BOOKS BY

MONROE ENGEL

NOVELS

FISH *1981*

VOYAGER BELSKY *1962*

THE VISIONS OF NICHOLAS SOLON *1959*

A LENGTH OF ROPE *1952*

CRITICISM

THE USES OF LITERATURE (*editor*) *1973*

THE MATURITY OF DICKENS *1959*

MONROE ENGEL

FISH

ATHENEUM NEW YORK
1981

Liberties have been taken with some of the names and arrangements of the actual places in which the story is set. The characters enjoy far fuller freedom.

Library of Congress cataloging in Publication Data

Engel, Monroe.
    Fish.

    I. Title.
PS3555.N388F5   1981   813'.54   81-7975
ISBN 0-689-11219-X   AACR2

Published simultaneously in Canada by McClelland and Stewart Ltd
Manufactured by American Book–Stratford Press,
Saddle Brook, New Jersey
Designed by Harry Ford
First Edition

FOR

B. S. E.

ONCE MORE

FISH

1

THE WALK from my apartment to Alfred London's house
takes me about a quarter of an hour, give or take a bit for
the state of my metabolism—an up or down that I can't
really account for but compare to the habits of a species of
sandworm I read about once that labors its way toward the
light some of the time and deeper into its medium at others
with so little discoverable reason for this shift that it seems
to move only by profound whim. I can of course hypothe-
size any number of possible reasons for the heavy sinkage I
feel in my thighs and behind my knees this evening. The
damp August heat, my interrupted sleep last night, even the
chronic thinness of the air on Brattle Street out beyond the
Episcopal Theological Seminary—each of these could be
assigned blame. But no more certainly than I can assign the
same symptoms to my reluctance to undertake the witness
I know is in store for me.

It isn't the activity of witness itself that makes me apprehensive. At the balanced age of forty-two, observation and
witness seem to be the talents I can use with least inhibition.
Only I favor detached observation—spectacle that's objec-
tive even if part of its interest comes from my knowledge
that under sustained observation it may turn reflexive. Even
the most detached spectacle can take that at once expansive
and reductive turn after a while, but the witness I've been
summoned to by Gretta this evening—Alf had summoned
me first, but to perform a different, simpler function—
won't be detached even from the outset, and I'll be impli-
cated in what I'm observing without being certain of either
the extent of my implication or even really what it is I'm
witnessing. Enough to make anyone sluggish. What I do

know of course is that Michael has been unwell again, and that Gretta has given up her guise of torpor.

I know too by now that Gretta isn't really lazy at all. Torpor is a style she cultivates, and then abandons by choice when Michael is agitated. On these occasions she becomes Michael's completer I think, translating his discomforts into action to keep him from going turbid with issueless troubles. But if it takes Michael to activate her, her resourcefulness once she is activated suggests that she's acting then also on her own behalf. It's taken me a while to perceive this symbiotic system, but even now, however familiar I've become with some of its forms and manifestations, I don't understand it very much better than I did the first time I ever saw Gretta and Michael, from the window of David Yoshalem's office.

That first view was from a special perspective. Yoshalem is more than my doctor though I wouldn't say he was exactly a friend. I'm one of his charges, one of a group of privileged patients who don't earn but are granted election because they interest him in some way. In the last three or four years, my interest for Yoshalem has quite obviously increased, and the place from which I'd seen Gretta first wasn't Yoshalem's actual or main office, which is in a drab yellow-brick professional building in Brookline, but the library of his apartment on the second floor of a converted carriage house behind the large square Brattle Street Victorian in which Gretta lives with her brother. It's her brother's house and the carriage house belongs to it, but Yoshalem had lived in the carriage house long before London acquired the main house. The elect are summoned or admitted to the library of Yoshalem's apartment sometimes evenings or weekends for general surveillance as well as more limited or specific medical care, and this room overlooks the garden of the main house.

One August Sunday morning just about a year ago now, Yoshalem, still in his pajamas though it was almost noon, let me into the library, then excused himself and retired to shave, shower, and dress. A lax way for a doctor to receive a patient, perhaps, but I wasn't exactly a patient even though I had come by appointment. I'd run into Yoshalem in the Square the previous afternoon coming out of a secondhand book store where he'd spent a couple of hours surveying the contents of a library the store had just purchased—and found, he said, nothing he'd have wanted that he didn't have already in better editions. An announcement of failure that was also a boast. Yoshalem's interests as a bibliophile have been established for a long time, and he spends a substantial portion of his income on books. The smile that went with this announcement then communicated self-satisfaction, his pleasure in knowing his own powers which even as we talked went into play with me now as their object. He hadn't seen me for a while, he remarked, and when he then suggested a visit the following morning, I knew that something about my appearance had made him decide a more protracted look at me was in order. Yoshalem doesn't play amateur shrink, but he is a rabbi manqué as well as an internist. Having given up rabbinical studies for medicine when he was nineteen—when his father died and left him a widowed mother and a feeble-minded sister to support—he'd found then in medicine a way to continue his pastoral vocation, and had also, when and as he could, continued his Semitic studies. He'd been reading in bed when I arrived. Flavius Josephus' history of the Jews he told me, which he'd been reading for months. Having refused to take on any new patients for a number of years, he kept thinking that his practice must therefore be sufficiently reduced to let him undertake reading projects on this scale. But it wasn't. His old patients kept getting older instead of dying.

Yoshalem's apartment, though extensively remodeled, retains something of the character and shape of its earlier existence. His bedroom, bathroom, and kitchen, which had been the stableman's quarters, are disproportionately small, while the L-shaped library, occupying what had once been an attic and hayloft, is huge. The ceiling of the library, following the lines of the mansard roof, slopes at the perimeters to small leaded windows that look into trees and to the tops of pine bookshelves painted a murky green over alligatored varnish. Leaves crowd against the window screens in summer, and their green and the green of the bookshelves gave the room the atmosphere of a jungle clearing this morning. With almost no air stirring through the leaf-choked windows, I sniffed an acrid odor of old hay or wood rot, and iridescent shafts of sunlight entering the room below eye level writhed in the elaborate patterns of the oriental rugs like mirages.

Waiting for Yoshalem to return, I knew from experience that I'd find nothing for quick browsing among the Judaica, medical texts, and medical histories that made up most of the library, and was ready therefore to be diverted when I heard voices under the windows on the long side of the room and water sluicing onto grass. From one of the windows, across a hedge of rank shrubs, I looked down at a woman spread-eagled in a small, round, red plastic swimming pool, her head, legs, and arms over the inflated tube that made the doughnut, and a boy who stood above her with his toes pressed into the doughnut watching her. Thick, sun-ruddied, the woman's hide was dappled by a blue bikini and the shadows of leaves. There was something intimidating as well as attractive about this substantial near-naked body so nearly filling the plastic pool that most of the water had overflowed onto the grass. Far more of her was out of the water than in it, but residual droplets stood on her sun-oiled arms and shoulders, iridescent and discrete. The boy observed her with fixed stolid attention, his thighs pressed one against the other and his feet bogged into the water-soaked ground. "You shouldn't be doing that," he said after a time. "You ought to be in some real pool."

"Oh? Like at a country club?" Her voice was unexpectedly small.

"I guess so," he said.

"Places like that make me uncomfortable," she said. "Just like they do you."

"I know," he said, "but aren't you getting too old to still feel that way? Scared, I mean?"

"Probably. How old do you think I am?"

"You were thirty-four last February twelfth, on Lincoln's birthday."

"I might have known you wouldn't forget that," the woman said. "But I'm not exactly scared, I don't think. What I feel in places like that is more like repugnance. You know. My flesh crawls, or shrinks."

"Practically, it amounts to the same thing."

"Okay," she said, "I guess that's true."

Preparing to cede the pool to him then—conceding to his tenacity, and, I thought, to the justice of his claim—she raised herself bottom first, her hands pushing against the floor of the pool, then shifted her weight to her legs. The blue loincloth baled, bellied, and retracted, and when she stepped onto the grass, the water sluicing off her torso marbled her thighs. Then she lowered herself again onto a cot of nylon tapes woven across an aluminum frame, and closed her eyes. Her face, which had looked indolent when they were open, was unexpectedly alert now. Her long upper lids created a crease at the outer corners about which lesser lines radiated in a structure of sentience like the mock eyes that sled dogs, huskies and malamutes, show in sleep, and this feral face, broad across the cheekbones and tapered below, poised ironically above her full somnolent body. Meanwhile the boy was refilling the pool, holding a hose from a limp arm, the nozzle just above his knee, doing this labor with the least possible exertion.

Watching, listening to the conversation between the woman and the boy, I didn't know Yoshalem had entered the room until I was spoken to. "Interesting."

He'd placed himself next to me to see what I was seeing, and this might have been either a statement or a question. Working from the inside with digestion and peristaltic action, inhalation and obstruction, blood clots and leaky valves, the input-output of the physical economy, Yoshalem is learned as well as canny about how people live, but I don't think his knowledge ever either quite makes the spectacle actual for him or relieves him of an essential distaste for it. "Who is she?" I asked.

"An ex-wife. An indifferent sister so far as I can see. A conscientious mother, obviously. Her maiden name, which she's resumed, is London. Gretta London. She keeps house after a fashion for her brother Alfred London who, like me, has so far eschewed the married state."

This summary was given without hesitation, what she was first and then who, findings of which he was confident but that didn't seem to engage him. The boy got into the refilled pool while we were talking. He shifted for a moment for a smooth place on the grass under the plastic floor, and then, leaning against the edge with the soles of his feet together so that his legs formed a diamond, he lifted water first in one hand then in the other to funnel it in a fine stream over his chest. "Some metabolic disorder, I would think," Yoshalem said. "The son, I mean. The mother's ailment would be harder to ascertain and must, in any event, be out of my line. The brother is a State Street lawyer with an interest in philanthropy. He apparently likes both making money and giving it away—an unobjectionable combination. He bought the house this spring, and I still owe them some sort of hospitality. I think I should have a small party, to which you'll now be invited."

Yoshalem's syntax had been exact when he talked about the party he would have—that I would be invited to it, not that he would invite me. The invitation came from his secretary, Mrs. Rosen, who in addition to managing his office life on Beacon Street also manages certain aspects of his Brattle Street life that he has neither disposition nor talent to manage for himself. Mrs. Rosen not only drives his car to a supermarket once a week to shop for him, sees to his laundry, reminds him of family birthdays, and pays all his bills except those from the booksellers in New York, London, Amsterdam, and Jerusalem with whom he indulges his only vice, but she also administers most of his limited social life.

Yoshalem really is, I believe, a transparent person. The only mystery about him is his simplicity—what allows him to be so transparent. But Gretta retains most of the opacity for me still after a year that she had this first time I saw her or when I met her at Yoshalem's party where, as Yoshalem had I guess anticipated, we became friends. What I've found out about her in the past year doesn't really reduce this opacity much at all. Even seeing that Michael and Gretta act for each other, for example, that it is not simply that Gretta acts for Michael, is only a beginning, and it was months before I knew even this.

One damp, cold, late afternoon in March though I went into the Square after I left Hillside, to get a haircut, and heading home again, I was too far gone vagueing to recognize the boy blocking my way suddenly in front of Woolworth's, but not sufficiently gone not to know that I knew him. The drawstrings of the hood of a maroon parka were pulled so tight around the head facing me at chest level that only eyes, nose, and a portion of the cheeks were visible. Circling just over the eyebrows and under the lower lip, the hood made the axis of the face horizontal, and there was plenty of time for me to see that the boy expected to be recognized and knew that he wasn't before I realized who it was. Time too for him to say, "It's me, Michael."

"Of course," I said, audibly dismayed. "I was in a fog."

"I guess my hood makes me hard to recognize," he said, to excuse my lapse, and brushed a nylon-covered cheek with the back of his left wrist while continuing to press a number of small parcels and slippery paper bags between his mittened hands.

The tighter he pressed, the more likely it seemed that the parcels might erupt. When I removed a couple of bags from the center of the clutch though, he readjusted the others, securing them in one hand or the other. He'd been shopping, getting some things that he needed and some that Gretta needed, he said. Hearing him say this finished clearing my head, for I hadn't seen or heard from Gretta then in over a week. When I called her at the gallery where she worked on an irregular basis, I was told she wasn't in, and when I called at home during the day, when Michael was in school, no one answered. I'd been pretty sure she was at home the whole time though, giving substantial test, as I'd known her to do before, to Pascal's notion that all man's unhappiness comes from not knowing how to stay at rest in one place. Only Pascal also said that life was movement, and she seemed to be testing this too, by contravention, and that was a test I could see my way into sufficiently to let her phone ring twelve or fifteen times each time I called. But it was picked up only once, when it was picked up only to be replaced at once on the cradle. And when I'd driven the president of the Hillside Film Club into Cambridge one early afternoon to the film library and stopped on the way back to ring Gretta's bell four or five long rings, there'd been no answer then either. When we were almost back at Hillside, however, the student, John Groppi, told me hesitantly that as I'd been pushing the bell a woman had drawn aside a curtain at a second-floor window, looked down at me, and quickly dropped the curtain again. A woman with a white streak in the front of her hair. It seemed peculiar enough to him to mention, he said.

Michael had been able to get everything he needed, he said now, and everything Gretta needed except a pot of paste—the kind that had a brush built into the top of the pot, he explained, and described the pinched aluminum tube that projected from the center of the cap to form the handle of the brush. That kind cost more than some other kinds that were also for sale in Woolworth's and might have been just as good, he said, but that was the kind Gretta used and he had fifteen cents less than he needed to buy it.

II

I discovered that I knew what kind of paste she used too. The sun porch down the hall from her bedroom had windows on three sides, a green tiled floor, and a rubber tree which, growing high without gaining much strength along the way, had assumed the posture of an inverted J. Gretta sunbathed here and also, at certain times, maintained an enterprise. Intermittently, but very intensely when she did it, she had I knew for years been making a scrapbook of articles, advertisements, and pictures cut from newspapers and magazines that in one way or another met her mood at these times and I found that it took only Michael's mention of the paste pot for me to picture with remarkable particularity the lettuce green quilted pad on the jade green, heat-absorbent tiled floor on which she sunbathed, and the orange-handled, left-handed scissors suspended apparently in space next to the paste pot and a telephone on the glass-topped metal-framed garden table. And the piles of newspapers and magazines under the table waiting to be plundered for the corrupt yield that substantiated Gretta's apprehension of what was happening "out there." When I'd asked once to be allowed to look at the scrapbook, she'd said maybe some day but not yet, though she'd be happy to share some of the more amusing items with me at any time. The scrapbook as a whole was a heavy dose, she said, and so far she'd shown it only to Christine Kaplan who could manage anything and to Michael. She wanted Michael to know everything anyway, she said, in time for the knowledge to do him some good.

It seemed only fitting therefore that Michael felt obliged to buy her the kind of paste she favored. I relieved him of the rest of his packages, gave him fifteen cents, and waited for him on the sidewalk, and when I saw that I'd been spotted by the Process woman with twiggy eyes and a Superman cape who worked this stretch of the Square, I turned my back on her and concentrated on a group of tinny electric heaters and a portable dishwasher in Woolworth's strangely disordered display window. She hovered behind me briefly, then gave me up as a poor prospect and moved up the sidewalk toward Nini's Corner where a young man in a fisherman knit sweater and pegged jeans had just dismounted from a ten-speed bike, removed the front wheel, and was yoking the frame to the metal post of a no-parking sign.

When Michael reappeared and I told him I'd help him carry his packages home, he said he didn't need help but said it without conviction, and I assured him that I'd enjoy the walk and really needed the exercise. We set off at a brisk pace with the damp air leaving a film of harsh fire clinging to the insides of my lungs and Michael, below me, moving through the steam of his breath, saying very little to each other until, several blocks out Brattle Street, we saw four men in drab dark clothing clustered in conference on the sidewalk. Domestic missionaries, their faces balanced between their dark stiff coats and narrow-brimmed fedoras, they were dividing territory for a house-to-house canvas— a bleaker form of persuasion than that practiced by the Process woman I'd just avoided, but a similar enterprise nevertheless. An extraordinary range of people are selling salvation or seeking it in this city at all times, and it's remarkable to me with what near-perfect consistency the sellers and the seekers don't get together.

The missionaries peeled off in pairs now as we approached them, one pair setting off away from us, and the other coming toward us and falling into single file to pass. After they'd gone by a distance, Michael said, "They ring our bell sometimes, but Gretta won't let them come into the house. She says they give her the creeps."

"The two who came to see me last fall sure gave me the creeps," I said.

"I guess you and Gretta must agree about a lot of things," Michael said.

Looking up at me as he said this, he'd also jostled against me, his body following his eyes. "I suppose we do," I said, and watching him through the steam of his breath, I thought as he continued to push against me that he might be delivering some message, not simply experiencing delayed transmission of the message he should have been getting from his neural sentries.

He veered off abruptly though and turned his face forward again, the disposition of his torso to resolve into a single lumpy mass exaggerated by the way the hood of his parka joined his head to his shoulders. "Do you think it's funny, my getting things for Gretta?" he asked.

"Funny?"

"You know, generally it's the mother who does the errands."

"Sure," I said, "but I don't think it's funny, anyway."

"I don't mind, even if I don't like it either," he said.

"Don't like what?"

"Going into the stores and asking for things. That's one of the ways me and Gretta agree. Lots of people make us uncomfortable." Looking up at me again, he ran into me again but bounced off promptly this time. "I don't know which one of us is worse," he said.

When we got to the house then I put the paper bags inside the front door but didn't go in, and almost a week later Gretta had called to thank me. She called in the early morning, waking me, but said nothing about either the time, or that she was thanking me for something done days ago, or about her stretch in isolation. She spoke slowly, as if unaccustomed to speech, but seemed to be moving past or through her words anyway and leaving them to make their way behind her so that my responses were always to something said in a time zone she was no longer in.

Night calls and the scrapbook are both by now similar signs, and my most recent call, last night, had been mostly about the scrapbooks. That at least was what it had been about immediately, though Gretta had been a little high too, which she'd announced. "I've been boozing," she said. "Only white wine of course and only to keep me happy while I'm working, but it's also true that I've been working ever since Michael went to sleep, which was some time ago."

She interrupted herself with a soft, wet sound between a giggle and a laugh, then said, "Poor Fish, you were asleep too."

"It's okay," I said. "What's up?"

"I've been attending to my annals," she said. "Don't you think that's a perfect title, by the way? I mean as I've described this project to you. And if I mispronounce the word once in a while, because I've been drinking, that's all right too."

"Sure, it's a great title," I said. "But how come you're working so late?"

"I've got to get up to date, and I have a terrible lot of newspapers and magazines to dig my way through before I'll be there. I've let things slide for months—out of false optimism, I guess. In the *New York Times*, where I find most of what I'm looking for, I'm only up to early spring, and that's just far enough to see that if I'd been up there in early spring, there's no telling where I might be by now. Someone down there was writing stuff for me the whole time, and I wasn't paying attention, which is sad for us both. Would you believe he was even running ads for me? 'Will your winter bulge be showing this summer? Shame on you. Don't just sit there. You still have time to do something about it.' I was losing messages like that, and now here it is deep summer, and my bulge is certainly showing."

She paused, but because anything said to Gretta about weight is a mistake, I made no intrusion into the silence. Only this wasn't entirely successful either. "You're being very careful," she said after a moment of waiting.

"Where are you, in the sun porch?" I asked, hearing that she hadn't had too much to drink to remember that Michael was asleep, since her voice was more suppressed even than usual.

"In the conservatory, you mean," she said. "That's what the real estate agent told Alfred it was the very first time he showed him the house. To make it clear that the place had class. Only it does my bulge no good to sit hour after hour boozing and cutting clippings out of the *New York Times* even in a conservatory, so I thought if I talked to you I might drink less for a while, which would help. I also thought it might be nice to share one or two of my less noxious finds with you as I think I once promised I would, providing you're not too tired to listen."

"I'm wide awake," I said. "I only sleep when I have nothing worse to do."

"Don't joke," she said. "Just listen and be appreciative. I missed more than just the chance to slim down by falling so far behind. Could there really have been a rerun of Julie Andrews and Carol Burnett in a two-woman hour of song and comedy called *The Six Wives of Henry the Eighth?*"

"Never, I don't think," I said.

"That's good—I hardly thought so. I must just have booted that one. But there's one item I'm sure of that I particularly wanted to tell you about. Did you know that uncertain spaghetti-eaters can now relax, thanks to a forty-eight-year-old mechanical engineer named Israel Robert Smuts, who's been granted U.S. patent number 3,552,017 for an automatic spaghetti fork that Rome's ambassador in Washington says should be reassuring for foreigners who wish to travel in Italy but aren't certain they have the know-how? No know-how now necessary."

"Are you okay?" I hazarded.

"Always," she said. "After all, when Alf takes care of somebody, they're provided for. I'm by no means even the only person he takes care of. You're going to meet Mona finally this evening, and it's because you're coming to dinner this evening that I wanted you to know about the automatic spaghetti fork. Alf isn't going to have spaghetti on the menu of course but I thought it might be encouraging just the same."

One thing at least did come through. I was being told that the occasion I'm now headed for was to be Alf's party, and I've known such occasions before—when Gretta was present mostly to serve Alf's plans, and when I found myself serving them too by playing audience to Alf's special and important guests. This was a way for Alf to recognize me as a familiar of the house. But there was something more on Gretta's mind too that she was neither telling me nor giving me better than a long chance to guess. She was testing me, and I was probably expected to flunk the test and thereby confirm her sense of the limitations of possibility. Only I couldn't overlook the possibility that there was something she wanted me to understand, since she's told me on several occasions that though she creates confusion about her programmatically, she also depends on me not to be confused. "Look," I said, "do you want to come over here? Or I can walk over there if that's all right."

"Poor Fish," she said, saying it this time over a suppressed giggle. "I must be sending out false signals. Maybe we ought to just be good friends again after all. Should we talk about that some time? Not now though, and not this evening of course either. I think you'd better just go back to sleep."

It was only a little after two I discovered, but I never really got to sleep again. Each time I was on the point of falling off, I'd suddenly be convinced I'd grasped something and was about to discover what Gretta had on her mind. That conviction would bring me fully awake, and I'd then discover that I actually had nothing at all, not even any reason to believe that Gretta had been doing any more than creating an atmosphere of possibility. A low-pressure area into which almost anything might flow.

One way and another therefore, I'm not really fit now for my assigned part at Alf's party, and having dragged along the way more than I realized, I arrive somewhat late to begin with. Alf greets me by telling me that he's glad to see me, and this emphasis on my visibility is his way to tell me I'm late. A continuous strong presence, he expects me to be as prompt and alert as he is himself. Or nearly so at least.

The family resemblance between Alf and Gretta is striking but limited. They have the same general coloration, the same contrast of dark hair and light skin, but their features are very different, and Alf's energy, unlike Gretta's which is chiefly latent, is always moving him into the world. He is not just lean but tight, and the keen nervous force that compresses his stomach and bows his shoulders also advances his nose and eyes from the plane of his face. Even the black wiry hair that rushes from his scalp, cheeks, knuckles, and the porches of his ears, seems compelled by this same force.

The glaze of his second shave of the day is only partially appeased by a thin scrim of talc, and he seems overcharged this evening even by his own standards. I follow him into the house and find four other guests in the den already, but Gretta is not among them, and though the guests have drinks, and a waitress wearing the crimson tunic of the student agency is passing a silver platter of jumbo shrimp, the room looks tentative and unsettled. Alf introduces me to each of the guests in turn—a former dean of the law school named Philip Cohen in whose class I'd sat for a term a few years back and whom I'd also met several times before socially, a couple in their sixties named Thorndyke whom I don't know but place as people of importance, and Mona Schwab whom I don't know either except as I've heard Gretta bad-mouth her. Mona is a law student and Alf's most recent girl—more serious possibly according to Gretta than most of his girls because, she says, there's a lot more iron in her construction than meets the eye. A five-guest party is small for this house, and even the den, which is the smallest room downstairs, looks uncomfortably empty with so few people in it. The Thorndykes and Mona are standing just inside the door, and Cohen is standing alone on the other side of the room.

He is ostensibly looking at the pictures on the far wall,

but I figure that neither he nor Thorndyke can lend himself easily to the other's ambiance, and each is waiting instead therefore to be approached on his own ground. When Alf has given me a drink, I feel compelled to join the solitary though I don't really want to, anticipating that Cohen will once more not remember me. Short, dark, ruddy-skinned, and burly, all of a piece, Cohen has the shiny cheeks and large eyes of a kewpie doll, and in those keen and vividly sad eyes, I see as I approach him that this failure of recognition is also genuine. The questions that he asks me when I've joined him and told him my name also indicate that he really does think he's never seen me before. Do I live hereabouts he asks, and, when I've said "yes," where? These are openers that are unlikely to lead to much, and don't, and it's obvious that he doesn't want to be asking me questions at all. What he really wants is to be questioned, but since I know what he does and even where he lives, my openers will have to be somewhat less perfunctory and none comes to me at once. What comes instead though, right away, is a wave of negative sympathy. Cohen is standing under a mezzotint of Mont-Saint-Michel, and though he might not have placed himself there for that reason, the brown of the engraving virtually matches his brushed-denim suit. His oversized head with its cover of patent leather hair appears detached above a large, maroon velvet bowtie, and his eyes are not just sad, but loony. They are also craving eyes, however, and though an appropriate question from me can't be what they crave most, it might help. Finally I try the travel-vacation gambit, and Cohen then tells me about a week he'd spent that winter in Barbados, in a small hotel run by natives that had been quite remarkably fine. The proprietors had been both gracious and efficient, he said, and through them he'd also been invited to be a guest or observer in one of the local courts and that too had been a gratifying experience.

Whatever the gratification of this vacation however, he gets only limited pleasure from telling me about it. I'm not,

I think, the audience he requires. A persistent absence of ocular focus suggests this unassuaged need, but just as he's winding up and I'm trying to think of what to ask him next, Gretta appears, and circling the room, holding a half empty glass, she eases everything. She tells Cohen his suit is pretty and tells the Thorndykes she's heard about them for so long without meeting them that she's granted them mythic existence. I can't hear what she says to Mona Schwab when she leans against her and whispers to her, but whatever it is causes them both to laugh into each other's faces, and since I know how little she likes Mona, this apparent complicity makes clear to me once more how little Gretta has just fallen into the life she now neither quite leads nor doesn't lead, how much it is the life she'd been brought up to occupy.

I am as exempted from her hospitable attentions, however, as Alf is. She neither talks to me nor looks at me, and this exemption continues even when she leads us into the dining room and seats us by a plan that she appears to devise on the spur of the moment, but that I suspect Alf had worked out in advance. This seating arrangement allows Mona to give Cohen the opportunity I haven't given him—and couldn't have given him I soon see in anything like similar fashion. Mona is seated to my left, between me and Thorndyke, with Cohen across the table from her, to Mrs. Thorndyke's right and Gretta's left, and though the table, too, is too large for so few people, she isn't intimidated by its width. Part of Alf's interest in Mona may be philanthropic, for he likes people who afford him the opportunity to do them some good, but it's apparent that she will not be anyone's charity case for long. She's still fresh enough out of the boondocks to play the wide-eyed belle at a party, but she is also watching herself with those wide eyes, and watching herself comparatively. At a certain moment she is going to change, and this change, when it comes, will be decisive. Tall, thin if not skinny, her underdevelopment is accentuated by a pink knit dress that her mother might have knitted for her, but what distinguishes her far more decisively than her dress or even her accent is the damp heat of expectation on her forehead, temples, and cheekbones as she leans across her plate and partway across the table to tell Cohen that an amicus curiae brief that he'd filed years ago in a textile industry case in Haverhill, which she'd read in her junior year in college for an American history research paper, had given her first cause to think about going to law school. "You see, I had everything to learn," she says. "Where I come from, people don't believe in women lawyers and don't much believe in labor lawyers either. So the idea of a woman labor lawyer isn't an idea you just come on."

Cohen's dark skin takes on eggplant lustre now, and as he tells Mona that he picks her for a quick learner, his eyes, from which the light had been notably withheld while he was talking to me, are brilliant, relighted with a belief in possibility. The craving that had looked loony to me must have been for just this illumination, and since Mona evidently entertains a related if less tested view of the world as a place in which desire solicits event—a belief that feeds desire—within minutes Cohen is baiting the conversation with the prospect of a research assistantship for her for the coming year that she allows she'd just love to have.

I am, for the moment, off duty—expected to talk neither to Mona at my left nor to Alf to my right at the foot of the table who is overextended between his obligation to be attentive to Mrs. Thorndyke to his right, even if her diffident reserve suggests she doesn't require attention, and his interest in the conversation between Cohen and Mona. His attention drifts toward Cohen and Mona as he talks to Mrs. Thorndyke, and watching this it occurs to me that he might have intended to bring them together without quite anticipating what that could mean. That Alf's parties are purposeful though is what Gretta referred to this morning when she called them his parties.

At the head of the table, Gretta is entertaining Thorndyke who not only appears even larger sitting down than he had standing, but seems disposed chiefly in two dimensions as though hewn from a wall. The massive frontal plane of his broad-boned face suggests an Indian infusion, as does the sinkage of his temples and his cheeks. But his skin is both as pale and as dry as parchment, and he parts his lips repeatedly and inserts his tongue strongly between them to moisten them. This gesture seems also to be sight-linked, and it occurs equally when he inspects the food and when his pale, gray, deeply recessed eyes turn on the brooch that joins Gretta's low-cut black dress between her breasts. Her costume reflects what Gretta calls her "mother-lore," for her mother, whose knowledge, she says, was limited in range but unerring as far as it went, always made it a rule to wear black and show some chest when she was out of shape, and looking up the table at her I find myself also watching Thorndyke appraise her summer-ruddy, resiliently thick skin. She laughs several times as I watch her, and when she raises her head to do this, her neck swells luxuriously. Thorndyke inclines toward her each time she laughs or he says something—or when he refills her wine glass, his hand outsized against the wine bottle, the heel down near the base and the thumb at the neck, the tendons fanning out vividly from the wrist. Drinking, talking, laughing, eating, Gretta continues to seem unaware of my presence, but it would be difficult to fail so consistently to meet my eyes by accident.

After a while a door creaks somewhere in the distance, and looking into the hall I see Michael's feet and then his legs in light summer sleepers descending the stairs. When the swell of his thighs becomes visible, he halts, hesitates, then turns and withdraws up the stairs again and again a door creaks. Gretta, seated with her back to the hall, cannot see this, but she holds a piece of filet on her fork for a moment, considers it, then returns meat and fork together still to her plate where they remain unmoved until the course is cleared. She and Thorndyke find less to say to each other now. When the dessert is served, a chocolate soufflé, she divides a portion of it a couple of times with the tined spoon but doesn't taste it, and she disappears when everybody else adjourns for coffee.

In the living room then Cohen and Mona gravitate together again and Alf seats himself next to Thorndyke, and this leaves me and Mrs. Thorndyke to each other. She finds a place for herself on a hard, isolated loveseat and I sit down next to her and only then remember how this seat imposes intimacy on its occupants. Thirty feet away by contrast, across a deep, mulberry carpet, Thorndyke and London are half turned toward each other from the opposite ends of a low, white, nubbly couch that really leaves too much space between them for easy talk. Somewhat less distant, near a monumental fireplace with tile facings and a double-railed brass fender, Cohen is perched on a leather hassock with Mona at his feet in a semi-lotus position. The coffee table directly in front of me is shingled with magazines, and with a pile of WGBH programs going back to January, and I am thinking about how difficult this room is to occupy, when Mrs. Thorndyke begins, quite easily it seems, to talk to me. Her voice is cheerful and relaxed, and, grateful, I look as she directs me at the ceiling-to-floor draperies that cover the wall of French doors at the far end of the room. Central to their design is a tree of life that shelters a menagerie of brilliantly detailed small animals, and this large tree is attended by smaller, green lollipop trees with bright fruit suspended from their green rounds. The ground of the cloth is a glazed golden beige. Her interest in these draperies is somewhat special, Mrs. Thorndyke says apologetically, since it has to do entirely with their fauna, and she wishes to disabuse me first of all of any assumption I might entertain that these animals are mythic, creatures that nature has never or not yet gotten around to. They are all actually stylized approximations of real animals, she says, though only someone who was both an amateur naturalist and a travel nut would be likely to know this. Someone like herself.

Her face, which had looked guarded to me at dinner, is remarkably open now as she talks—round, earnest, modest, bordered by frizzed gray hair and friendly glints of light off her gold-rimmed eyeglasses. The Hindu artist who wove that cloth had to have had specific animals in mind, she says, even though there are quite a number of them he couldn't have seen in India. "Like that little fellow in the upper right-hand corner who looks like Eddie Cantor," she says. "You're not too young to know about Eddie Cantor, are you?"

I assure her that I'm not, and that my father had been an Eddie Cantor fan. "You mean the monkey with the big eyes and mod glasses," I say, to make this certain.

"That's the one," she says, "only he's not a monkey. He's a galago, a bush baby, and they don't exist except in Africa. Not monkeys exactly, though they are primates. More like lemurs, or loris. Nocturnals. Those popeyes gather more light than ordinary eyes, which makes them an advantage at night though they might be painful in full sunlight. I have a friend in New York City who once kept a bush baby loose in her apartment. She's a bachelor lady, which is why she could do it. You see, the bush baby urinates on his paws to make them sticky so he can hang onto things, curtains for instance, but that also means that just about anything he touches is going to smell like urine. Eventually even my friend had to give up and donate the pretty little fellow to the Bronx Zoo."

I say I can understand that this must have been a hard decision for her friend to make, and Mrs. Thorndyke goes on to point out a loris and a ring-tailed monkey to me, and to indicate how they are like and unlike the galago. Each is a species with which she's had personal experience, she tells me, and I think I'd like to know better what this means if my attention were not being drawn elsewhere. Alf's attention too, I notice. Though he still seems to be trying to find out something from Thorndyke, asking questions and getting answers that look to be less than full, he also glances across the room from time to time over my head toward the hall and stairs. Unreadable sounds float from that direction, Gretta's voice and Michael's. Hers is generally the initiator and his then follows and seems to parody hers, imitating but simplifying the line of sound. "Is something wrong?" Mrs. Thorndyke asks.

"He's probably having trouble getting to sleep," I say.

"A boy?"

"Twelve years old."

"So hard to tell with children what is bothering them," she says, and though her concern sounds genuine, it's apparent that she talks more certainly about bush babies.

Looking down from the shallow, iron-hard loveseat, I see her toes reciprocating inside her black shoes lying one next to the other in the deep carpet like rafted boats, expensive, no-nonsense shoes with bright steel buckles, and over the jamming and unjamming of her toes inside them, the rasp of nylon against leather, her stomach issues sounds of stress. Restive odors drift through an open window behind the draperies, the heavy, figured fabric swells and collapses, and a lurid light attenuates the colors of the draperies and is followed by the boom of thunder and, immediately, the sound of heavy rain. I know that Gretta has come downstairs when I see Thorndyke place his hands on his knees to raise himself from his slump in the corner of the white couch. When she comes into the living room where I can see her myself, her face is more definite than it had been earlier, more concentrated. And less ingratiating, I think. The streak of white hair an inch wide over her forehead and diminishing as it goes back bifurcates her head with the severity of a wedge, and her blue eyes isolated by her high ruddy cheekbones fix me now finally as though they'd just discovered my presence. "You were up there a long time," Alf says. Concern and annoyance jostle for place in his voice, and he takes his wristwatch in the finger-tips of his right hand, brings it out from under the sleeve of his jacket, but doesn't look at it.

"It took a while to decide it would be friendlier to come down," Gretta says. "Michael's just brushing his hair and putting on his bathrobe, but he'll be here in a moment."

She is generating something, and the air that I hear escape between Alf's teeth is too harsh for a sigh. Hazard hangs in the room, palpable as a cramp. "He won't go to sleep?" Alf says.

"He hasn't gone," Gretta says. "I expect he will go eventually."

Fingering his left eye now with the middle finger of his left hand, Alf stretches first the lower and then the upper lid as though they were sticky, and Thorndyke, who is still holding himself up by his knees, moistens the hole in his lips with his tongue. The utterances that issue from Mrs. Thorndyke's stomach are no longer entirely digestive, but include elements of speech, expletives or explanations that aren't quite completed, and Michael's arrival is announced by the dry scrape of the plastic soles of his sleepers on the wooden floor of the hall, which becomes only an intimation of sound then when he shuffles onto the living room carpet. The belt of his terry-cloth bathrobe is untied, and the open panels of the robe frame a belly which is not small-boy chubby but a middle-aged resolution of slippage that pulls on his shoulders and weighs on his legs. His face though is Roman—square, clear-eyed, the mouth wide and thin-lipped, the nose definite, dark hair low on his forehead in loose, imperial ringlets.

He trundles across the room, conveying himself to Gretta who is seated on the floor in front of the fireplace where he turns and backs between her and Cohen and Mona until he has his heels at the brass fender, his hands joined over his stomach, and the panels of his robe over his arms. "How are you boy?" Mona asks him when he has settled.

"I'm okay," he says.

"That's good," she says. "But you know, if there was a fire in that fireplace, honey, you'd cook. And be pretty toothsome, too."

"What does that mean, toothsome?"

"It means good enough to eat."

"Well, Mona," Gretta says, "that's the first time I ever heard you talk pure nigger."

Mona's face, stretched to laugh, holds as Mrs. Thorndyke says, "Do you speak Gullah by any chance, Miss Schwab? I hadn't known until last spring when I went to the Sea Islands that there were still people who spoke Gullah."

Mona's "huh" now, delayed and truncated, has to be as much a preview of her future as her exchange with Michael had been a vestige of her past. "To tell you the truth, ma'am," she says after a moment of recovery, "down where they do speak Gullah, I pass for a Yankee."

Cohen makes a placative sound, and Alf stands up abruptly and asks if anyone will have a drink. The rain has cooled the big room, made it almost chilly, and for this reason too drinking is an attractive idea. Thorndyke asks for a Scotch and soda and Gretta for a brandy, and Alf walks around behind the white couch to a table where bottles, glasses, a silver ice bucket, and a silver pitcher are in readiness. "Why aren't you in bed, young man?" Cohen asks Michael.

"There's no point if I'm not going to sleep," Michael says.

"Nolo contendere," Cohen says to the room at large.

Alfred gives Thorndyke his Scotch and soda in a highball glass, then leans down to give Gretta her brandy in a snifter, and as the crystal globe with its half-inch of viscous amber changes hands, the light through the amber dissolves their fingers. Looking away from Gretta toward Michael, Alf says, "You must be tired."

"I'm not," Michael says with stolid poise.

Watching Gretta assessing the room through the snifter as though it were a lens, I try to enter her mind—to imagine first of all how this might change her perception. Does it, I wonder, bring out hidden structure like a dye in microscopy? "I'd like you to go back to bed," Alf says, his voice carefully unthreatening.

"If Gretta will come back up with me," Michael says, reasonable too in his own way.

"I'd like you to go up alone," Alf says, his tone unchanged, but with greater strain in his articulation now as he leaves safe ground.

"Even if I don't want to?" Michael asks.

"Even so."

He intends apparently to persist, but his persistence is also audibly reluctant and Michael's face continues to be impassive, and waiting for one of them to say something more, for the crisis to take shape or recede, I hear Cohen speak next instead. "Everybody has to learn to do some things he doesn't want to do," he says. "Your uncle's right."

"In order to do the world's work?" Gretta says, so quickly that she has to have been waiting for something like this to be said, and far too quickly for the look of pain on Alf's face to make any difference.

"Amen," Thorndyke says.

A cramp continues to possess Alf's face as Gretta raises the snifter to her mouth and drains it, and as she bends her head back to do this, her neck swells even more than it had to Thorndyke's flatteries earlier at dinner, and less attractively. Then she raises herself to her feet, pushing against the floor with one hand and holding the glass in the other, and places the glass carefully on the mantel. Her head swings the arc of the company like a panoramic camera, making a record but no statement, and completes its survey on my face once more. For a moment she raises her eyebrows into high arches that stretch the long upper lids across the bony hollows like drumskins. "Let's go, pal!" she says to Michael, though at first I think she may be talking to me.

She crosses the hall and begins to climb the stairs, then

waits for Michael on the landing under the arched window. When he catches up to her she shuffles her feet in a kind of soft-shoe that matches her step to his, places her left arm across his shoulders and starts up the second flight of stairs with him at his slow, considered pace, and something closes around the center of my body like a cold collar.

2

IN THE SUMMER, when I'm not teaching, the stretch and yawn of the day can sometimes tax my powers to stay lively. Or even, I've discovered, to stay alive. In June, returning from a conference with a lawyer in Stamford about my father's estate, I cracked up my car alongside the Connecticut Turnpike in an autonomous one-car accident. I must have been vagueing for miles before I actually slipped off the road and fetched up against an entirely material Norway maple that was unavoidable by the time I saw it. Luckily I'd been driving in the outside lane, luckily I'd drifted right and not left, and luckily the grassy margin alongside the Turnpike gave me time to wake up and start braking before impact. When I came to again in a hospital a couple of hours later, I was uninjured except for a gash on my face that was of only cosmetic consequence. And though the car was totaled, even this had its lucky aspect. I took a job then rewriting and editing reports for a research company called Municipal Systems, Inc., for the summer, partly to help pay for a new car in September, but partly also in the hope of what I've discovered to be true—that there are distinct advantages to having to get to a bright air-conditioned office five mornings a week for a day's work that requires to be thought about continuously while it's being done but that scarcely requires to be thought about at all before or after. And that also requires me while I'm working to remember or at least assume that the material world exists.

Work even of this order requires the daily restoration of sleep though, and by Friday morning I'm making do with too little sleep for two nights running. It seems apparent to me that Gretta's call early Thursday morning and her disruption of Alf's party in the evening have to be elements of the same incident. But the incident is still inconclusive, and listening to Percy talk now—and with the surface of the coffee cup in my hand not much warmer than the damp air against my face—I don't feel recharged for the day. In fact, I have the willies, and the lobes of my brain feel defined and interleafed inside my head like processed cheese slices. The interleafing though seems to be air, since my face is not only surface tender but also spongy. When I touch a cheek with a finger, the feeling of indentation persists after I've withdrawn my finger again. This is in marked contrast to the integument of Percy's face which is so thin that in the early morning sunlight I see systems of veins behind it, count his pulse in his temples, see a nerve working a different pulse in the hollow under his right eye.

Percy had taught at Hillside the year after Janet and I split, and in the course of that year we'd had a lot in common and seen a lot of each other and Percy had made a finding against teaching by which I wasn't unaffected. Since then he's tried several different jobs against which he's also made negative findings, but since February he's been an orderly at Mt. Auburn Hospital and seems to like that better than anything he's done before. He works the night shift, and sometimes on the way to the subway, going home in the morning, he catches me at breakfast to have a cup of coffee or fry an egg, but mostly to talk—pent-up and garrulous because he hasn't had the chances he counts on to talk to insomniac patients during the night. In the winter when he's come in this way though he's always kept track of the clock no matter how hard he was talking—always remembered when it was time for me to set out for Hillside—and it has to be an implicit judgment that work at Municipal Systems is even less real than teaching that now when he makes these early morning visits, he keeps on talking until I cut him off.

This morning he comes to what I think he really wants to

talk about by way of various preliminary diversions. Highly distractable, he'll talk about anything that occurs to him for a while, resuscitating a faculty that has been suffering from disuse as though it were the resuscitation itself that chiefly mattered to him, and what he actually said was of only secondary importance. But when he tells me that he'd played fiddle in Charlestown the previous evening with some people he'd never played with before, I hear a different order of interest. Percy's fiddle-playing is out of the league of most of the musicians he gets a chance to play with, and he's always on the lookout for better players. But moving around a lot as a consequence, playing with different groups two or three times a week, he has also been working up a kind of ethnography.

The previous evening's players, he reports, live and work together in a cabinetmakers' commune. There are five of them, three men and two women, and they have a couple of fine old houses on Main Street, one of which they've fixed up to live and work in, and the other of which they're about to start fixing up on spec—which suggests, he says, that they belong to the left capitalist wing of the craft.

This is a trap I know already and don't much need to negotiate again. The perception that people fail to put the different parts of their lives together, or regard their lives as discontinuous history, supplies Percy with a lot of his most dependable amusement. Idling amuses him too, human engines turning in neutral, and he doesn't exempt me altogether from the scrutiny that affords him these laughs. What makes this a trap though is my susceptibility to his point of view. Part of the secret of our queer friendship is that Percy represents a certain extreme of possibility for me—that his way of seeing things is a way I wish to resist. The trade-off, I think, is that Percy in turn has a stake in my resistance, that he depends on me to be skeptical about his skepticism. Only a trade-off of sorts of course, and when I'm feeling somewhat feeble, as I am this morning, it seems best for both of us that I not let my capacity for resistance be too severely tested. "How good are they?" I ask therefore, backing up to a less arduous track. "I mean as musicians?"

"Not very," Percy says. "But one of the men has constructed a remarkable bass out of an eight-foot two-by-four bolted at one end to an empty oil barrel. You lay the other end over a chair back or anything else that will hold it about waist high. It has two strings to bow or pluck, and you can also kick the barrel when you're working at that end for percussion. Not bad. I stayed out there so long mauling that rascal, I was almost late to work."

Percy's amusement always intensifies when he can make himself its object, but he doesn't allow himself to be diverted now even by this opportunity. "I really would like to tell you what I think about those birds in Charlestown," he says. "It doesn't matter of course but it wouldn't take forever either."

"It's going to have to be under way then," I say.

"Of course," Percy says. "I seem to forget how attached you are to your new office life."

Bland irony is the only form of dissimulation he allows himself, and he uses it now to let me know again what he thinks about Municipal Systems and of my assertion repeated several times that I get a kick out of making a good enough or even a poor piece of writing better of its kind and that I like entering unknown frames of reference. Most of the research undertaken at Municipal Systems is team research, and the prose of the reports I've edited has more often than not been collective—a possibility of which I'd had no experience eight weeks ago but to which I can now testify. The plan for consolidating the high schools of two adjacent townships in the Berkshires that I've been working on for the past several days comes to me in a team prose absolutely uncontaminated by personality. It had caused me great disorientation at first, but now, when I think I've mastered its intentions, I experience the special freshening of finding my way in an unfamiliar idiom. A feeling of expansion. I have to finish editing the report though by the end of the day if it's to be retyped and clear the office as scheduled by the beginning of the following week. And knowing that Hans Scherman, who'd taken the last part of the draft home with him the previous evening to ready it for me has probably been back in the office with it since eight o'clock or earlier, makes me additionally determined not to stay at the breakfast table while Percy pursues his inquisition.

In the bedroom tying my tie, I hear him through the wall placing the breakfast dishes in the sink and returning the milk and butter to the refrigerator, being helpful while he prepares himself to develop a judgment that will not I think, for all its specificity, be unique. Percy holds to the idea of an existence all of whose parts make sense together, at any moment or over any period of time, and he holds to this not just as a radiant and encouraging concept to be thought about or aspired to, but as a standard to be met. As such it's devastating, and persistent practice in its application has made him adept at wreaking the widest possible devastation with it. That he doesn't spare himself this lash he wields doesn't inhibit him in wielding it either, and as we leave the house a couple of minutes later, I detect his readiness to raise welts. The cooling effect of the previous night's storm hasn't lasted even into the early morning, and in the treeless glare of Mt. Auburn Street, Percy's head produces its own counterglare. His eyes, nearly blinded by concentration, project an inward gaze so deep that what I am seeing is only their backshine or brilliant exhaust.

He starts slowly and carefully, even effortfully I'd say, for Percy too uses an invented rather than inherited idiom just as my report writers do, except that his could scarcely be called communal. "There's something not just ethically wrong," he says, "but something pragmatically wrong too —I mean something that plain won't work—about the games those folks are playing over there. They wouldn't say boo to a goose and don't think they have to. Wherever they've been before, their money has made good enough clearing noises for them. But they're surrounded by angry people this time, and that's something new. Even the kids cruising the streets out there are looking for trouble rather than just hopscotch or kick the can. It's what you might call ontological deprivation—and right in the boil, these folks are acting out a kind of surfeit that may also be ontological deprivation, only it's of a kind so different the two parties have no way to recognize each other."

This isn't exactly conversation or even explanation. It's more like homiletic, and I take what comfort I can from the fact that he's at least developing it rapidly this time. A summary version meant to make up in compression what it sacrifices in accumulation. But as he hesitates again, poised for total delivery, the driver of a trash truck engages its compactor, and the air is torn by the scream of gears and the smashing of wood, glass, and metal. Percy laughs, and with his attention forced outward, his strained face relaxes. "That has to be the effect I was after," he shouts over the sustained din.

When the compactor has completed its cycle the street is relatively hushed again, though the heat translates even the hum of a car engine or the slap of a foot against the pavement into pressure. Laughter departs from Percy's face quickly and he is inside himself again. "I guess I'd about finished anyway," he says. "I'll just walk the rest of the way to the kiosk with you in friendly silence, because suddenly I'm pooped."

Though he speaks with resignation, the resolute line of his lips suggests that he hasn't really altogether abandoned the idea of communication yet, and I can only hope that this persisting mental simmer won't come to a boil before we part. I could use a few quiet minutes now to ready myself for work. Even if I don't have to think about the substance of what I do at Municipal Systems in advance, it takes concentration to get into the state of mind—it might even be a state of existence really—that the work requires. The prose I edit, collective and without any history of use,

is located in an absolute present that requires me to be in a
neutral state of being if I am to improve it without changing its spirit. An easier state to attain I suppose than Percy's
coherence, but it's demanding enough nonetheless in its
own way, and it would be a help, therefore, if Percy didn't
have too much more to say to me. Right now though not
only is he saying nothing, but no one seeing us could even,
I think, be certain that we were together. No one else on
the street seems very surely together though either, which
suggests that isolation is an atmospheric phenomenon.

We continue apart this way until we reach the kiosk and
actually part, and Percy heads downstairs into the subway.
Watching him for a moment before I continue across to
Mass. Avenue, I can see that he really has run out. With his
thin high shoulder blades winging through his tee-shirt
and his baggy white hospital pants bunched and pleated
under a black leather belt, he's an indeterminate presence,
even a different subspecies from the other grosser figures
abroad at this hour. The more differentiated life of the
Square tends not to appear until later, and there is little to
see on the street now in addition to gross life except the
previous day's accumulation of empty cigarette packs, her-
niated newspapers, and heat-prostrated ice-cream cones.
Except that to my surprise the quarter-cadger has already
taken up his position, earlier than I've ever seen him there
before, in the doorway of Leavitt & Pierce under the suspended figure of the Indian woman in the gold-trimmed,
blue Mother Hubbard. The fixed wooden waves of her hair
are dressed with a pair of feathers in a V, one gold and the
other maroon, and she announces the store's trade by prof-
fering a bunch of cigars grouped like fasces in her right
hand and a jug of tobacco in her left, and the man under
her nearly equals her in immobility but is considerably less
colorful.

I've been aware of him here for several weeks now, not
every day but many days, and though I can't figure out
either where he comes from or what he's really up to aside

from cadging, the way he goes about this single limited activity is no more ordinary than his appearance. His flat face and flared nostrils could be Negroid, but his skin, deprived of pigment as though by some genetic accident, is insistently ambiguous—opaque, foggy, utterly neutral. Neatly built and of medium height, he's nodding in the doorway now as though he might have spent the night there, asleep on his feet like a horse, with the frayed and stained collar of an ancient poplin raincoat still turned up around his neck and under his chin for warmth even though the air on the street is by now oven warm. "Spare a quarter?" he asks a woman walking fifteen or twenty feet in front of me, but doesn't ask this question until she is well within the limited range of his flat, breathy voice.

He speaks only the three words, and his face remains immobile, and though I've watched him for days with increasing curiosity, I've been unable to discover the criteria by which he tries one man or woman and not another, makes or withholds this minimal pitch. His arms hang against his sides, elbows back, the four fingers of each hand down into the pockets of his raincoat with the thumbs hooked over, and his only move is the withdrawal of one hand or the other from a pocket to take money, which only occurs when some proffer has already been made. He receives it then with the four fingers still together, the thumb splayed out, the rosy gray palm soft as chamois. "God bless you, sir," he says, or "God bless you, ma'am"— but with no fervor.

Since he never mistakes the sex of the donor though, he must be somewhat attentive, have some way to determine what it is to his interest to know. His three-quarters closed eyes must be doing something that is to limit or select what they see, though it may be a trick of projection rather than mere selection he's practicing, some form of optical reversal by which he keeps the world distant but keeps it clear. A good trick, moreover, since he's been loose and happy every time I've seen him. The critical evidence of this cheerful condition otherwise denied by his appearance is an indentation like a navel in the left corner of his mouth that is always about to open to a grin but never does. Though he's touched me three times already this week he touches me again now without recognition—the way Bogart does John Huston having his shoes shined and reading a newspaper in *The Treasure of the Sierra Madre*, except that my face is in plain view and has been each time. "Spare a quarter?"

Only the mouth moves, and even it moves so little that the rosette in the left corner remains unchanged, not even saying "spare," really, but something more like "spah," which requires less effort of articulation. A small difference, except that the phrase is repeated several hundred times a day. I've already given him a quarter, been blessed, and gone by when it occurs to me to test this subtle economy. Fully alert suddenly for the first time this morning and wondering why I haven't tried this before, I continue half a block along Mass. Avenue and then reverse direction, and again I'm asked for a quarter and blessed when I give it. The repetition seems absolute, with no energy wasted on improvisation. The third time, however, after I've gone half a block once more and re-reversed direction and the quarter has been solicited and given once more, an emanation of recognition that could also be complicity flits across the dun cheeks. It's too swift for sure identification and too swift certainly to be called a smile, but this stroboscopic flash of satisfaction is enough nonetheless to cause me satisfaction too, and I continue on my way now on a palpable adrenal surge.

There's nothing else to look at or think about until I turn into Bow Street which is short and bowed, and at its midpoint then into Arrow Street which is slightly longer but straight, and laid out at an angle to terminate on Mass. Avenue again. The namers of these streets had seen the city as potential text, and Municipal Systems is housed in what had once been a mill on Arrow Street that reflects a similar view of possibility. The first story, which is of brick and could have been a complete structure, has a two-story wooden building, also potentially complete, perched on top of it like an oversized hat, the only apparent connection between the two structures a brick cornice supported by five brick corbels just above the first floor that looks like a safety edge or girdle to keep the upper, wooden building in place. Each of these structures is in itself handsome but the unlikely conjunction is absolutely distinctive, and a developer had bought the rundown and underused building for next to nothing a few years back, gutted its interior, and created dramatic new spaces meant to attract glamour businesses—architects, designers, public relations firms. The plan has turned out, however, not to be sound, possibly because the building isn't really in the Square but on its fringe. Most of the glamour businesses that had moved in initially have moved out again, and some of the present tenants are far too ordinary for the spaces they occupy.

The two floors under Municipal Systems, for example, now house a bindery, and there is the usual strong, animal smell of glue this morning on the stairs floated in space like Jacob's Ladder that I mount to the glass-walled studio on the third floor in which the Municipal Systems staff, seven of us this week, work all together flooded in light from a series of glass domes in the roof and high windows over the street. The room had been designed as a drafting room and could have been an aviary, a clear cube of space with Hans Scherman's office a glass box inset in the far right corner. Everyone works visible to everyone else here at all times, a condition I'd learned first to tolerate and then quickly to like. I had a moist summer cold in late June shortly after I took the job here that the air conditioning had made explosive, and at first I'd kept a box of Kleenex in the center drawer of my desk that I bent to use, trying to blow my increasingly tender nose as nearly inside the drawer as possible because it made me uneasy to blow it under surveillance. But I'd gotten over this inhibition in a few days, and I could now blow my nose, scratch, or readjust my clothing in open view with no more than a slight residual sense that these should be privileged or shielded activities. I meant but had so far forgotten to tell Percy that one of the secondary advantages of working at Municipal Systems this summer is a growing suspicion that the need for private being can be exaggerated.

No one has arrived yet in the big room, but Hans Scherman is as I'd anticipated at his desk in his glassed-off corner, his crew cut standing like an oatmeal brush over the broad, clear-eyed, canvas-skinned face that conveys undistracted intelligence—the look of a man who knows he's helping to keep the world in order. Reading a typescript and with a succession of other papers in orderly piles or folders to either side of him waiting for attention, he welcomes me when I come to the door of his office with a wrinkling and unwrinkling of his high forehead, a kind of skin wink, and holds up his left hand in an easy gesture that assumes abeyance. You will surely be patient, it says, until I've reached a more convenient halting place. How he can know who is waiting to talk to him is a mystery, since he hasn't looked up once. But I'm nonetheless certain that he does know and that I—Harry Karp—am identified, even placed.

3

WALKING INTO THE SQUARE again in the evening, I cut across
the alley from Mt. Auburn Street and come out on Brattle
under the glass walls of Design Research. Closed but fully
lighted, its goods brilliantly visible, this transparent building both dominates and is emblematic of the stretch of the
Square to which other evening walkers come as I do to do
errands or tongue ice-cream cones possibly, but primarily
to look into the shop windows and at each other, to be
observers.

There was no answer when I called Gretta in the afternoon, and no answer again when I called once more in the
evening, and feeling too restless then to read, I headed for
the Square where I can almost always count on something
to take my attention for a while and keep me lively. The
way in which this city is spectacular isn't at all the way of,
say, Los Angeles, which Janet had shown me when I visited
her the previous winter. There are no movie stars to gawk
at and there's nothing in any way comparable to the line-up
of Silver Clouds and XKE's I'd seen bumper to bumper on
Sunset Boulevard. Money is shown here in more sober fashion and the city is more or less consistently dour in fact
except during the few weeks in spring when the lilacs are
in bloom. But even in winter when dog turds are preserved
in ice over the brick sidewalks as though in amber and the
air is a liquid refrigerant, the streets offer a variety of legible
spectacles.

This is still, that is, an articulated city, and though the
tourist and specialty shops of Harvard Square have begun
to proliferate into Central Square and several of the old
frame buildings on the commercial blocks of Brattle Street

have been replaced by glass and reinforced concrete buildings that are handsome in such an unparticular way that they might as well be in Los Angeles—or in Mexico City or Dakar, for that matter—the rate of dissolution isn't rapid, and Harvard Square is still as distinct from Central Square as each is from Inman and Kendall or Technology Square, a new lunar terrain that indicates where we might be going but aren't yet. I think of these squares as informing nodes distinguishable from each other not only architecturally and by what they offer in the way of commerce and entertainment, but also by the expectations they arouse and the consequent life they attract. By the last particularly, though in this way Harvard Square is composed really of several distinct subzones with areas of runover or mix between them like the portions of a painting on unsized canvas where adjacent colors merge by osmosis. Areas of unstable chemistry that might be dramatic but tend in fact to be relatively characterless.

I head for the Square evenings when the weather is favorable and I have nothing better to do, to stop vagueing—or, preferably, to forestall it. By now, these chronic, accelerated slippages of attention from which you start with only a schematic notion—an outline deprived of detail—of what's been going on for the past ten, twenty, or thirty minutes scare the bejesus out of me. They aren't painful exactly, but I know that some kinds of internal hemorrhage are painless too and issue no warning until the bleeder discovers that what he thought was a bass drum thumping outside his window is actually his heart making do as it can with decreasing working supplies. And the analogy is reasonable. Vagueing is also a symptom of deficiency, of the failure of the environment to provide circumstances to keep the registering instrument occupied, or of the instrument to register, and I actually thought I heard something like a drumbeat or tattoo just before I hit the Norway maple alongside the Connecticut Turnpike in June, though impact and sound could also have been concurrent. It's hard to be sure about the order now, since neither my vagueing before the accident nor the concussion I received when the car stopped faster than I could make for distinct remembering.

I walk into the Square evenings, I guess, to give the world's thingishness a chance to assert itself. To be reminded of the particularity of substance. And though the frequency with which I need such reminding may be increasing, I can certainly remember earlier times too when I suffered from social-sensory deprivation. The summer in Virginia, for example, when I was a draftee getting amphibious training. At least amphibious training was what I was told I was being sent to Virginia for, though before the week spent on the Chesapeake climbing cargo nets and piling out of the maws of landing craft in simulated combat conditions I spent six weeks waiting to do this and not doing a whole lot else. Several companies of us waited together, quartered in a hollow square of vacation cottages on the grounds of the Nansequod Inn in Miramar. Mold Village we called it, and even the name Miramar was a deception, since the town wasn't at any point on its perimeter less than two miles from the ocean. It was as nearly nowhere as any place I'd ever been before or have been since however so a view of the ocean might well have been its most probable aspiration.

There wasn't much to do but rest, read, and turn out for drill once a day on the oblong of sand and beach grass on which the cottages fronted, and the hot, sticky wind across the parade and the uselessness of the activity made even drill pretty desultory. Day by day I was winding down, feeling my lines going limp, and after a while, along with three other trainees who were ad hoc friends, I began frequenting the Miramar amusement park late afternoons just before dinner to rush down a few beers and then buy a string of tickets for the Dragon Loop and settle down to really try my lassitude. The ride climaxed on the far side of the highest climb, at the beginning of the descent, where it was actually also possible for an instant to see the gray, flat miasma of the ocean. But after the first ride or two, even that made no difference, and all four of us would be reading newspapers or magazines as we climbed and dipped as though the Dragon Loop were a commuter train, though we could hear the school kids around us in the other cars— who didn't have the money, time, or need to ride as assiduously as we did—screaming piously on every drop.

By the time my company finally got onto the Chesapeake, I was just about semi-comatose, and the first day of the exercise I climbed down the side of a transport ship on a limp, spineless net into a leftover World War II LCVP and then cruised onto the beach and waded ashore in the bath-warm water without ever quite realizing what I was doing. Follow the leader was presumably the game I was being trained to, but I was overdoing my education. I'd succumbed too far it turned out even to follow instructions. On the return, climbing from the LCVP onto the transport, I mounted the net from the trough instead of the crest of the swell as we'd been instructed, and only a scream from below got me to haul myself up as far as I could by the hold my hands had on the net. That was just high enough to have the gunwales of the LCVP graze the soles of my boots when it rose from the trough on the succeeding swell and careened against the hull of the transport. The memory of that crunch of metal against metal can probably still lower my blood temperature, but at the time even fear was a removed emotion. It was as though someone I knew reasonably well, but who was not myself, had had a close call— which was oddly the way I felt too going off the Connecticut Turnpike in June.

Tonight though I'm not quite vagueing, or not yet. I'm still only at the stage when my attention keeps falling off images it can't find its way into and yawing around, and I head for the Square therefore looking for simple incontrovertible things to bump against and nose at. In my dynamic scheme of the Square, the stretch of Brattle Street I enter and where I do most of my evening walking is the subzone of the observers—men and women with whom I have at least this much in common, that they too come here to see what there is to see and return then wherever they've come from without having done anything more than that. By my exact cartography, this zone extends from the mini-plaza at the inner end of the education school library around the ninety degree bend as far as Woolworth's.

This is a tourist zone essentially, even if few of the people who walk here on an average evening come from any further away than Belmont or Natick. In summer though, some part of the tourist composition is likely to be exotic, and I've already heard Italian and German spoken when I spot a group of Japanese businessmen in shiny permanent-press suits looking into the window of Reliable Camera. Each has at least one camera and one camera case slung separately over his neck and several have second cameras or accessories as well, and they're comparing the cameras they're wearing with the cameras in the store window most of which are also Japanese. One of them has his camera turned up as though to take his own picture though it's actually his view of the camera I think and not the camera's view of him that he's trying to arrange. He's pushing the black box hard against the limits of the straps to get it to more comfortable range, and his expression of surprise must be caused not by what he sees, but by the difficulty he's experiencing in seeing anything at all. His head strains back and his lower lip protrudes effortfully as he looks past the neat, round swell of his belly under a white nylon shirt at the telescopic lens of his Nikon, and the other men are making animated conversation and laughing at his difficulty. Both the talk and the laughter are convivial and unboisterous, and as I watch, one of the men steps back from the group and takes a flash picture of the entire incident—the puzzled man straining to look down into the erect lens, the other laughing men watching him, and in the background the shop window in which still other cameras are dispersed on square velvet-covered pillars of different heights like performing seals.

I slow to watch but don't stop and stare, and once I've gone by I'm pretty close to the limit of the zone. The couple of hundred feet between Woolworth's and the Harvard Square Theater around the corner on Mass. Avenue is an overlap area, and the liquor store diagonally across the Square on the other reach of Mass. Avenue, the front of which is a cops' rendezvous point, marks the beginning of the subzone of those frequenters of the Square whom I think of as having intentions more active than observation. Men and women who seek something. Interested persons, whether their interest is general and social or individual and personal—or even some combination of the two as it is presumably for the army of hawkers of sectarian and underground newspapers who fan out from here all over the city. These ideological entrepreneurs seem to know pretty well what it is they're up to or looking for. And the cruisers too, even if they're somewhat more programmatically scruffy here than on most other cruising grounds, also seem to operate from understood needs. Most of the solicitors though appear to be considerably less defined persons who may be seeking nothing less or more definite than transformation.

Nothing else of sufficient interest to stop or even slow me turns up in this area where observers and solicitors mix, so that I soon find myself standing on the curb at Nini's Corner facing across the traffic into the next zone and observing its guardians, the pair of cops who stand outside the liquor store. The cops actually do nothing, but they are always there, always a pair, and generally a contrasting pair. Tonight one of them is white and one black, but they can also be fat and thin, tall and short, or benign and threatening—and sometimes recently one has been a woman. I pause hard at the corner then, considering whether to cross over or turn back, aware already even here in the borderland between the two zones of a taint in the air of unclear appetite, of relentless and unfocused inclination to consumption.

Consumption is on my mind these days, not as a global problem but in its more immediate manifestations. My own consumption to begin with. I don't give a thought to broad ecological questions, not even to the approaching exhaustion of fossil fuels, but I can't help thinking about how many pounds of hamburger I've consumed in forty-two years and how much toilet tissue I've flushed down the hopper along with the unassimilable portions of all that carnage, and those thoughts can give me the willies. It's the inefficacy of my consumption that gets me—or, you might say, the space I've preempted and not then really been able to occupy. When I'm asked why I don't remarry—and that's a question I'm asked with more frequency than I'd have imagined possible—I can't quite bring myself to say it's because I've consumed one marriage already, but I certainly think something like that. That for better and worse I'd had my chosen portion and lost the capacity to be nourished by it, and that to marry again therefore would be blatant excess. Even if I tell myself that Janet's remarriage modifies my actual consumption, I'm stuck still with the admonitory notion that what I'd used once poorly, I'd do well now to forego. My very appetite for this kind of sustenance may, it appears, be too ambiguous to promise much.

Most of the time at least, the discomforts and hazards of going it alone seem a fair enough trade-off for what I remember as an increasing and increasingly unmeetable need to forgive Janet not her sins and vices, neither of which she really had, but styles and ideas of being—ways particularly of thinking of herself in the world—against which I have even now little more to say than that they're not my own. That little more though is that they also stir my itchiest skepticism. My disbelief in them is so entire that I find it almost impossible to credit anyone else's belief as being more than assertion, and alone, I'm spared all such rub of two different dispositions making forced accommodation at close range. But it isn't as though these large differences in the ways in which Janet and I saw ourselves in the world necessarily or always created the most humiliating needs for accommodation either. The smaller, less dignified rubs were in fact worse. After a while, to cite one dreadful example, the compensating bob of Janet's somewhat top-heavy body as she walked or, worse still, ran, could put me on the borders of true rage, and it didn't help a bit to remember that an only slightly less developed version of that same motion was once likely to draw me to a very different heat. I'm now spared a whole range of such rubs large and small, but the other side of this forgiveness is that I experience very little heat of any kind, and can lapse altogether easily and at almost any moment, into a cool vague. I don't suppose, come to think of it, that there is any such thing as a hot vague.

Anyway, a large part of my current attachment to the Square depends on the regular possibilities it offers, particularly in the evening, of a kind of consumption in which nothing is actually consumed. Even if, discovering some evening that I've run out of toothpaste, I take this as an excuse to walk to the Square, I'm really happier to find that the drugstore has closed before I get there and to take my turn and come back with nothing more in my hands or pockets than I'd started off with.

Looking across now at the black cop and the white cop side by side in front of the narrow front of the liquor store that diminishes almost to a point in the rear—a near pie-shaped wedge of interstitial space between the shoe store and the quick food bar to either side of the curved corner—and seeing that each cop sports an extravagant mustache and long, full sideburns and that neither could tip the scales at less than two twenty-five, I discover that though I don't really want to return home yet, I want even less to cross over into the zone overseen appropriately by these two excessive figures. Reluctantly therefore I reverse direction, and find nothing more of any particular interest as I re-walk my route. The Japanese tourists are no longer in view anywhere along the street, and when I come through the alley onto Mt. Auburn again and look at my watch, the fact that it isn't yet ten o'clock indicates how little my outing has turned up. As I reach my corner though a Peugeot with an open sunroof, a man and woman in white tennis clothes in the front seat, turns in ahead of me and draws to the curb. Mona Schwab emerges through the sunroof and as I approach proffers an open can of beer. "Have some," she says.

I wave off the invitation. I see that Alf must wish to talk to me, but I don't want our conversation to take place here. "Come on up," I say, "if you have time."

"You're sure?" Alf asks. He's never been inside my apartment though he's come this far before a couple of times, and I attribute this avoidance to sympathetic shame at the modesty of my quarters.

"I'm sure."

"Okay," he says. "After four sets under lights, I certainly don't have any other plans for a while."

Mona, who'd started to get out of the car as soon as I tendered my invitation, laughs and says, "Come on, Alfred, don't play the feeb."

She says this with audible glee, and I feel a tug between them that's on the edge of a tug of war as I climb the three steps of the stoop to open the door for her, and Alf, stiffly intentional, gets out of the car pressing another open can of beer and the rest of a six-pack against his side with one hand so that he can lock the car with the other. "Two flights up," I say, and after inhaling the sweet pungencies of sweat and beer as Mona squeezes past me, I notice that the backs of her legs hanging out of her shorts from the lean lower curve of the haunch to the pompons of sneaker liners just over her heels are not only smooth and brown but seem inexplicably vulnerable.

I hold the door until Alf has passed me too and preceded me up the stairs, then have to squeeze between them in turn on the narrow landing to get my key into the apartment door. Alf pulls in his stomach and holds the open can of beer over his head in one hand and the six-pack behind him in the other, and I feel the intensity of his hesitation then as Mona and I step into the apartment. A reluctance to follow us into the entrance hall, which is even smaller than the landing. The only real space in sight is up and out through the windows of the dark living room to the red beacon on top of 1010 Memorial Drive in the middle distance, but as I turn on the lights in the living room Mona, who's already looking into the bedroom and kitchen, pleases me once more. "Not bad at all," she says.

I moved into this apartment about six months after Janet and I separated and after having lived in the interim in a sublet that was a true rathole, and in that six months too, I'd gotten rid of everything I owned that I wasn't sure I liked or needed. I sold most of the furniture I acquired in the division of property that Janet and I conducted exactly, and justly, and remarkably without rancor, and gave a lot of clothes too to Morgan Memorial. I even donated at least half of my books to the Hillside library, and though this was a hedging way to not quite get rid of them, it meant at least that all the books in my immediate possession fitted into two sets of shelves, one in the living room and one in the bedroom. Each of these rooms under the eaves on the third floor of an end house in a row of five attached houses is small, neat, and very bright during the day, and despite its miniature scale, the apartment is open and uncluttered. I buy nothing anymore without using up, giving, or throwing away something first, and I know what I have, where it is, and why I have it. Moreover, everything I have works or is usable, so that there are no dead goods at all. A lot of the goods Janet and I had acquired died during our last couple of years together, and our apartment became something between a warehouse and a morgue. Nothing in my apartment now looks either stored or in disuse, but it also occurs to me from time to time that I create so little detritus only because I'm creating very little history.

There's a couch, a soft chair, and a couple of straight

chairs in the living room, and Alf chooses to sit on one of the straight chairs and to place the six-pack on the table between them that serves me both as a desk and as a dining table. When I remove a can from its slot, more to be friendly than because I want to drink beer, the three remaining cans in the cardboard pack are obvious excess. Alf never takes more than one drink, and Mona, who's removed a cushion from the couch, placed it on the floor next to an open window, and seated herself on it knees up so that I have to practice avoidance not to look down her legs, shows no interest even in the can she's carried up the stairs with her and placed on the windowsill. "We weren't just playing tennis," she says, smiling but talking away from Alf and me out the window. "Alfred was giving me lessons. My form would be an acute embarrassment if I were allowed to play mixed doubles with his friends—or even ladies' singles."

"Not true," Alf says.

"Oh, come on, Alfred," she says. "It sure is."

Her persistence reminds me of Gretta's contention that she always knows the end is in sight when Alf's women begin to kid him, since anyone who knows Alf at all has to know how hard he kids. Mona isn't to be shrugged off though, but finding myself liking her a lot better than I had the previous evening, I also wonder whether this new liking is really based on anything much more than her appreciation of my apartment and a touch of compassionate lust roused by the exposed backs of her thighs. She'd climbed the stairs like a kid, knees thrusting sideways and feet hanging loose, making the pompons wobble on the backs of her ankles. An unexpectedly tender motion, but she may nonetheless be hard as nails, since the physiology of character, however powerful its suggestions, is not to be trusted. I've switched from thinking about this though to thinking about when to ask about Gretta and how or what to ask when Alf asks me if I know where she's gone. Holding the welted edge of the beer can poised at his lips, he's watching me intently over it, and knowing whether he's testing me or simply nervous is no easier than knowing whether Mona really is more likeable than I'd first judged her to be. "She took off with Michael some time in the middle of the day while I was at the office," he continues. "There was a note when I got home saying she didn't know how long they'd be gone."

"She didn't tell me anything," I say, and am aware as soon as I've said it that this statement is too simple—that Gretta has certainly been telling me something. Telling me at the very least that something was about to happen.

Alf continues to watch me over the can a moment longer, then takes a drink from it, puts it on the desk, and asks where the bathroom is. I point him the way through the bedroom, and though he closes the door firmly behind him, the sound of his urine hitting the bowl in short bursts before it steadies is altogether audible. "Gretta's probably the only person in the world who could get him this way," Mona says, "which has to be a distinction of sorts. We didn't call on you by chance. The only accident was that you happened to be on the street when we arrived."

"I imagined so," I say.

"Alfred had it all figured," Mona says. "We'd come here, and if she wasn't here and you were, at least you'd know where she was. But he half expected she would be here, and didn't like that idea. He has very serious opinions about what's good for his sister, and her well-being really concerns him. Gretta must have some peculiar quality I don't get that elicits this protective response from men. From you too. You were paying pretty careful attention to her yourself last night."

When the bathroom door opens, she pauses, but her voice is slightly louder then when she continues. "I was just talking about the old-fashioned treatment your sister gets from both you guys," she says.

"I'd prefer that you didn't," Alf says, and sits back down again so tentatively that I suspect he doesn't intend to sit for long.

"It's okay," she says. "There are no gentiles present."

Alf's mouth clamps shut in distaste, and his evident determination to say nothing should be taken I think as cautionary. He's holding himself so tight over the edge of the hard wooden chair that his vertabrae show as a line of knobs under the elastic white of his Lacoste shirt, and his nose and eyes really loom now from the plane of his face. "If you do hear from Gretta," he says to me, "I'd appreciate it if you'd ask her to get in touch with me. She doesn't have a history of doing very well on her own."

This expression of a wish creates the opportunity of a response but doesn't require it, and as he waits to see if I'll take it up, on the floor next to the window, her arms around her legs hugging them to her thin chest, Mona watches us both and waits too. "Okay," he says after an interval, "I'm really asking, I guess, whether you'll let me know where she is if you do hear from her?"

"And I guess that depends," I say, wishing to be no more evasive than necessary.

"Okay," he says, in a way not to settle things but to put them in suspension as he picks up the half-empty six-pack and prepares to leave. An admonitory farewell.

4

WHATEVER THE INTENTION of Gretta's disappearance, one of its unexpected effects is to force me for a time Saturday morning to a remarkably precise sympathy for Alf. "Since she hasn't apparently chosen to tell you herself," Christine Kaplan says, "I don't think I should tell you where she is. You can understand that. But I'll tell her that you came to see me. That you were concerned about her."

She is being correct and even consolatory but not tentative, and the memory of my own reticence with Alf on very similar grounds only about twelve hours before makes me indisposed to try to change her mind. Like Alf too, coming to see Christine without much expectation that she'd tell me anything, I'd come without telephoning first —made the hot trip across the river with the distinct chance of not even finding her at home because I knew that on the telephone I'd certainly have short shrift. I'd also believed though that face to face there was a chance to gain something from Christine's rather antique courtesy, but what this actually comes to now that we are face to face, is a kidglove brush-off. This lack of success doesn't surprise me however, and I wouldn't have come to Christine for help at all except under duress.

I'd gone to bed the night before a couple of hours after Alf and Mona had left and gone promptly to sleep, but been awakened only minutes later by my own stifled call for assistance. I woke to the sound of an actual smothered cry, and though this wasn't the first time I'd been startled awake by dream-induced fears that throttled their own expression, I couldn't remember having dreamed this time and, perhaps for this reason, waking up was no relief. But I wasn't experiencing fear exactly either. It was rather more like a conviction of oversight—that I'd neglected to do something that required to be done at once. Even with this sense of deadline though, I didn't act quickly. The idea of talking to Christine occurred to me at some point during the night, but it was late morning before I worked up sufficient belief in this idea to make my way to the Square and then underground into the subway.

After six minutes underground, when the train surfaces to cross the river, a wash of sails flutters and bellies below me in the basin and up ahead a jet black crease splits the green shimmering end of the new Hancock Building. The spire of its predecessor, the monument of an earlier dinkier city, slides across its façade at the same rate of deceleration at which the train slows into the station. These images are fixed then when the train stops, and in this bright world of replication, I'm suddenly and inexplicably larky. Such fecklessness is always irrational, but it's particularly irrational now when it's induced by illusions that don't even pretend to be more than illusions, and by the time I've walked through the station and descended by a series of grilled passages like dog runs to the narrow sidewalk between the access to the Drive and the Charles Street Jail, the shimmer in the air is once more mostly carbon monoxide.

With my eyes and nose smarting and the traffic dinning in my ears, I bring a narrower, less imperial attention to bear on a middle-aged black woman waiting on the steps of the jail and a middle-aged white woman getting out of a taxi in front of the Mass. Eye and Ear each one holding a brown paper shopping bag containing, I conjecture, a week's supply of somebody's underwear and socks. But I deliberate this constrained possibility until I've made my way around the protuberance of the concrete addition to the hospital that has encapsulated the old brick front like a carcinoma, a smooth sheath over the old, more articulated hide. Once on the other side, my attention can broaden again to take in a vista of pastel-striped, buff and oyster apartment buildings on the plain that was reconstituted here a couple of decades ago after the swarm of the old West End had been wiped away. A total replacement ambiance has been created too—stores, restaurants, movie theaters, even, I've discovered recently, a semi-underground synagogue that is remarkably and confusingly like a miniature of the great temple at Karnak. Somehow everything that's been done here though still leaves the area so desolated that I can't pass it on the Drive, much less walk through it, without a flagging of my vital signs. Reminding myself of the utility of all this—that Christine, for example, can walk from her apartment to her lab at Mass. General in ten minutes, or drive in two or three minutes from parking garage to parking garage at night or when the weather's bad—isn't restorative at all, maybe because the banded cubes dingy against the heat-hazy sky, whatever the facts, still look uninhabited.

Though I've been here often enough with Gretta to know my way, I miss it this time, and having walked right past the street named for a great American transcendentalist into which I should have turned, I have to find my way back between the ranks of redwood cabanas screening the swimming pool. Real heart sinkers these, and a uniformed guard, posted next to the underground garage entrance, watches me with obvious suspicion until I identify Christine's building by the number in gold script over the doorway, and make a point of walking like a man who knows where he's going. I've anticipated the possibility of challenge though, and don't discount it entirely even after I've managed this purposeful motion. In the past few weeks I've been subjected to discriminatory challenge on several occasions, and haven't in the same time been smiled at once on the street by a woman I don't know. Both these changes seem attributable to the long cut on the left side of my face that I've carried away from my crack-up. The scar still hasn't paled much, and with this alteration of my emblematic self, I have to act what I'd simply seemed before, and haven't yet gotten my act very securely together. It works this time though, and I don't have to wait at the guard's post as I'd already pictured myself doing, while Christine is phoned and asked whether she's expecting a visit from someone named Harry Karp. My name in the guard's correctly neutral voice would I knew sound improbable even to my own ears.

The lobby of Christine's building isn't wearing well. The carpet is more scuffed than it had been the last time I was here, the imitation grass wallpaper loose in more places along the seams, and more names, telephone numbers, and political and sexual exhortations have been scratched into the enamel of the elevator doors. The doors themselves moreover have developed a stutter. But the gloom of the windowless third floor hall hides all such minor change, and its odor is familiar. A mixture, perhaps, of armpit and cauliflower. The button I push on Christine's door activates muffled, distant chimes—a sequence of notes that continues well after I've lifted my finger. I hear no footsteps then from the carpeted apartment, and the next sound I do hear is the drawing of a bolt. "Well, Harry," Christine says then calmly, "what a nice surprise."

She's wearing a yellow slack suit, her feet are bare, she holds her eyeglasses by one earpiece in her left hand with the end of the other earpiece in her mouth, and her face under its helmet of soft, pale blond curls shows no more surprise or pleasure either than her voice indicates. Since her courtesy is deliberate, and since she's always courteous, it's necessary to distinguish the forms of her courtesy. She's not being hostile, though she's capable of polite hostility too, but she is being effectively guarded. "Not at all," she says, when I ask her if I've come at a bad moment, and she opens the door further and takes her glasses from her mouth to wave me from the obscurity of the hall into the brightness behind her. The rank of windows on the far wall of the living room looks out into the glaring haze off the river from which I've just come and into which I anticipate a

quick return. This will not, I think, be a long visit. I'll ask
my questions, get what answers I can, and leave swiftly.

Christine precedes me into the living room, her bare feet
half hidden as she walks in the deep pile of the ash gray
carpet. The pair of couches to either side of the glass-
topped coffee table, one facing and one backed to the windows, are covered in a lighter gray tweed, and the walls are
off-white, and among all these close grays, the red and
purple anemones on the coffee table are a violent presence.
Even the cover of the medical journal open and face down
next to the anemones is gray. Christine places her glasses
on top of the journal, nosepiece on the spine, and we sit on
opposite sides of the table on the two couches. I face the
light, and Christine has her back to it so that stray hairs
form an aura around her head, and she doesn't wait for me
to question her. "I can imagine why you're here," she says.
"Nothing very much has really happened, though—not at
least yet."

Her equanimity is positive. She lays her cards on the
table, telling me at once and on her own all I think that she
intends to tell me, and doing it this way so that I needn't be
tempted to ask more. This can be taken as another aspect of
courtesy. But it is something more iron than courtesy too,
and her soft, virtually unlined face—the color of her skin,
hair, and even her clothing as close as are the coordinated
grays of the room—suggests such resolution as little as it
does her true age. I can no longer think what kind of a life
I'd imagine for Christine if I knew nothing about her.
Something more ordinary and genteel probably, but it
would be hard to specify. She looks I think like no one else
I've ever known. Sitting across from me now with her feet
folded under her on the couch, she manages this posture
with a kind of benign cockiness, her head straight up, neck
extended, and back stiff. But that erect and admirable torso
is also soft, buoyant, and reputedly knowing. Though she's
been divorced from a doctor named Max Kaplan for years,
according to Gretta she keeps the anomalous name of Chris-

tine Kaplan as a reminder that marriage is an unnatural condition. A heroic name therefore, and Gretta ascribes a heroically purposive career and freewheeling personal life to Christine also, though there's a trace of something in this ascription that I can't weigh accurately. On each of the occasions, for example, when Gretta has told me that I was making a mistake not getting to know Christine better, I've known that she was disappointed with me for some reason. Since Gretta makes no claims on me, such disappointments have to be expressed indirectly. Understanding this, however, doesn't much help me to understand what she's really saying about Christine who not only shows neither her age nor her mettle, but also looks, despite the varied history claimed for her, extraordinarily unused.

I'd watched the smooth, pink soles of her feet lifting through the pile of the carpet ahead of me as she showed me into the apartment, and even the skin over her Achilles' tendons was pink, as unblemished as if she'd never worn shoes. I'd observed this with particular attention, for I suspect there's something significant about the striking differences in structure and wear in this prominent thin-skinned cord—something that could in time allow me to make a judgment about women no less comprehensive, precise, or startling than the judgment I'd come on once in one of the minor journals of my beloved Stendhal, that the women of Angoulême have the finest eyebrows in France. Could, that is, if I did my research as Stendhal did his, which I don't. Christine's Achilles' tendons though are pristine, dropping without a fault in either texture or line from plump calves to pink, uncallused heels.

I thank her but say it's too early now when she offers me a beer, but that I'd appreciate a glass of water, and as she explains then why she doesn't feel she can tell me what Gretta's doing, I watch the tall, sweating glass travel on the thick, elliptical, sea green slab of the coffee table, a motion simultaneously circular and directional that leaves a wet, shiny trail, a snail's slick. Two ice cubes bob on the confined sway of the water inside the glass.

The visit seems to be ending even faster than I'd antici-pated, but as I contemplate my exit—seek a transition that will answer to the grace of her declaration of limitations—I notice that Christine doesn't really seem quite ready to have me leave yet. She seems to have something more on her mind and to be waiting for my full attention to tell me what it is—waiting out my interest in the errant glass that comes to a halt after a certain amount of circular motion but only a finger's width of progress. The rocking of the ice cubes has also slowed, and the surface of the water is almost still.

"Maybe I'm being overscrupulous," she says finally, "and should just tell you what I know and assume that you'll know what to do. Or what not to do really, since I'm cer-tain you shouldn't do anything. I don't share Gretta's love of mystery, and I have more confidence than she appears to have that you'd have her best interest at heart once you knew what that was. I don't assume that of Alf whom she's also left in the dark. He's earned her distrust, and you'd earn it too if you intervened in a situation she ought to handle herself. Part of the reason I'm tempted to tell you more is to make sure you don't do that."

I have to suppose she's levelling with me, and what makes this even more than ordinarily appealing is my unexpected discovery that she can be shy. Her pale skin has sanguined —her cheeks, her earlobes, and her throat where inner heat has also roughened the ordinarily smooth cool skin. This unexpected blemish seems part of her unexpected candor, and startles me. "I may know even less than you think," I say, meaning to be candid in return. "I'm not even sure I know what the problem is."

When Christine's eyes widen, her throat pales again as quickly as it had flushed. "Really?" she says.

"Really. Not only don't I know where she is, I don't even know why she went."

"How would you like to live under Alf's surveillance?"

My sudden optimism is reduced again by this question, the answer to which is too easy to tell me anything I don't know already. "I can find Alf hard to take even for an evening—or less," I say, adding the last two words when I remember that last night's visit hadn't lasted half an hour. "But Gretta's tolerated him for some time. Something must therefore have changed."

Something has changed here also though, and it's my candor that's now coming into question. Christine's skepticism asserts itself by stages. A flaring of her eyebrows that produces the beautiful reverse curve of classical architecture, and then a flaring also of the fine wings of her nostrils. These accumulating emphases actively question my good faith. If I really am as much in the dark as I claim to be, my ignorance, I'm being told, is at the very least peculiar. What I hear unsaid is that such ignorance must in some way be willed—that the skin of the world, its enchanting but also sparing veil, isn't as absolutely obdurate as I allow it to be.

The fact is that I'm perfectly ready to entertain such a charge or something like it, but at the same time that I don't find it necessarily accurate. I am, after all, confronted right now by strong contrary evidence. Christine herself may not be quite as she seems, but I have no real view of her beyond her veil, and that soft, lucent integument generates notions of touch and pleasure that are much more immediately convincing than any suspicions I have about her motives. "Gretta lives with the tick of the clock in her ears at all times," Christine is saying, "watching for signs that she'll have to catch right away when they do come and that can come at any moment."

If she's being forthcoming now, something critical is being withheld nonetheless. Presumably lightning has been discharged, but the air is still dark. "You really must know something I don't know," I say, and then add, not to sound unintentionally arrogant, "I mean something about Gretta."

To Christine now I apparently seem either persistently duplicitous or a fool. At least I assume that it is this constrained choice that makes her more nearly angry than I've ever seen her. "You puzzle me," she says. "You must know about Michael."

"Not necessarily."

"That he's an unclear case?"

"I really don't know what you mean."

"Not even that what must have been the onset occurred four years ago?"

She watches me for a moment before continuing. "I'm astonished," she says then. "It was right after the divorce, and Gretta and Michael were staying with me at the time. In Maine. The marriage had become such a mess before it was over that Gretta knew she was well out of it, but just when she was feeling better, Michael wasn't. Given the nature of what was happening to him, the divorce couldn't have had anything to do with it, but Gretta was of course sure it did. Michael was cranky, he was tired most of the time though he was also spending a lot of time sleeping, and he was eating or asking for something to eat whenever he wasn't asleep. He'd go through a box of Hydrox cookies in half an hour, then complain when there were no more, and at my place, where it's a six-mile drive to the nearest store, that was difficult. But Gretta was ready to make the trip to the store any number of times a day, and with her new energy of release, it didn't even bother her to spend that much time bouncing back and forth over a rough, dusty dirt road. The only thing that bothered her was Michael, and it didn't seem to occur to her that he might actually be sick."

Christine interrupts herself, to make sure I haven't heard this before. She continues to look surprised when I say I haven't, but she also looks pleased now, and her initial determination that I should know next to nothing has evidently become a determination that I'm to know all. "She hadn't noticed how frequently he was complaining of thirst, either," she says. "We couldn't take a walk without his complaining before we'd gone a quarter of a mile that he was hungry or thirsty or both. After two or three days this began to make me suspicious, and I told Gretta I thought we should take him into the local hospital for tests. Only the urgency I attached to this finally persuaded Gretta that we should do it. But, unfortunately, by conveying that same urgency to the resident who did the admitting, I alarmed him so much that he began treatment even before he took a simple sugar test and that made a certain diagnosis just about impossible. After a massive dose of insulin, Michael's symptoms cleared up in forty-eight hours and haven't reappeared since. The total state might develop any time from today to ten or twelve years from now however, and knowing that it's likely to come suddenly when it does come doesn't allow Gretta to relax much. Since she also doesn't want it to happen though, she tends to be skeptical about what she does see. The last few weeks she's been apprehensive but also suspicious of her alarm, and the combination has been driving her batty and was driving me batty too until I finally persuaded her yesterday to have him admitted to Children's for a workup. To answer the question you asked first, she's staying at the hospital motel and she'll stay there as long as Michael's in the hospital. If it turns out he's still okay and is discharged, which is possible but not what I expect, I might take them to Maine again for a few days. I have some vacation time coming, and though I hadn't planned to use it next week, I could arrange to. I don't think Gretta will want to move back into Alf's house right away in any event—or, probably, that she should."

I nod my head, and both the speed with which my perception has improved and the extent to which it has seem even to me to endorse the suspicion that I've known all this all along but kept the knowledge unacknowledged. That Gretta had already told it to me even if in her own way, or that Yoshalem had told me at the very beginning, or that I'd picked it all up myself from Michael's appearance and behavior. Yet I could also swear that I hadn't known, and even with this enlightenment I'm still uncertain of what I should or wish to do.

Christine however is willing to be clear about this for me. "I depend on you not to get in touch with her," she is saying, "or tell Alf what I've told you. The background of course he knows, but not where Gretta's gone or why she's there. He'd take over at once if he knew, and that wouldn't be at all good. She needs to act on her own, and even more to act for herself. What she needs also of course is a real job, instead of just being decorative in a gallery three or four hours a day while Michael's in school and quitting in the summer when he isn't. A real job would make her independent, and as long as she isn't that, she can't take help from anyone without risk of giving herself over entirely. That's what's happened to her in the past whenever she's asked for or accepted help—from men, that is. What little I can do is different. Women don't have much tradition of obligating themselves to other women. But if she asks help of Alf or you—and even more certainly if one of you presses help on her without waiting to be asked—historical bad habits are going to reassert themselves. She'll end up feeling grateful and betrayed, which is a rotten combination. You can understand that can't you?"

Of the two possible answers, it's certainly more accurate to say that I can understand than that I can't, but the constrained choice also feels bad. The way I've sometimes watched myself cause a student to feel when after a long explanation relatively uninterrupted by questions I ask whether whatever it is I've been explaining isn't now understood. In the still, cool, orderly room, the low hum of the air conditioner, a kind of white noise, is the only sound as Christine waits for me to signify my understanding and consent and, I guess, leave, but the dilemma her question poses has stymied my capacity for resolution. It seems difficult to say anything but "yes" or "no" so long as her question persists and equally difficult to go without saying anything. The dilemma dissolves though when the door chimes sound again, almost as muted and distant inside the apartment as they'd been from the hall earlier.

Christine's patient expectant smile is replaced by a grimace of disturbance. "Excuse me," she says, and she walks past and behind me to the door. Looking out the window then at the bright light over the river, withdrawing as far as I can, I hear Gretta's voice follow the sound of the door opening. "It looks like we jumped the gun," she says. "Unless something unexpected turns up, they're going to release him this afternoon. But I think I'll just keep my room at the motel for another day or two anyway if they do."

Her voice is charged, and when I stand up but don't turn around at once, to give Christine a chance to tell her I'm here, I hear the sibilance of what I take to be this warning before Gretta says, "My God, you called out the fire department!"

"I didn't call him, he came," Christine says, her voice dry.

When I do turn toward her now, Gretta looks unaccountably naked to me in a white Oxford man's shirt and denim skirt, and I also feel how she brings the heat of the street into the cool room with her. Broadcast, the impact of this caloric intrusion on my skin is startling and even abrasive.

5

GRETTA'S PACE until we actually get to the hospital doesn't give me much chance to say anything, and though I don't have a lot to say anyway in the way of statement, there are some questions I might ask her if given more opportunity. My call on Christine has left me needing to know why I've muddled around so long in a tricky half-light in which I've seen most of what there was to see but remained ignorant anyway. Paying attention is what I think I do even when I do little else, but bumping around in this obscure air, I'd remained persistently stupid for a remarkably long time. Wheeling out Storrow Drive now and through Kenmore Square in Gretta's VW, the top down and my head out in the hot, humid rush, I recall the contention of the old rag, junk, and bone collector in *Bleak House*, which I've just reread because I'm assigning it to my seniors this fall, that he didn't know how to read but wasn't going to be taught either because "they" might teach him wrong. I should know at least, I think, whether my own bum readings over the past year—functional illiteracy is, after all, what they've amounted to—are attributable to inattention or stupidity, or whether the text had been obscured for my benefit.

But if Gretta has managed to keep the nature of Michael's troubles from me all this time by intention and not mere inadvertence, it's hard to understand why she should wish to have me with her when she learns to what point these troubles have arrived. Her ruthless excitement suggests that she isn't quite as certain about this judgment as she'd told Christine she was. She's driving so fast that I keep expecting a police siren, and whatever the reason she's asked me to be with her when the authoritative report is delivered, I don't think it's in order to make amends. I've had an apology from her, but it's been an apology only of sorts. "Poor Fish, I've been mean to you," she said after Christine had explained the purpose of my visit to her—and told her also how astonished she'd been talking to me to discover how little I knew.

I'd taken this putative apology for amusement and not contrition, and watching Gretta behind the wheel of the red Beetle, which she likes driving I think partly because it's so obviously both too small for her and too humble, I'm convinced that she's behaving only as she wishes to, and that she's unlikely to do anything else right now. Her appearance in the low seat of the open car, with her skirt riding up over her thighs and the wind ruffling her casually buttoned shirt, is also a form of self-assertion. She doesn't even, I don't think, intend particularly to attract attention, and taking me with her to the hospital may not be something she's doing for me at all. It could be primarily a statement to Christine, who had not been at all happy that I was going with her.

The extent to which Gretta had tried Christine in a very few minutes couldn't have been inadvertent. Entering her apartment like a multiple counterforce—bringing heat into the cool, noise into the subdued quiet, disruption and contingency into its orderly arrangements—she'd announced at once that she could only stay a moment. Her car was illegally parked, she said, but that didn't actually matter since she had no time anyway. She never came past the vestibule even though Christine said that it would make whatever time she had to stay pleasanter for everybody if she came in and sat down, but fired off her news right there.

She'd come at all, she said, only because it was unlikely she'd be able to come for the late dinner for which Christine was expecting her. Nothing was sure yet, and she'd know more when she got back to the hospital, but it looked as though the tests were going to show up nothing new or decisive and that Michael would therefore be released that afternoon. This account was given with vindictive satisfaction. Her color was high, her eyes brilliant, and her attention kept moving out voraciously as she talked. The apartment was too contained for her, and I can see that this quick drive from the hospital and back again must, whatever its motives, also be a needed way to let off steam.

It would be hard for anyone to really meet her high charge now, but in the short time she'd been in Christine's apartment—not more than five minutes altogether—Christine had responded to it with mounting irritation that she both expressed and tried to suppress. Twice she asked Gretta to please stop twirling her keys, and each time Gretta stopped briefly and then started again. It made no sense, she remonstrated, for Gretta to drive all the way over from the hospital only to say something that could have been said just as easily on the telephone—and it was also just chance she'd been at home and not out doing the errands that she always saved for Saturday morning and that she'd been about to go out and do when I dropped in on her. Having deflected her rush of pique somewhat toward me, she'd then gone on to state more fully what she must have told Gretta in some abbreviated way already in their first whispered interchange at the door—why I'd come to see her, what she'd told me, and her discovery of my ignorance—and Gretta had then offered me her dubious apology.

She'd been too high to take in what either Christine or I might have thought or been feeling, and what Christine was very soon feeling as a consequence was distress. "I don't understand why you can't have dinner with me even if Michael is released this afternoon," she said.

"I guess I could if I brought him with me," Gretta said.

"That wouldn't, of course, be the same thing."

"I didn't think so, that's why I didn't propose it."

When Christine put a hand on Gretta's forearm, this might have been intended only to short-out her ruthless energy but it looked abject. "We do, after all, have some things we have to talk about," she said, "and it would be difficult to talk with Michael around. He insists on understanding everything."

"Of course," Gretta said.

Christine had then allowed herself to express some of the irritation that must have been her customary prerogative as the more executive of the two friends. "I can't plan to take you and Michael to Maine next week, and take time off from work on very short notice, unless I know what you have in mind," she said.

From irritation, her voice modulated back toward confidence, but this grasped advantage was fleeting and probably costly, for it seems likely to me that I'm on my way to the hospital now with Gretta mostly because Christine had made a false move. The only thing she had very certainly in mind right then, Gretta had replied, was that she had to be back at the hospital in about fifteen minutes for a conference at which she'd learn whatever there was to know. She could begin to think about other matters after that, she said, and she'd then turned to me and said, "Come with me, Fish. I can use moral support. And we know, because she's told us so, how busy Christine is."

"Oh, Lord!" Christine said, and there was an unexpected sound of pain under that strangely genteel complaint.

I had no prior claims on my time though, and welcomed the opportunity to find out more. Possibly even to come finally into a good light. I went down in the elevator with Gretta, therefore, without hesitation, and outside we found the guard who'd surveyed me on my way in surveying the red Beetle parked directly under a no-parking sign. Gretta said she'd been unable to find any other place to leave it for five minutes and thanked him for watching it, and he nodded and still seemed to be thinking about what to say when she started the car so fast that the squealing tires added a fresh whiff of burned rubber to the already burdened air.

Her rate of passage continues to be illegally swift until we have to make a left at the hospital motel, then a left

again in accordance with the arrow on the sign that says
HOSPITAL PARKING, and then a third left into the gloom of
the multi-level parking garage. Here she actually has to
stop the car and pull a ticket from a dispenser to lift the
black-and-white-striped barrier arm across the entrance
ramp, and the three left turns, the mandatory halt, and the
succession of tight loops by which we ascend the central
core of the garage, passing FULL signs at each level until we
emerge into the light again on the roof where there are still
some vacant places—all these together finally check her
momentum. When we've descended to the street then she's
less animated and seems to have forgotten about me as we
cross a congested intersection and go up a covered concrete ramp and through glass doors into the lobby of the
hospital.

Where we enter first, everything is familiar enough even
though I've never been in this particular hospital before—
the information desk directly ahead, and to the right the
gift shop bright with magazines, cards, and plastic potted
plants. But we don't linger in this familiarity. "Left," Gretta
says, signifying that she is at least somewhat aware of me
again, and I follow her through a long doglegged lobby
divided by couches, play equipment, and bulletin boards
into areas in which children play while adults watch them
or wait, each with unsettling intensity. Beyond this waiting
area, the lobby opens through two glass walls onto a multi-
levelled patio, an inner park with trees, shrubs, and grass
where some of the play equipment isn't easily distinguishable from the free-form sculpture with which the patio is
also furnished. Children on stretchers and wheelchairs are
taking the air on the patio, some accompanied by nurses,
and as we approach the elevators at the far end of the dog-
leg, two children cruise across the lower level of the patio
on scooters from which IV poles rise like masts. Plastic
bottles swing from the hooks at the tops of the poles, and
the plastic lines that drop from them flap like halyards as
the scooters bank around a curve. The two riders in their

white hospital robes are indistinguishably boys or girls.

I follow Gretta onto an elevator and then off again onto a corridor that belongs more readily once more to my hospital image, and the patients in the one-, two-, and three-bed rooms we pass are also distinguishable now as boys and girls, though their ages are less determinate. No longer children, they aren't grown yet either, and there's a lot more activity in these rooms than I remember from other hospital corridors, and more spillover into the corridors themselves. The atmosphere is neither hushed nor particularly orderly, and this absence of expected decorum is unsettling. I'm not convinced I should really be here—or that my curiosity about why a girl in one of the rooms inclined over a basin is blowing earnestly into a tube, is decent, since the two girls who share the room with her appear to have no interest in what she's doing at all. Then we turn off the corridor though into a private room not much larger than a closet, and Michael is sitting in a large chair beyond the bed that almost fills the room, wedged between it and the window. The broad flat wooden chair arms are both too high and too far apart for him, and his own arms are wedged between them with his elbows in his lap. He's been reading, and he's wearing blue-and-white broad-striped pajamas instead of the white hospital johnnies that all the other children I've seen have been wearing. "You're late," he says, and though he looks at me behind Gretta, he's talking to her.

"Come on, pal," Gretta says. "Five minutes?"

"Okay, but they came and left again."

"They?" Gretta says.

"The resident," Michael says, "the one who looks like Groucho Marx, and Dr. Yoshalem."

"They'll be back. I'm sure they haven't gone far," Gretta says. "I brought Fish along too."

"I see," Michael says. "It's going to be a big deal."

"For sure," Gretta says.

Michael can be no more surprised by my presence though than I am by the mention of Yoshalem, whom I'd thought

Gretta knew only casually as her brother's tenant. About this too I've evidently been in the dark, and when the resident who does have bushy black eyebrows, a black brush mustache, and a stiff inclination from the waist suggesting weight in the seat of the pants returns to the room with Yoshalem, Yoshalem is as unprepared for my presence as I am for his. "I didn't know you were going to be here," he says.

When I laugh he adds, "Yes, certainly," with a catch between the two words that is a tick of hesitation released when he raises his eyebrows, which further lengthens his long, flacid, putty gray face. "I'm not actually on the staff of this hospital," he says. "I'm only an invited visitor too. The case is Dr. Kornbluth's."

The resident, made uneasy by Yoshalem's deference, bends farther from the waist and paws his right foot. "There's an empty office next to the nurses' station where we could talk," he says.

"Why can't we talk right here?" Gretta asks.

Kornbluth looks to Yoshalem for adjudication, but Yoshalem only twitches his left eye and sucks his cheek, while Michael follows the exchange closely from his chair which is the only chair in the room. High-backed as well as broad-armed, enclosing as well as supporting, it is the presiding location. Gretta is sitting near him on the bed, Yoshalem stands at the foot of the bed with one long-fingered, soft hand on the rail, and Kornbluth stands next to him looking at a sheaf of papers on a clipboard but not, I notice, reading them. I've backed somewhat toward the door, to ease the jam but also to establish a more appropriate relationship for myself to what is to take place.

"Dr. Kornbluth tells me that the tests are not very decisive," Yoshalem says, and though he is talking unemphatically, his throat pulses and his words are accompanied by soft clicks and a light groan. "The results, that is, all fall within normal limits, but he thinks they support a finding of pathology anyway and suggests taking certain measures that a clearer finding would have necessitated."

"Because of the history," Kornbluth interjects. "The episode four years ago has to be considered a genuine onset, which means that he's been in remission. His symptoms in the last few weeks suggest strongly that that isn't going to hold much longer, and it would be prudent, therefore, particularly since he's already here, to begin proper management."

"Management?" Gretta says.

"I imagine the word has a bad sound to you," Yoshalem says. "But as we use it clinically, it's neutral. It recognizes that patient care has many aspects and that successful treatment is a product of a number of different measures. Dr. Kornbluth would like Michael to be put on a low-sugar diet, to begin small daily injections of insulin, and to test his urine regularly also."

"How would I do that?" Michael asks.

"It's very simple, really," Kornbluth says. "If we keep you in the hospital another two or three days, we can teach you everything you have to know about how to do urine tests, what to eat and what not to eat, and when and how to give yourself shots. A kid your age learns this stuff very fast."

"I wouldn't learn to give myself shots very fast," Michael says.

"Your mother could give them to you," Yoshalem says, "until you got used to them and decided you wanted to administer them yourself."

Gretta, who has been listening to Yoshalem and Kornbluth with keen but ambiguous attention, turns toward Michael now and smiles, but her smile isn't I don't think intended to encourage him—or not primarily to do that. It doesn't solicit anything from him either, and Michael's face remains unmoving except where in one corner of his mouth the lips roll in slightly, increasing his mouth's breadth. But this is a determining exchange nonetheless. "We could go on as we have been?" Gretta asks. "Doing nothing but being watchful?"

"I wouldn't advise it," Kornbluth says promptly.

"I understand," Gretta says. "But it would be possible?"

"Of course," Yoshalem says. "Dr. Kornbluth would consider the other course more prudent, however."

"I see," Gretta says. "What do you think, Michael?"

"I agree with you," Michael says.

"I haven't said what I think, have I?"

"Not exactly," Michael says irritably, "but I can tell what you think."

"I guess we wait then," Gretta says.

This time when Kornbluth looks to him for help, Yoshalem's face is already turned toward the floor and purposefully masked. "There's some risk in that procedure," Kornbluth says in distinct protest.

"Of course," Gretta says.

When Yoshalem continues to say nothing, Kornbluth says, "Okay, then. I'll take care of his papers and he can leave in about an hour. But you'll keep in touch with me—or with Dr. Yoshalem if you prefer?"

"She'll keep in touch with you," Yoshalem says, his diffidence giving way now to asperity.

The two doctors begin moving toward me, and I back through the door and into the corridor to make room for them. Kornbluth keeps behind Yoshalem, insisting that the older doctor precede him, but his deference is impatient and he seems to be pushing Yoshalem, who never moves quickly, through the door ahead of him. When we're all in the corridor—all except Michael, who watches us depart from his throne—we move four abreast, with me at one end of the line and Kornbluth at the other walking sideways, bent across our line of advance so that he can face and talk to Yoshalem. "You understand that I of course go along with this decision, but that it would not be my choice, and that it makes me uneasy," he says.

"I appreciate that—as well as your courtesy in allowing me to be here at all," Yoshalem says. "I'm sure you'll be kept in close touch with the situation."

"Messages can always be left for me here at the Adolescent Unit if I can't be reached directly, and I'll get back promptly."

"That's very good," Yoshalem says.

We part from Kornbluth at the nurses' station, and the resident, standing with his heels together, toes pointing out and bent stiffly from the waist, demonstrates an extraordinary reach as he extends his arm in its white sleeve past Yoshalem to shake Gretta's hand, then past Yoshalem and Gretta to shake mine.

Gretta isn't leaving, however. She only goes with us as far as the elevator where she asks Yoshalem if he can give me a ride back to Cambridge and he says he can. Something more pressing than my transportation obviously still concerns him though. "You're certain you want to do this?" he says to Gretta, his voice only barely interrogative.

"I'm sure," Gretta says.

"Why?" he asks, more decisively.

"Once it starts, he's going to be patiented all the rest of his life," Gretta says. "Soon enough, therefore, when he'll have to be."

"All right," Yoshalem says. "But you know it may come on, when it does, terribly quickly. You'll have to be vigilant."

"Haven't I been?" she asks—smiling broadly, almost laughing, but looking at Yoshalem with intense inquiry. "I'd say myself I've been grooving on vigilance for so long that I'm not sure I'd know how to kick the habit."

Yoshalem makes a wordless sound and looks at his feet again and when the elevator doors have opened, having stepped into the car with Yoshalem without saying anything because I feel supernumerary, I'm unprepared to have Gretta put one hand against the door to hold it back and the other on my shoulder. "I'd like to get Michael away for a few days," she says, "but I think I don't much want to take him to Maine with Christine. And not just because

Maine is farther than it may make sense to take him right now, though there's that too. Do you have any ideas?"

"I might be able to arrange something on the isthmus, the place I've told you about," I say, too startled to think until after I've said it about whether I really want to do this.

"That would be fantastic," Gretta says.

Her fingers loose their hold on my arm then and slide across my wrist, gratefully I think, and just before the doors that have been framing her face close across it, I say, "I'll go down and check it out tomorrow."

6

"HE HAD A GENIUS for making anything he talked about not matter," the girl says, "so that after a while we might as well have been reading telephone books. When one of the guys gave us a reading in the lunchroom one day from the *Guinness Book of Records*, stuff like someone hiccupping for nine days seemed a lot more exciting than transcendence in *Wuthering Heights*. You know, hiccupping had a lot more urgency."

I realize how emphatic my concurrence is when the girl, who has looked away from me most of the time even when she's been talking, turns toward me abruptly from the aisle seat, her eyes startled in the circumscribed portion of her face visible within the two panels of hair closed in her fist at chin level. The weight of these resilient yellow falls overcomes their disposition to kink or curl, creating two cascades of shallow waves instead that just leave her eyes, nose, and mouth uncovered before coming together in her hand. Meanwhile her other hand keeps touch with a white Angora cat inside the leather satchel in her lap. The cat had been entirely covered, invisible, until somewhere near New Bedford when it had raised its flat face to a breathing slit left unzipped in the bag, and the girl, her own hair held then too in one hand, had used the other hand to part the hair from around the cat's eyes and peer into them.

Before she took the seat next to me, while the bus was still at its berth in the terminal, she'd asked me whether I was allergic to cats, but we hadn't talked again then until we were approaching Jericho when she asked me, without turning toward me and without preface, what I did, and when I told her after the moment it took to be certain she

was talking to me that I was a teacher, she'd talked about
the nursing school she was going to that required her to
take general education courses in the summer, and about the
summer term she'd just finished, and how she was going to
spend the last couple of weeks of summer that remained
now until the regular term began with her family at Jericho.
The panels of hair drawn taut still alongside her mouth
muffled her speech, and her body was muffled too by the
granny dress that covered even her feet when she was
seated, a net shawl across her shoulders secured over her
chest with a gold diaper pin, and a neckerchief the ends of
which were drawn through a gold ring that she fiddled with
as she talked, slid up or down. Even before we began to
talk I'd found myself wondering about that obscured body,
imagining the quality of the warmth produced by the soft
weight of the cat in her lap to which I attributed the faint
mossy fragrance I'd been breathing under a stronger fragrance of patchouli. The combination, alerting as well as
agreeable, had worked against my disposition to sink into
the soft buoyancy of the ride and fall asleep, and her conversation then had really been alerting. Listening to her talk
about her teacher's failures of urgency—the word obtruded
from her generally easier idiom—I felt the harsh tingle of
hyperventilation.

The girl settles back into her seat again after checking
my emphatic response and remains settled until the ocean
makes its appearance between the two sawed-off hills above
Jericho when she leans forward to look past me out of the
green tinted window. Across an undistinctive landscape of
residual farms, split-level houses, isolated strips of roadside
shops and quick food restaurants, the ocean asserts a commanding presence, and the girl's response to it is even transmitted to the cat, which raises its obscured face through the
slit now and revolves its head to look back and up at her.
"What's her name?" I ask.

"His," she says. "Everyone makes the same mistake
though, I guess because he's so soft and silky. It's Nicholas,

and I don't know another guy I'd trade him for."

Because she's no longer closing the panels of her hair in her hand, I both hear and see her more clearly, and hear and see too the mixture of complaint and amusement in this assertion. She's younger than I'd thought, and her face, once her hair has fallen away from her cheeks, is unexpectedly and pleasingly round. "Here we come," she says to the cat, pointing it still in its bag toward the windows and the channel visible a half mile ahead and to our left now before the road turns left, where what I know to be a dozen or so cottages jammed together on stilts appears at this distance to be a continuous, unidentifiable, skeletal structure. "Have you been here before?" I ask.

"This is the first summer of my life I haven't been here," she says. "When I was in high school I even worked summers waiting on table at Barney's. You know Barney's?"

"I've seen it from the road."

"It's the pits," she says. "But anyway, it's here."

The bus slows, its brakes exhaling plaintively, and before it's actually come to a halt at the approach to the causeway in front of the bait shop, she's said goodbye and has the pack off the overhead rack and slung over her shoulder, over the net shawl and the granny dress, and the bag with the cat in it under her other arm, and is moving down the aisle of the bus with a complex gait, her weight shifting laterally as well as forward. Once she's climbed from the bus then, crossed the excrescent sidewalk, and passed between the bait shop and Christy's Take-Out onto the sand, she stops to lift her feet behind her one at a time out of her sandals that she slips into the bag with the cat through the breathe-hole. She works her feet in the sand a moment, flexing her toes, then sets off to walk the couple of hundred yards to the head of the channel where, with the tide near dead low, she can cross the flats and come back again along the other shore. The channel is about fifty yards across at this widest point where the bus, a few minutes ahead of schedule, idles at the curb.

Though the cottages have devolved now into separate structures, it's also a fact that the decks reach farther and farther across the short stretches of sand between them each year and diminish their separation, and in the year since my last visit, tv antennas, flower boxes, weather vanes, wind bells, and picture windows have also proliferated. The new windows are bordered irregularly by pristine shingles, their brightness slow to fade even here along the water's edge where weathering is rapid, and the raw oiled boards of the new stretches of deck also glisten conspicuously in the sun. The decks are sparsely populated now in the late morning, mostly by the old and infirm who can't take a full day out on the beaches or fishing. Directly across from me, four geezers in swimming trunks are playing cards at a round picnic table under a striped umbrella, three of them shirtless, their smooth slack torsos tobacco-colored, and the fourth sporting a Harry Truman shirt with large red flowers twined in glossy green leaves unbuttoned and open across folds of belly. When the girl has crossed the flats and come most of the way back, one of the shirtless players looks up from his cards and waves to her.

The number of bungalows stilted over this unstable sand has remained just about constant for all the years I've been coming through here, but the bungalows themselves have changed—not only grown, but sometimes also shifted location, lowered onto rollers and dragged some limited number of feet or yards along the sand by a tractor to be raised then by jacks and have another set of piles built under them in order to achieve a change of view or reorientation of neighbors but no real change of ambiance or even intimacy. Intimacy has to be the condition of relationship here, for the houses are clustered so close that it's actually possible now, with the expansion of decks, to jump in some places from one to another. Any radio or plangent bedspring will be heard in half a dozen houses at once, and coming by at night the previous summer I'd seen the blue glow of a tv in a house toward the back of the settlement through a series of aligned picture windows.

But this is also the way anyone would choose to live I think if they could tolerate it—cheek by jowl, flank by flank, every body at the same communicated temperature. Such tolerance is no longer, if it ever was, a general human capacity however, and I don't imagine even the families in Jericho as living in an unfailing harmony of warm somnolence. I think of them rather as having an acquired or developed capacity to shout and clobber in full view and hearing of neighbors who also shout and clobber—a public venting which because it is public is also relatively shameless and harmless, perhaps even positively salutary. Such at least is the possibility I try to hang onto, and the girl with her goods on her back and her white cat bagged under her arm who can hardly wait to return for more seems to bear out this comforting notion.

It's frustrating therefore to have the bus roll away from the curb and cross onto the causeway before she's made her way fully back into the settlement and I can discover under which particular set of antennas and weathercocks her taste for urgency has been nurtured, or through which picture window she's viewed the restive bay which has never in all the many times I've seen it looked quite the same twice. The causeway is two narrow lanes of concrete bordered at its shoulderless extremes by a low barrier of steel posts and cables. This built-up ribbon is a battered survivor, its edges chewed, crumbled, and crenelated by the water's frequent assaults, and its surface is so pitted and wavy from inundation that we sway and pitch even at half speed. The slow motion—and the fact that slumped in my seat I overlook the edge of the causeway from the window next to me and see only beyond it—creates an illusion of marine travel, and I can easily believe that we are moving on the choppy surface of the water itself.

Gulls bob in the weedy shallows, and farther off a tuxedoed kingfisher rises from a weir pole, flies a wide arc with rapid wing beats, then folds its wings and dives and is lost

in reflected brightness somewhere on its way down. With
the midday sun warm as well as bright on my face and
without the girl to alert me any longer, I feel myself turning drowsy, the passing view out the window less and less
compelling. Losing urgency is in fact the way this feels as I
watch five figures of assorted sizes, probably a family, grub-
bing for clams along the crescent shore, a bushel basket on
an inner tube drawn along behind them to store their haul
cool. Having glided past rearward, they are succeeded by
what might be a green heron poised in the marsh grass,
though at the distance from which I view it, and viewing it
lazily, I could be seeing only a stone with a reed behind it.
Then the heron, if it is a heron, is gone also and there are
clammers again, several groups of different sizes, each coherent but vague against the broad expanse of the flats,
drawn together by the universal-ubiquitous constructive
principle which is more or less balanced in my experience
however by an also powerful principle of repulsion. A
strenuous dynamic that actually produces, I suppose, an
equilibrium of sorts.

As I begin to drowse, my attention reverts, slides away
from the scene in front of me to the conversation just behind me first, and then, from the girl's talk about her teacher's failed grasp on urgency, it slides still farther back until
it fetches up on the petulant face of Steve Randolph who,
even though I'm not actually going to have to see him again
this year, has apparently kept a clear place in my mind.
Perversely but not inexplicably, Randolph's face has remained with me this way when the faces of most of the
students I taught last year have sunk along with their names
into the benevolent semi-oblivion that is a teacher's counter
to mental population glut.

The student who causes uneasiness or discomfort though
is at least as likely to evade this general oblivion as the one
who gratifies, and Randolph's fitness for mnemonic survival
depends entirely on nongratifying attributes. Tall, with a
broad soft body and ruddy cheeks, he projects a clear air

of entitlement, and he'd come to see me the very first day of school last September to make an appointment to talk about the books he'd read over the summer. I'd suggested to my junior class the previous spring that each of them talk to me about a summer reading list of their own choosing and then talk to me again in the fall about what they'd actually read, and most of them, after coming around promptly enough in the spring, had been a lot slower in the fall. But not Randolph. After presenting a more ambitious list than anyone else, he'd gone on to read most of the books he'd listed and he wanted to talk about them. He'd read enough to take quite a bit of time just citing titles—novels mostly, but many of them long novels—and making brief remarks about each that were consistently intelligent if also a little bland. All I had to do was draw him out occasionally or express approval, but we were talking at the end of the school day and in mid-September in mid-afternoon the low sun suffuses my room at Hillside with viscous warmth. The air has the thickness of liquid but no buoyancy, and I was soon so heavy-headed that I knew it was lucky Randolph required no more response from me than I could manage by now, after having taught at Hillside for over a decade, virtually asleep. I felt benevolently grateful to him for doing so much reading, for talking about it with such spontaneous ease, and for requiring so infrequently to be corrected or even shown where he was missing something. He required, in fact, not much more than a semblance of audition—or that was all he required at least until, approaching the end of his list, he said as though it were an afterthought but with the guise of accident so unconvincing that it was obvious to me even half asleep that this was his predetermined destination, "Oh, I almost forgot, I read another book we didn't put on the list. My first Dostoievsky novel, *Crime and Punishment.*"

The rise in intensity as he said this promised an increase in demand that I knew I was going to find it hard to meet, and just the need to pull myself together to try to meet it made me resentful. "That's quite an extra," I said. "What did you think of it?"

"I don't know," Randolph said, balking finally at taking the burden for intelligence entirely on himself. "I don't seem to want to think about it in any of the ways I'm used to thinking about other novels I've read, ways you've taught me and Mr. Johnson and Miss Brower. The book bothers me. Isn't Dostoievsky saying that virtue is meaningless unless God exists?"

"Let's say he has Raskolnikov thinking about that," I said, and falling back on this pedagogic old chestnut, I reached hard into memory at the same time to try to meet Randolph's question more particularly. "As Ivan does of course in *The Brothers Karamazov*," I added, when this came to me next.

"I haven't read *The Brothers Karamazov*," Randolph said, "but does that really make any difference? A lot of what bothers me is that I can't think about *Crime and Punishment* the way I can about other novels."

Some additional heat spread across the back of my neck now which, unlike the sun's heat, came from inside. "Tell me better what you mean—what you can't or don't want to think about," I said.

"Well, I don't see that it makes any difference to know or remember that it's Raskolnikov who thinks this in *Crime and Punishment* and some other character who thinks it in some other novel. I'm sure it's what Dostoievsky believes. He doesn't keep any edge over Raskolnikov the way you showed us last year that Dickens did over Pip. He doesn't use that kind of irony. That's what you said it was, didn't you, in *Great Expectations*, an ironic view? But I don't think this is anything like the same, even though I know Dostoievsky is supposed to have learned a lot from Dickens. Since reading *Crime and Punishment*, I haven't been able to figure out if I believe in virtue myself if God doesn't exist, and no other novel's ever done anything like that to me before." He finished decisively, looked past my shoulder out the window behind me though he didn't appear to be looking at anything out there, then started again. "I stopped believing in God when I was nine years old," he said, "but I didn't think that not believing in God might mean that it was silly to try to lead a good life. I always used to think I'd be a doctor some day, but I don't know about that anymore. The end of the summer was pretty bad."

If he'd only managed to look just the least bit tormented, something more might have gotten to me even through my torpor and the conversation might have opened up. But he didn't look tormented at all. He looked querulous, and, along with the touch of whine in his voice there was also, I thought, a certain sound of satisfaction at having achieved this difficulty. His physique counted against him—the large, soft, well-proportioned body and the ruddy cheeks—and even though his madras shirt and chinos were sweated through in places, he still looked meticulously dressed at the end of a hot day. In class the previous year, conscientious and ambitious but never incisive, his intelligence had seemed something he possessed but didn't quite inhabit, an instrument placed at his disposition, entitlement too. Sometime around Christmas he'd started coming to class with prepared questions or topics for discussion that generally had either a biographical or a moral bent. Could Dickens have written *David Copperfield* if he hadn't worked in the blacking factory? Was the class assigned a Shakespeare play to read because Shakespeare was supposed to give them more human understanding, or were they only reading him for pleasure? The questions, though generally addressed to me, were public questions and their simultaneous ambition and blandness made me dread seeing his hand go up—not waving or pumping but just moving slightly from side to side, patient and steady because he was certain no one else in the class was capable of asking his question before he asked it himself. Which was correct. No one else in the class would even begin to think of Randolph's questions.

His question this time wasn't quite the same though. It

had edge whether or not it was felt, and it wasn't foolish. But the difference only made it harder to tolerate. It felt outrageous to me to have Randolph question me this way without even a class as audience to make it possible to think of the question as a piece of civic virtue or philanthropy— to be asked to believe that this ultimate question didn't just interest Randolph, but that it possessed him more or less the way it had possessed Dostoievsky. Possession was after all an absolute.

But the very idea of possession is foreign to my homey classroom at Hillside. After years of mid-morning snacks, the air of the entire school smells of grape jelly when it's hot, and in this fruity medium, my head and eyes weighty, my difficulties in dealing with Randolph were physical first of all. That I couldn't just put my head on my desk and take a nap was evidence enough of his capacity for bland imposition, and inclined toward me across the desk, pressing me in this way too though he was still looking out the window, his soft firm face close up was clear-skinned and smooth, unmarred by a single hickey. His eyes were clear too, the whites uniformly opaque and unveined, the pupils dark blue with flecks of golden brown, and it was this unblemished health as much as anything else I think that I was finding intolerable, that his capacity for imposition, for pressing, for taking himself at utmost weight, should leave him so clear-eyed and unworn. If my own eyes hadn't been so heavy and the gravitational attraction of the surface of the desk to my head so strong, my response to Randolph might nonetheless have been more kindly, better disposed, but these very physical facts insisted that there was some essential disparity between intense health and moral intensity of which Randolph had no inkling. Dostoievsky, after all, was an epileptic whose body had been half shot before he was thirty—and also a gambler drawn obsessively to ruin. "You have to remember," I said, "that Dostoievsky's intelligence was as extreme as his life. In his fiction he doesn't seem much interested in any intelligence that isn't exacerbated.

Do you know what I mean?"

"The word means something like aggravated, doesn't it?" Randolph said.

Correct without being addressed to what I'd wished to ask, this answer in the form of a question couldn't temper my impatience at all. "That's right," I said, "and unaggravated people ought to be able to live with a lot of the dilemmas that Dostoievsky's aggravated characters find it hard to live with. I've managed not to believe in God myself for a long time now without murdering anyone. But also, wasn't Raskolnikov a little mixed up about just why he had to kill the lady pawnbroker?"

"Yes," Randolph said.

He'd looked sulky on his way out then. Not morally let down, I thought, but rather as though he felt he hadn't gotten his money's worth. This impression however was too interested to be depended on. There had after all been a suicide at Hillside a couple of years before and psychic blowups of various degrees of earnestness were recurrent features of the school's life. Before going home therefore I stopped in the office to find out where Randolph lived and then drove some miles out of my way into the broadlawned back regions of Belmont to attempt the conversation we should have had already but hadn't. Only when I found the right street and cruised it looking for the right house, I spotted Randolph under a backboard attached above the doors of a three-car garage playing rotation basketball on the blacktop with a couple of other boys both of whom were also Hillside students. The sharp pop of the ball against the backboard sounded unmistakably derisive to me, and I accelerated again and kept going, and the next morning in class Randolph was clear-skinned and cleareyed as ever in a fresh madras shirt and fresh chinos.

A single incident and it had had no perceptible consequences, but I'd been having a recurrent dream for several years by then, starting the year I'd returned to Hillside from law school which was also the year Janet and I had split. In the dream, which has only insignificant variations, I'm standing in front of a class of fresh-skinned glossy-haired students all of whose faces show intense embarrassed confusion. It's the first class of the year and none of the faces is very well known to me. I'm telling them what I think we'll be doing together this year and what I hope to have happen, and I think I'm talking simply and clearly and not saying anything I haven't said so many times before that I shouldn't even have to think about it, when one of the students—and each time so far this has been a girl—raises a hand. "Sir," she says when I stop and recognize her, "we're finding it hard to understand what you're saying."

That is the teacher dream, and it's displaced another dream that goes back at least to sometime when I was in high school, which was a student dream—having to take an examination in a room with the windows open and the wind blowing, holding down the examination with one hand and the blue book with the other and having no way therefore to write the answers to the questions that are racing through my head. Once I'd had the teacher dream I never had the examination dream again, but the two dreams are also very different. The first was a dream of frustrated ability, and the second is a dream of loss.

7

THE LAST STRETCH of the trip after the causeway is high-speed travel once more on a good blacktop road bordered by gravel shoulders that warps its way in long gentle bends through flat bottom land—meadows mostly, spotted with fawn-and-white and brown-and-white Jerseys and Guernseys and an occasional black-and-white Holstein, and lush still even in August. Off to the right the meadows extend to salt marsh first and then, in a middle distance, to tidal river. The green is punctuated too by well-maintained barns and silos and by occasional high trees with sloppy crows' nests in their upper branches, flattish clutters of dead leaves and twigs, and in this easy country the bus doesn't have to slow again until we approach the stop at Solway's garage where Dolly, lounging by the jeep on the cement apron beyond the gas tanks with her beam against the near fender, doesn't even budge when she sees me, though her solid weathered face does open into a grin. An ironic grin, I think, which may have some immediate cause or may not, and when I dismount, kiss her, and tell her how good she looks—by which I also mean how good her full, soft, dry cheek feels to my lips—she replies that she always takes good care of herself. The dry tone of this has a sound of admonition, but for the next few minutes then, in the jeep, we make no attempt to say anything more over the furor of the engine and the more amiable body rattles. But the hard suspension, however much it deters speech, puts me in another kind of communication with every bump or hole in the road. What would be punishing over any long distance is for the short run to the camp only one more aspect of the benevolent particularity I associate with the isthmus, and

it's my tenaciously held-to notion that the isthmus is altogether particular. That it has its own landscape and smells,
its own limited but emphatic spectrum of colors, and its
own weather. I can tell myself with real conviction that
every day here is distinctive—not always good, but char-
acterizable—unlike most other places I know where days are
simply all right or not all right, and are largely lost as a
consequence.

Never having vagued on the isthmus, I believe that I
never would, and that this advantage derives directly from
its special character. Even its discomforts have value, and
the shocks against my coccyx now seem obviously preferable to the cushioned ride I've just concluded in the bus.
Each neural twinge is response to a touch from wherever
we are at the moment. The Greyhound's insulating float
had me nowhere, and sliding toward sleep as a consequence
as soon as the girl with the cat got off at Jericho, but now,
bumping and knocking along and with the engine hot and
redolent as well as noisy, I'm happily alert. Not so alert
though that when we swerve into a driveway the sudden-
ness of the turn doesn't compel me to grab the dashboard
with one hand and the door frame with the other not to
pitch out the space where a door should or could be but
isn't. "What's up?" I ask into the immediate area of quiet
when the engine noise seems not to die but to jump away
from us up a hillside to where a backhoe is trenching the
slope below a big, square, yellow Victorian house.

"He was at home shingling the roof with Stevie when I
left," Dolly says, and I realize that the man on top of the
green and yellow John Deere, only his head and shoulders
visible over a high unclipped privet hedge in late heavy
bloom, must be Les.

The arm of the machine, jointed like a grasshopper's leg,
shudders now and then lifts and extends, raising the bucket
too over the top of the hedge, and when Dolly says she's
going to find out what's going on, I get out of the jeep too
and follow her up the hill and through a gapway in the

hedge into the yard. The rank odor of the privet, the blossoms mostly gone by and brown, almost covers the exhaust fumes from the backhoe which has its two downhill wheels off the ground and its weight braced on the stabilizers as the bucket strikes into hardpan. The seat is turned to the rear, facing the hoe, and with his back to the larger bucket that acts as a counterbalance, Les is manipulating a brace of short canted levers with ball handles. When he lowers the inverted bucket of the hoe again and brings it back toward him, its teeth clank through the stone-packed dirt and the long jointed arm curls on itself at the wrist and elbow with nervous delicacy.

"He keeps his touch," I say.

"He'll still offer to shave you with it," Dolly says, "but less and less is it a picnic for him anyway, sitting up there in that noise and stink making a bunch of linked elephants act tactful."

Complaint, boast, and amusement are audible in this statement in indeterminate proportions, but when Les lets the engine idle and stands up to turn the seat around, I can see that he's diminished again and that his face has undergone further erosion. He spots us and salutes with his left hand, but his runnelled cheeks remain stiff and unexpressive as though their erosion limited mobility. Then he turns the key in the ignition and the machine, which had settled back on its wheels taking all weight off its stabilizers, shudders and goes inert though it continues to issue cracklings and small pressure noises.

"You made it," he says.

"No trouble," I say.

"You won't see much of him though if you're working," Dolly says. "I thought you were going to knock off for the day—except maybe for helping Stevie some."

"I was, until the man's crapper backed up." Gesturing negligently behind him with his thumb, he specifies the incontrovertible.

"Okay," Dolly says, "we'll go along. But we'll be waiting

for you for lunch."

"I'll take a break as soon as I uncover the cap," he says. "Shouldn't be more than half an hour."

Following Dolly down the hill again, I decide that they're probably all right still even though Les looks shorter to me as well as thinner than the last time I saw him and Dolly, from the rear, is as broad as a mare. It's hard to see how a system by which one wanes as the other waxes can operate indefinitely, but so far at least they've both retained swagger, and this similarity within difference seems to make for some kind of equity. Neither of them can ever have been exactly pretty, but each has a swarthy knowing glamour that can even cause strangers to take them for cousins or sometimes brother and sister. Each goes his own way too without much effort to be ingratiating, though for Les this has become a somewhat dogged procedure I think that generates a lot of impatience. He shows his impatience for us to leave now by the ostentation with which he watches us down the hill and into the jeep before restarting the backhoe. Coming back to life then though, retracting its stabilizers like a giant beetle and moving around to approach its work from a different angle, it wheels with unanticipatible speed and agility on the steep hillside.

"We play a game," Dolly says, easing the jeep back onto the road. "I do what I can to keep track of him without making it too obvious that that's what I'm up to and he does his best to keep me in the dark about his whereabouts without making it too obvious that that's what he's up to."

The noise as she accelerates now excuses me from response, and after another short stretch of speechless driving, we're onto the isthmus proper, a corridor of sand and scrubby vegetation between the large breached pond and the ocean. Soon then we turn off the hardtop onto a couple of tire tracks over sand and coarse beach grass that pass a line of cottages before reaching what Les, harking back to his boyhood in Alaska, calls the Camp, though the house he's building here is going to be appreciably larger than any of the cottages along the way and solid enough to be comfortable as they are not even during a February nor'-easter. A certain working mess or squalor also distinguishes the Camp from its neighbors. Heading for a white flagpole with a gold ball at the top, the flag stiff out to the northeast now in a good southwest breeze, we pass the cabin, the outhouse, and the toolhouse before we park just behind the large new shell which was still being framed when I'd been here last but is now closed in. Windows and doors are in place and primed, and the back wall is almost half-shingled. Bricks, cement blocks, shingles, two-by-fours, and tongue and groove boards are stacked in orderly piles in the yard and a cement mixer covered with a green plastic tarp stands near the back door, but there are curtains behind several of the windows.

"You're really in?" I say.

"Sort of," Dolly says. "We moved in officially a little more than three weeks ago."

"And the cabin's empty?"

"Not exactly. We've left most of the furniture in it because just about any of it we tried in the house looked like hell. That means that it's the house that's just about empty. I go back to the cabin whenever I need to be cozy—or even if I just want to get away from all the constructive activity."

She looks up as she says this toward a boy in bathing trunks with a nail apron around his middle who's appeared over the ridge from the far side of the roof and walked part way down toward us. "Gramps had to go out on the backhoe," he says. "Somebody's septic tank backed up."

"So I gather," Dolly says. "We ran into him on the way back from Solway's. Do you remember Harry?"

"I think so," he says, but he doesn't make much of it, and turns quickly and climbs the roof to disappear again over the ridge.

"One of Mary's boys?" I ask.

"Stevie," Dolly says. "I told Les I'd gotten too fat to

climb a roof, so Stevie's helping him shingle up there at two fifty an hour while I work on the side walls. He's saving to buy himself a motorcycle. When he's old enough to get a license, that is—but you'd think the bike was going to be waiting for him at the end of the last course, the way he goes at those shingles."

"I wouldn't mind doing some shingling again myself while I'm here," I say. "I don't think I've forgotten how since last year."

"Fine," Dolly says, "with me. But you're not going up on that roof either—not with your accident record."

"Oh, that," I say.

"Yup, that," she says. "Let's have a look at you head-on."

When she moves closer to me now, her eyes are no longer taking me in as myself, making a whole from the parts. Instead, they examine a discrete portion of my face only, and when she places her blunt fingers on my left cheekbone, they feel dangerous to the still tender scar even though she's fingering me lightly. "It's not so bad," she says ultimately.

"So I've been told."

"It even looks familiar."

"Hmmm," I say, but not skeptically.

There have been a lot of reactions to my new look in past weeks, most of which I can't recognize, but this is one I think I do recognize but haven't heard before. Dolly squinches her thick-lidded eyes and observes me more generally again. "Okay, more later," she says. "I've gotta do something about lunch though now so it'll be ready when the work force arrives."

"I'll give you a hand," I say.

"Don't," she says. "Take a look around the mansion instead so you can tell Les how beautiful it is when he gets here."

8

WAKING UP to the scratch of bird nails on shingle, I know where I am. The cabin is the only place I've ever heard this ultimately dry sound before, but on the cot in the loft, inside the V of the exposed rafters, the accumulation of trapped warm mid-afternoon air makes it difficult to wake decisively. Inert, I find time to listen not only to the birds' scratching close above my nose but also to the unexpectedly decisive impact of their feet, the electronic whine of bees working the honeysuckle behind and below my head on the other side of the wall, and two hammers tapping across the yard, shingling.

The hammers would indeed have made it difficult to sleep inside the house, and a lunch of meat loaf sandwiches, apricot pie, and ice tea, eaten at high speed, had completed my need for a nap. Less than half an hour elapsed between the time Les drove up on the backhoe, climbed off and slouched across the yard looking as though he needed oiling, and Stevie climbed down from the roof and reported how many bundles of shingles he'd laid that morning to the time Les was gone again and Stevie was once more on the roof. The sturdy food was packed away without ceremony and almost without conversation, except when I remarked as Dolly had suggested I might on the progress made on the house since my last visit. When Dolly remained at the table to smoke a cigarette after Les and Stevie had departed though, I stayed with her.

"You don't have to hang around to help me clean up if that's what you're doing," she said. "I don't find kitchen work a hardship, maybe because I don't do that much of it. I don't altogether work half as hard as Les does."

"He's okay, though?" I asked.

"More or less," she said, "or would be if he'd let up some."

"Could he?" I asked.

The question had caused a soft contraction in one side of Dolly's face. "I'd have been pig happy in the cabin indefinitely," she said. "But Les figures that settling for anything less than a real house is settling cheap, and that has to mean thirty or forty hours a week on the backhoe and pounding nails evenings and weekends."

She took a last drag at the end of her cigarette, and, as she stubbed it out, smoke drifted densely from her mouth and nostrils. "He doesn't figure things very well," she continued, "but whenever I think about telling him that he ought to cut down I remember that we've made it for thirty-seven years now, sometimes just barely, and neither of us has ever been able to tell the other one what to do in all that time. When we've tried it's never helped, and it's sometimes also caused a lot of grief. What I do let myself do now though as I told you, that I wouldn't have done before, is try to keep an eye on him. I don't like him to be working Sundays because Sundays he has no helper, and works alone. That's why I pulled in before to check up, and I'll find some excuse to drive by there again later if he doesn't get back early. Evenings too when he goes onto the beach to fish if he doesn't go with somebody I go along and sit in the jeep and pretend to be watching the birds, though I still don't know a sanderling from a yellowlegs and couldn't care less."

Her concern was laced with an exasperated consciousness of easier possibilities, but she kept her manner inexorably laconic and turned away from further strain to this control by telling me that I'd probably better go take a nap if I was to be of any use to her shingling later. "You'd better nap in the cabin too for now," she said. "With Stevie knocking on the roof and me then after a while on the wall, it wouldn't be very peaceful in the house no matter how splendid it might be. Which reminds me—that was nice what you said about the house at lunch and I'm sure Les was paying more attention than he pretended to."

Effectively dismissed, I went over to the cabin where I ignored the old sagging double bed downstairs and climbed into the loft where I'd slept on both the past occasions when I was here. I must have fallen asleep within seconds of hitting the cot, so that it isn't until, awake again now, I notice the mirror fastened between a pair of rafters over the head of the cot, that I remember Dolly's remark that the change my face had undergone hadn't made it unfamiliar. Looking up, I see my face framed inside the chrome edging of the cheap glass, and though I've looked at myself too attentively in the past few weeks to be surprised by what I see, I find it freshly interesting. Shaving every morning has taken particular attention, to work alongside and not across the long scar that starts near the outer corner of my left eye and descends in an easy curve to the left corner of my mouth, and the way the scar is defined still by small hairs projecting to either side of it is evidence of this respect. In fact the scar has dimmed and faded enough to owe a lot of its definition now to these bristly borders. The assiduousness with which the surgeon had closed the gap torn by the broken windshield, however, has changed the left side of my face even more significantly than a more prominent scar alone could change it, by drawing the skin tighter over its bony underpinnings. In effect, I've lost binary symmetry. It's conjecturable that the left half of my face has evolved from the right, but to think about it this way is also to reverse the historical process by which the smooth-masked right half, the face of the well-nourished but deracinated American Jew, evolved from the highly articulated faces of my European forebears.

I assume Dolly has noticed specifically what I've been noticing myself but no one else apparently has, that less than six months after his death, my father, Irving Karp, is being reincarnated. I detect ways in which my body too is

becoming more like his—veins emerging from the concealing flesh of my legs as they had from his legs in middle age,
striations appearing in my thumb nails that I remember
seeing on his thumb nails, even liver blotches appearing in
the same proportions in the same places I remember them
on his torso: to the left of my navel, over the right breast,
on the lower curve of the right buttock. Twice in the past
month I've even been awakened at night by my body's en-
actment of a gesture that I identified as I awoke as one of
his gestures, though one I hadn't recalled before—a neural
twinge of shoulder, neck, and face—and this memory being
incorporated in me by violence, is reclaiming me from the
estrangement of the last couple of years of his life.

Actually though this is more than reclamation, since it
affects emblematically an intimacy that never quite existed.
We Karps had been a constrained family, and when first
my older brother, Ben, and then I slipped away, to college,
neither of us ever really came back. Our departures had
been quiet but decisive, and the same could be said for my
mother's departure a decade later, though the mode of her
departure at the age of forty-eight, by way of a massive
unpredictable coronary, was even more clearly decisive.
Thin, dark, and rather pretty in a distracted way, she was
the most suppressed member of the family, and she had
seemed to me to entertain a more or less perpetual suspicion
that there was something she wished to do that she couldn't
remember. This might have been because she'd really had
less and less to do most of the time I'd known her, deprived
progressively by my father's financial success of the only
way of life she probably wanted, or at least the only work
or function for which she was prepared. She was always a
somewhat more vivid presence during the intervals when
we didn't have a live-in maid—those black, Irish, or displaced Polish women, generally young, each of whom,
whatever their differences, became a disgruntled, slovenly,
obtrusive presence in the house after a longer or shorter
time—and I remember too a characteristic injection of rest-

lessness into her lassitude that I associate with late afternoon, and particularly with winter afternoons when early
darkness brought me into the house well before dinner. My
father habitually took a 5:32 train from Grand Central and
was home an hour later, and my mother's restlessness began,
I came gradually to realize, when she could imagine him
emerging from a grilled elevator and then from a narrow marble-walled lobby onto Seventh Avenue south of
Twenty-ninth Street to walk to Grand Central—a walk
which, along with the same walk in the opposite direction
in the morning, constituted his chief exercise and recre-
ation.

I was in the army and Ben was already in Alaska when
my mother's coronary took her off. Took her off, it seemed,
like a willing passenger, bewildering my father who was
prepared to accept anything that came his way but expected always that it would come on schedule. I have little
idea even now what his feelings for my mother were, but
I'm pretty sure he'd been unthinkingly faithful to her and
certain he'd expected to spend the rest of his life with her.
When that expectation was destroyed, he sold the house in
New Rochelle and moved to the city that he'd left twenty
years before on his way up in the world, except that he
didn't return to the Bronx but moved to Manhattan, to a
two-room apartment with a closet kitchen in a West Side
residential hotel. Visiting him there, I slept on a daybed in
the living room, except when I visited with Janet, when he
took another room in the hotel for us. Most of my visits
had been made alone though even after I was married, and
they were quite regular, but though we were closer to each
other in these years than we'd ever been before, our closeness was still without intimacy. One of its few avenues of
expression, however inadequate, was swimming together in
a pool in the hotel basement—a dark, booming place with a
mirrored ceiling in which you could follow yourself and
dodge traffic if you swam on your back as I always did after
a while for relief from the rigors of the crawl. I'd start by

doing as many laps of the crawl as I could for my father's benefit, which was generally a number more than I'd have done for my own pleasure. My father swam only breast-stroke—the appropriate stroke for his short, thick, muscular body—and he took a lot of satisfaction in my classy crawl. It was probably a demonstrable return on his investment in three years of expensive summer camp, but there was more to his satisfaction I think than just seeing this return on his money. His own body had been made strong by the stringencies of his early life, but he did little to keep it that way—partly on principle or prejudice. He judged team sports brutal and possibly overdeveloping, and games like golf and tennis stupid, or effeminate, or both. Walking and swimming were the only forms of exercise he approved of for thinking men, and he'd encouraged Ben and me to swim long before he sent us to camp. I was about four when he took us swimming in a ship's pool on our way to Bermuda. The ship was, I suppose, one of the round-bottomed Furness Line cruisers designed to traverse the shallow water of Hamilton Harbour and consequently not at its best in a rough sea, and this was an Easter vacation—a time for equinoctial storms, though it was also more specifically, the first time in our family's way up in the world that we took a winter vacation. The other, more knowing passengers let us have the pool to ourselves one day for reasons that became abruptly apparent, but that my father, never having been on a pleasure ship before, couldn't have anticipated. The sea was rough and the ship was rolling, and as we climbed into the pool on one side, the body of water retreated from us, piled up on the other side leaving us all but dry, and then combed over on the return roll and crashed onto our heads. Irving Karp grabbed his two small sons before we could be washed away from him, and securing us against his hard round torso under water, each under one arm, carried us to the surface and pushed us—first me and then Ben—up the ladder we'd just climbed down. But I can't, curiously, remember being frightened at any time.

What I remember instead is my intense comfort even under water in that embrace I'd never experienced in anything like that way before or was to again.

Our closeness certainly had no such access in the years my father lived alone in The Granger where his two rooms didn't any more belong to him at the end of his time there than they had at the beginning, and I recall with particular dread the flowered cretonne draperies and slipcovers that went to the cleaners regularly once a year though they never looked as though they'd been used. I visited arduously in those rooms every couple of months all the time my father lived there. Somewhat less arduously when Janet was with me, since she would find things to talk to my father about, or do a crossword puzzle with him—but her absence then made the lack of access between us even more marked.

When I visited alone, I'd generally fly to New York in the early morning and fly back again the same evening, and though my father and I would say little to each other in the course of one of these long days, we observed each other so closely that on one early spring visit I knew almost as soon as I arrived that something had changed. My father was wearing a camel's hair jacket without lapels over a blue sport shirt, gray flannels, and desert boots. Desert boots! Even in shorts he'd always worn lisle socks with garters and the blunt-toed black shoes he bought two pair at a time once a year at a Rogers Peet sale. His yellow-streaked Bismarck hair that grew low on his forehead crowding his eyebrows, and which he'd had cut in the same shop in the Graybar building next to Grand Central Station every other Monday morning for years, taking the 8:05 when we were still living in New Rochelle instead of the 8:36 those mornings in order to arrive at the office as usual at 9:30, was full behind his temples now, scissored rather than clipped, and his nails were manicured—not just shaped but buffed too. When I detected the odor of some expensive aftershave as well, I guessed the nature of what had happened even though it had never occurred to me before that it might. Not to my father. Not at least in anything like the way in which it apparently had happened. For he was obviously in the transforming grip of passion.

It took me most of the day though, a Saturday, to be told anything. I left Boston on an eight o'clock flight and was in The Granger before ten, and we sat for a couple of hours on floral cretonne, had several cups of coffee, and said nothing significant. When we decided to take a swim before lunch then, I managed only a couple of fast laps before I had to turn over on my back, and watching myself lolling in the mirrored ceiling I also watched my father swim up alongside me, head high and feet low, lunging up out of the water with each frog kick and then pulling himself down as well as forward with his arms.

"You don't swim like you used to," he said, dropping his feet to tread water, his massive head with the new, fuller wings of hair at the sides only inches from my eyes. "Are you okay?"

"I'm fine, Pop," I said.

"You pooped out awful fast. I can remember you used to do ten, twelves laps anyway."

"I know, Pop, I'm getting old," I said.

Jets of air from his scornful nostrils drilled holes in the water. "You got up in the middle of the night to get on that flight," he said. His short body was still thick, hard, and all of a piece now in his middle sixties, and when he breast-stroked off again, rising and sliding back, he made a lot of motion in the water without much strain but achieved low forward efficiency.

After lunch we walked across the park to the zoo, but breakthrough still didn't come even though we stood around the seal pool for a long time in the warm spring air both, I think, waiting for it. We were most of the way back to the hotel before he said he hoped I'd stay in town into the evening and join him for dinner with a friend, and that was the closest he ever came to an announcement.

I stayed, of course, though I'd come in early that morning meaning to leave before dinner, and I had my first view of Sophie in a French restaurant on lower Sixth Avenue that had been at the same location for years and still retained a lot of old-fashioned lustre. The walls of the several large connecting dining rooms were paneled in dark wood, the white table linen was heavily starched, and a cut-glass bowl of black and green olives, scallions, radishes, and celery over ice glittered prismatically on each table, the colors of the vegetables intensified by both the glass and the ice.

My father was obviously known here, and when the head waiter informed him that "the lady" had already arrived, I was encouraged by the fact that his friend wasn't too guarded to arrive before he did and wait for him. When I saw a woman with slanting eyes and a high-cheekboned face then watching our progress through the intervening dining rooms with candid interest, her appearance encouraged me too for similar reasons. Our passage behind the head waiter was slow, for though the tables were generously spaced, waiters and bus boys with large trays exercised their claims on that space without undue deference, which gave me time to begin to absorb the situation. It seemed neither inappropriate nor disagreeable to me though it was a surprise that my father should have a still desirable friend, a dusky-skinned woman with Chinese eyes and black bobbed hair, and it wasn't until we neared her that I detected the slight sag of the flesh under her strong chin and that there were wrinkles around the corners of her eyes that must have taken time to be engraved there. When we'd almost reached the table she stood up, a distinctly sumptuous figure in a high-necked black crepe dress, and I saw that she was also half a head taller than my father.

She was a model on Seventh Avenue where the idea for models was not the illusion of flesh, as it was for photographic models, but flesh itself. I learned in the course of the evening that she was in her early forties and that she came from Iowa City where she'd married a dentist, had a child, lost the child, and gotten a divorce. She'd been in New York for a number of years supporting herself by work that was both disagreeable and poorly paid, and when my father had met her the previous winter she was taking night-school courses in design, but she'd since given them up. She and my father had had an arrangement for some time already, and they were married the following fall, right after Thanksgiving, and lived together in the same two rooms in The Granger until April when they moved into an eighteenth-century saltbox house in Connecticut.

Their life there was obscure to me even when I was still seeing them regularly. The house, though small, was larger and a lot more attractive and comfortable than the two rooms at The Granger, but it never looked much more as though it belonged to them. Most of the furniture had been bought with the house, including some good antiques and a lot of heavily upholstered couches and chairs with good linen slipcovers. It was a congenial enough setting, but I couldn't imagine what it was a setting for—what my father and Sophie did there, how they used up their time. Along with the house they'd acquired the services of Les and Dolly who lived a couple of miles down the road but across the tracks. Dolly cleaned and did some cooking and Les, who worked five days a week for a heavy-equipment company in Bridgeport, cared for the grounds after working hours or on weekends. But Les and Dolly also became my father's and Sophie's friends—the only friends they had in Connecticut so far as I could tell, though they had a lot of cocktail party acquaintances. Semi-retired, my father went to New York only two or three days a week. Sophie either went in with him or met him there for part of the time—and they kept one room in The Granger, and went to the theater in the evening and ate at expensive restaurants.

But in Connecticut where they were most of the time, so far as I could tell they did next to nothing. My father acquired a dog and a thorn stick and he walked the acreage of his modest estate in corduroy trousers and heavy shoes, deciding with Les where second growth should be cleared and where new trees were to be planted, squiring. He also maintained a correspondence with the State Department of Agriculture and did some business with a nurseryman in Newtown. One fall he took up shooting, but when he caught his thumb in the breech of a shotgun, tearing the tendon, he decided hunting had been a mistake. And Sophie kept a horse and some chickens and took piano lessons. That, so far as I could tell, was all they did. Or had done. For in the last couple of years when I'd seen very little of them—because my divorce had been incomprehensible to my father and made him intensely uncomfortable, and I'd found it too hard to manage this discomfort—even this activity must have been reduced. Les and Dolly retired to the isthmus about the time I was divorced, and though my father had made their move there possible by selling them the piece of property for what he'd paid for it just after the war, which by then was a fraction of its worth, their going must have been a deprivation for him and Sophie. Another couple had been found to do the work Les and Dolly had done, but they didn't replace them as friends, and my father had begun to slow down about then too—become dimmer, stiffer, more nervous. He continued to assert when I talked to him, which I did less and less frequently, that he was happy, and I didn't doubt that this was, in some way, true. But the quality of this happiness, as I could imagine it, enforced our isolation from each other. I acquired very little direct knowledge of him during this last couple of years before his death in April, and his death had been a strange reversion—a remarkable duplication of the coronary that had carried off my mother, whose name, Leah, he called out just before he died. The only word, Sophie told me, that passed his lips in the course of his swift flight. Sophie had been awakened by the noise of his labored breathing next to her in bed, and he'd been dead then within minutes, before the doctor she called could reach the house.

9

AFTER A FEW MINUTES I'm enough awake to swing my legs off the cot and climb down the ladder into the cooler air below where I can come to more fully. Waiting then for this to happen, I admire the cabin's ingenious comforts, which gives me occasion to wonder also that the new house promises to be so different. It had seemed inexorably bleak when I'd walked through it before lunch, and however premature that impression may be when the walls and ceilings are still untaped panels of Sheetrock and I'm walking on plywood subfloors, the new sectional sofa facing a new twenty-four-inch television in the new, otherwise empty living-dining room doesn't suggest much help from finish. If the cabin is on the small side for comfort, the house is even more plainly too large. I'd wondered particularly about the three upstairs bedrooms, empty also except for Stevie's sleeping bag and pack in one of them. These are in addition to the master bedroom downstairs which contains only a brand new king-size bed and an assortment of cardboard boxes.

The cabin is of course unfinished, but unfinished is its style. Built as a garage to be camped in until there was a house, its interim use had been almost too successful. A larger two-car garage is under construction below the house, and the cabin is to remain a cabin. That it's to be an income producer justifies leaving it furnished as well, and though it's probably true that none of the battered goods around me would look right in the house, they might do something for it just by looking inappropriate. In addition to the four bedrooms with their associated bathrooms and the living-dining room with a fireplace and a bay over the water, there's a large up-to-the-minute kitchen and a smaller room that's fated to be called the den.

Put to its makeshift purposes, the garage and its loft are too crowded to accommodate any notions but need and use. Comfortable notions. The sink, stove, and refrigerator along the east wall have counters between and cabinets above them and the workbench along the opposite wall has shelves under it. An ordinary double bed and a painted bureau in intimate proximity jam the low end of the room under the loft floor, a mini-television hangs from the edge of the loft over a wooden table and four wooden chairs, two nonmatching splayed easy chairs that resemble slipcovered mushrooms sprawl on an oblong island of worn maroon carpet, and a potbelly stove squats behind the chairs and is vented through a tin panel replacing one of the glass lights of the garage door. Nothing here is gratuitous unless it's the silhouettes of tools on the wall above the bench to either side of the single window from which the tools they once located have been removed.

I'd visited here last with Les and Dolly about a year ago. Les had taught me to shingle and we'd shingled a couple of walls of the outhouse, but mostly we'd loafed—beaching ourselves stupid in the sun, fishing, and doing a lot of sociable eating and drinking. I was hardly ever alone, and never felt much wish to be either. Even when I woke on the cot in the loft at night and heard the two of them breathing, snoring, or turning over just below me, those sounds were so reassuring that after a while I was waking simply to hear them and go back to sleep.

The foundation for the new house had been poured only a few weeks before, and the walls, framed but not yet boarded, were a skeletal cube, a lacework of possibility through which even the ocean was still entirely visible. Now most of those possibilities have been foreclosed, and the large empty actual house that stands in their place also obscures a large piece of water. The difference feels bad to me. Will Dolly say any more about it than she has already?

She likes to talk, and particularly to gossip, and I have some number of things I'd like to have conversation with her about that might or might not be considered gossip.

When I come out of the cabin now, she's sitting with her back toward me, legs hanging over a plank suspended between two ladder jacks set along the near wall of the house, shingling. Stevie is at it too, the regular triplets of his hammer audible from the far side of the roof—a tentative stroke to start a nail and two quick ones to set it. Two of these triplets in rapid succession are followed by a brief pause to place the next shingle, and though Dolly's hammer makes the same pattern of sound, her pauses are noticeably longer. Working surely but without his enthusiasm, each time she reaches for another shingle she allows herself a slump that could be principled self-sparingness but might also be simple sloth.

This invisible difference interests me, and my interest in both Les and Dolly is pretty consistently more than casual, though I also entertain some skeptical questions about it. The world I perceive is inhabited by discrete persons no two of whom seem to behave or manage themselves in significantly similar fashion, but for a few years now I've held to the conviction that there was something exemplary about Les and Dolly that made them deserving of special attention. The very unlikeliness of this conviction may be part of course of what makes it so attractive, and when I cross the scruffy yard to the stage now to tell Dolly I'm reporting, I'm nervy with attention.

She on the other hand takes my presence here at nothing but face value. "Okay," she says, "there's a hammer for you next to that ladder."

What could be simpler? When she points to her right without turning around, this shift causes the stage to dip and rise, and she puts her hands down to either side of her and holds onto the plank until I climb on and slide a bundle of shingles to the center between us.

"Move easy," she says. "It'll hold us all right, but it behaves like a trampoline."

"Don't worry," I say. "I'll be gentle."

The wall we're to shingle jogs back about a foot from the main wall and is only one story high. It's a run of about fifteen feet, and starting from opposite ends we'll work until we meet, then slide back to our respective ends with a handful of shingles, raise the firring strip five inches, and start again. On my first course—I wait to begin until Dolly has finished the course she's on—it takes concentration to remember what I'd learned first a year ago and not done since. I both see and hear that I'm not being very efficient, and when I meet Dolly I'm still well on my side of the middle. After a couple of courses though I set up a rhythm, and I can even generally pick up a next shingle of the right size on the first or second try. I'd liked this dumb, repetitive, self-justifying work when I'd tried it first a year ago, and though Les had told me then that everyone enjoyed shingling once, I find myself liking it again in much the same way. On the fourth course I meet Dolly at midpoint, and when I've moved back to my end of the stage and helped raise the firring strip once more, I'm relaxed enough to stop work for a moment and look past the corner of the building along the shallow curve of the beach that extends more than a mile south to the harbor. The southwest wind, piling up the haze, has confused the distinctions between sand, sky, and water, and the old, white hotel on the hill behind the town—long and low as an ocean liner, and with a superstructure like a ship too—floats on a cushion of haze. Three stories high except at its center where a short fourth floor is surmounted at its center in turn by a cupola, its windows are arranged symmetrically, in vertical as well as horizontal ranks, though a porch roof separates the first- and second-floor windows, and those on the third floor are roof dormers except at the center where the roof jogs up another floor. Dormers are cut into this roof too, extending the vertical lines of the windows on the three floors below. Serene and ghostly, the white-walled silver-roofed structure is twenty-two windows long, and twenty-two white, wooden columns, each centered on a window, support the porch roof. I was still a boy when I'd counted them first, and though each time I return I expect the hotel to have burned or evanesced in some other manner in my absence, it is once more still here today, neither more nor less spectral than I remember it.

The town too at this distance is ghostly and unchanged, but there are houses on the intervening dunes now where there was only fluted sand and a fine whiskering of beach grass when I first came here, some of which are prepossessing as well as new. The nearest one is a pickled wood box, blind on the back side except for a clerestory under the eaves, though the side facing the ocean which I can't see is, I know, all glass.

We spent a succession of vacations when I was a boy in the cool, breezy frame hotel that smells still in my memory of iodine from the sea and of the damp coco matting runners in the halls. The isthmus is in fact the one memorable place of my childhood. The very frequency of the limited daily events of my existence in New Rochelle has long since all but wiped that life from my mind, but the events I associate with the isthmus were just repetitive enough to be poignant. The three or four month-long vacations we spent here—and there were also shorter ones later—persist for me as my one keen experience of family life, whether despite or because I'd been here most of the time only with Ben and my mother I don't know. My father had joined us only weekends, and my mother had I think had a weekday admirer—the nice but I knew even then ineffectual eldest son of the proprietor of the hotel. The wrinkled droop of the skin under Arthur Weber's quiet eyes suggested defeat, and it must have been a very limited flirtation he conducted with my mother. But at the time it caused me vivifying sensations to know when there was dancing for the adults in the living room evenings—there would be puzzles and games in the dining room for the children at the same time—that through the glass doors separating dining room and living room I would see Arthur as his duties allowed dancing with my mother, his flaccid right cheek on her thin silky cap of black hair, eyes closed, the visible portion of his face radiating contentment.

Contemplating the beach delays me though, and when I finally galvanize myself and meet Dolly again, I meet her once more at dead center but she's gotten there well ahead of me and stopped to wait. This course is just about at eye level, and she announces that we're going to have to raise the stage if we're to continue to work sitting down and since she's only going to work sitting down, it's a good time to take a break. Elbows on her thighs, head almost against the wall, at maximum rest, she cups her cigarette against the wind in her right hand and watches me rummage for a shingle to fit the gap between the meeting ranks without trimming, find it, and place the two nails carefully, six inches up and an inch from each edge.

"I thought you might have forgotten," she says.

"I get a kick out of it," I say.

"Even those little cedar splinters sticking in your hands?"

"Sure. Why not? They make my palms feel acute."

She laughs, but the need to talk that had been exacerbated each time we approached the center of the stage—where the dip of the plank drew us toward intimacy the way the hollow in the middle of a mattress draws two sleepers—but had then been sufficiently appeased by small talk to allow us to draw apart again without saying anything isn't appeased this time. We're thigh by thigh in the low of the dip, and the sustained nag of this finally compels a question. "When did you see my father last?" I ask, knowing that she'll know I don't mean the cosmeticized face in the satin-lined casket we'd both seen in April in the funeral parlor in Stamford.

"February," she says. "At the annual party."

"I wasn't even sure they'd given it this year," I say. "That's how out of touch we were."

III

She takes a drag of the cigarette, holds it, then clenches her mouth and expels the smoke from her nostrils, thin and mostly air. Where the smooth, browned flesh settles into her jaw, the harsh line of the bone is broken by small dewlaps, and she turns this warrior head toward me now, but not so far that we're actually looking at each other. "It was bigger than ever," she says, "but they seemed to know even fewer of the guests. You should have been there even if he was giving you a hard time."

"That wasn't exactly it," I say, but don't say that what had kept me away was my perception of the hard time I was giving my father, and not by anything I did or said that might have been remediable, but by the nature of my existence. I'd become essentially troubling to him and decided, seeing this, that staying away would at least keep the trouble less fresh. Though this couldn't mend the situation, it might I thought make it easier, but I'm not sure any longer that it really was easier this way either for him or for me. My perception of the trouble I was causing him had been determining, however—and that we could find no way to talk about it. Staying away though had only made the trouble more diffuse, not less pervasive, and I have to wait now for it to wear itself out through the inevitable but unexhilarating offices of attrition.

"Okay," Dolly says. "I'm sure I don't understand. But do you want me to tell you about the party?"

When I assure her that I do, she takes off her glasses that she's been wearing to shingle with the earpieces pushed up through her hair to cock the lenses so that she can look down through them or out over them, and lets them fall onto her chest from the short chain that links the ends of the earpieces. "You know pretty much what it was like even though you weren't there," she says, beginning conventionally. "Those parties never changed much, except that as your father got older most of the guests got younger. Not many of them could have been within twenty years of him this time. The men were mostly lawyers or stockbrokers or in advertising, and they almost all worked in New York. Close to half of them must have been wearing those fruity plaid pants, and their wives, most of them blonde one way or another, favored good wool skirts that showed their tennis legs. You know the type, and you can imagine how your old man stood out in a crowd like that. Sophie too but him particularly. He was wearing a checked sport coat and gray flannels, and he circulated but was having a hard time I thought remembering names. Sophie stood in front of the fireplace looking friendly and waited for people to come talk to her. Sound familiar?"

"Entirely," I say, knowing also that Sophie's dress had been either the same high-necked black dress she'd worn the first time I saw her or one so much like it I wouldn't have known the difference except for the triple string of pearls my father had given her after they were married which she wore tied to fall with the knot between her breasts, pressing the resilient black cloth taut across them. She wouldn't just have stood in front of the fireplace either, but she'd have taken a stance there, one foot heading forward and the other a half step off to the side, the height of the heel creating a continuous gleaming line on the forward leg down the shin to where the toes began and disappeared into her shoe. Her foot tendons stood out through the sheer black of her stockings, sharp and not quite parallel extrusions that intensified the black of the nylon where they pressed, and her weight was disposed in a sequence of reverse sweeps—the swell of the full calf, the bow of the thigh, the hollow of the drawn buttock—resolving in the concavity between the dips of her rib cage. And my father would have been looking at her with abject pride whenever he wasn't making earnest attempts at conviviality or even as he made them, observing her from different vantages as he moved around the room.

"Everything was more or less the same, then?" I say.

"I wouldn't quite say that. Not everything."

"What then?"

"It's hard to say," she says, and the impatience in her voice is accompanied by a slight thickening of her jaw muscles, a reflex of opposition because I've urged her to finer discrimination than she's inclined to. "It wasn't change exactly, because it was all familiar, but there was more of it. Your old man was always high-strung, but this time he was more so. They didn't really need me to help them with that party at all, and Sophie only called me because he'd been after her for days, worried that she and Marge, the woman who worked for them after I left, wouldn't be able to manage alone. I got there the afternoon before the party and Sophie, Marge, and I spent the whole evening making hors d'oeuvres with your father wandering into the kitchen every little while to see how we were doing. He'd come in scratching his seat the way he did when he was jumpy—you remember how the skin would be twitching all over his face —and ask us what it was we were making or how many we were making of each kind. Then, during the night, just after I'd gone to bed in the sewing room, I heard him come into the kitchen again. I knew who it was because of the shuffle. He'd stopped lifting his feet much, the last couple of years. I heard him open the refrigerator door, and when he kept it open a long time I figured he was checking to see if we'd made what we said we were going to make. Whenever we told him how many of any kind we were going to make, he thought we should make more, and I guess he was afraid we hadn't done it. We mostly had though and they must have been eating hors d'oeuvres three times a day for a week after the party."

"That all sounds familiar enough," I say.

She holds up her right hand now instead of continuing, pointing with her index finger, and I hear the steps coming toward us across the roof before Stevie appears at the edge, first the toes of his sneakers and then his trunk and face. He still has a boy's smooth skinny body, but where knots are beginning to form in his forearms and biceps the veins stand out thick and blue against the fine skin as he leans over and the blood rushes into them. The wind whips his lank hair across his face and he paws at it to keep it away from his eyes. "You guys getting ready to knock off?" he asks.

"We're just taking a break," Dolly says. "Don't tell the boss we were goofing off when he gets back, and don't please go walking around on that roof as though you were on flat ground. The only way I got your mother to lend you to us was by promising we'd send you back in one piece."

"I'm not going to fall," he says, and disappears, though we hear the sound of his feet moving up the roof again.

"I guess we could slap on a few more courses," Dolly says, "and then if Les hasn't gotten back I'll take a spin to see how he's doing."

"Okay," I say. "But was it only the business about the hors d'oeuvres that you noticed? Or that and the shuffling? None of that sounds too bad."

She puts on her glasses again, sliding the earpieces back up through her hair until the jeweled nosepiece is propped across the bridge of her nose, and I remember how she'd looked sometimes in the kitchen with Sophie checking a complicated recipe that intimidated her. Her face has gone blank or hidden that way again now. "I'd say he was a little jumpy about Sophie too," she says finally.

"With cause?"

"I doubt it. Sophie isn't any spring chicken herself, and I don't think that kind of thing was ever something she went in for much. Even if it were, she was just as much off her turf in Northtown as your father. But I'd say he had it on his mind just the same."

"That doesn't sound too happy."

I can see that she's still thinking because her face is still distant, but all she says is, "Let's get down and raise the stage."

"Okay," I say. "You first."

When she's climbed down the ladder at her end, I swing

my legs over and drop to the ground, and as we face each other to lift the plank evenly and not dump the stacked shingles, she says, "I don't think it was so bad, really. I think maybe it helped keep them both going."

The rush of ease, that I know even as I feel it won't last, makes me want to touch her while it does, hug her perhaps, but my hands are occupied. "Tell me, Dolly," I say instead, "how can I get to be like you when I grow up?"

She only grunts at the other end of the plank, straining to reach the hook of the jack over the proper rung of the ladder.

10

"WITH THE WIND coming out of the east," Les says, "we can cast half way across the pond and still never get a bump."

This is his third or fourth version of the same judgment, which can be intended I assume only to temper my efforts, since his own are already moderate. Even with the wind behind us he's been casting short, and his plug has just splashed down a few yards beyond me and to my left though he's standing behind me on the beach to my right. It pops back through the mild chop now on a diagonal that I have to sidestep to avoid, placing my waders cautiously between the smooth, shifting stones that cobble the bottom.

The previous summer he'd still just about made up on skill what he no longer had in the way of strength, but now the eleven-foot rod is clearly too much for him. Pushing it, he gets little action, and the high lob of the plug is short both on distance and on control. He's in fact a menace to be near, but each time I move to keep clear of him, he squints into the low sun to see where I'm going and then closes the gap, keeping up a steady stream of statement that it takes effort to hear over the light wash of the surf through the breach. What I do hear clearly though is the threatening whir each time his plug goes over my head. Once the monofilament settles in a faint whisper across my shoulder, but since he's nearsighted yet insists that squinting does him as much good as glasses, he fails even to see me brush it off.

The only bluefish caught on an east wind, he reiterates, closing on me once more, are singles—strays too dumb to know the weather. Even a cod knows the east wind's no good and swallows stones when it blows to stay on the bottom. Fish have built-in weather detectors, and the bluefish act like they have some kind of radio communication too. "They may not open their mouths for hours or even days," he says, "except to take in water. But then some boss fish gives a signal, and every blue for miles around is slashing at any goddamn thing that moves."

After being virtually mute at lunch and not much more talkative at dinner, he'd begun talking his head off on the way to the beach. Mostly to talk down our chances. He was absolutely certain that the wind's shift from southwest to east in the late afternoon that had cleared the diffuse haze but put the feel of rain in the air had also encouraged the blues to take off for other parts. The shift had come just about the time Dolly and I stopped shingling. She quit first, around three, to take the jeep and check up on Les, and I worked on alone until she got back. By that time, because of the change in the wind, it was hot for the first time all day, and I quit too and we took a swim. We'd even managed to persuade Stevie to come with us, pointing out to him that he was wearing swimming trunks already. He'd only taken a quick plunge and gone back "to earn a full day's pay," but by then, settled down to dry and warm in the fine iron-streaked sand, Dolly and I had lost the will to work. The sun was really hot, and baking through from both sides I found myself able for the first time to imagine Gretta and Michael here—and to think that I was imagining this comfortably.

Would it be possible, I asked Dolly, for a friend of mine, a woman friend with a twelve-year-old son, to rent the cabin for a week or so? A perfectly reasonable question that I'd actually committed myself to ask, but it took just the interval of time required for Dolly to say she'd have to talk to Les about it but didn't see why it shouldn't be possible for the undefined hesitations I'd left behind me to overtake me again. "I'd better check the idea out again then with my friend," I said, and felt the partially relieved fright of a close squeak.

Dolly must certainly have expected me to say more, but she asked me nothing as we continued to laze in the sun a while longer. Only in this nervy aftermath of avoidance, I wasn't exactly lazing any longer though I was still taking in warmth all the way round. Then when we went up to the house, Les had returned and was impatient to get to the beach before the last fish had departed. Dolly hustled supper onto the table, and we ate with no more interruption for conversation than there'd been at lunch.

It seems now though that that last fish may in fact have departed already, for we've been fishing for close to an hour without a bump, and the lower edge of the sun is beginning to flatten off over the horizon. The day is running out visibly, and casting directly into this oversized deforming red disk, I discover with some surprise that I'm unready to have it run out altogether. I seem to be counting on at least one fish, and the simplicity of this unchecked expectation and the attention required by the various matters I have to keep track of in trying to satisfy it—watching my casts, watching the water, watching Les's casts to make sure I'm not stigmatized, and listening to him with whatever attention I can spare from listening to the sound of my reel—has me shamefully nerved up. The reel is an old Ru-Mer to which I have strong sentimental attachment, and it too has aged badly since my last visit to the isthmus. If the lure snags even on light weed now, the gears clack by and the handle bumps in my fingers.

Les though really seems to have given up. Even the focus of his talk has changed, from fish to not seeing how he can do all that remains to be done before the snow flies if he and Dolly are to be okay in the house this winter. "Why not cut down on the time you spend on the backhoe for a while?" I suggest, shouting but not turning my head.

"What?" he says, his voice louder with irritation.

This time I do turn my head, eager to keep him from coming any closer. "The backhoe," I say. "Couldn't you do only three or four days of work a week on it for a while and have more time that way to work on the house?"

"I could if I got paid what a backhoe operator gets in the United States," he says. "If pay on the strip wasn't ten years behind. Except if it comes to that, there's nowhere else I'd still get a chance to operate heavy equipment. They'd have retired me in Connecticut."

"You can always move back into the cabin when the weather turns," I say. "Would that be bad for one more winter?"

"It wouldn't be too great for Dolly," he says. "I'm hardly home more than to eat and sleep anyway, but a woman needs a place to live."

"Maybe," I shout, but don't take time to say that I don't think it really would make Dolly very unhappy either because I've just located the patch of water I've been looking for but not previously seen. However debatable it may be that Dolly requires a big house, it's demonstrable that bluefish don't much like slack water, and the water I've been casting into for the past hour has been unpromisingly quiet. Now though suddenly just beyond where I've been casting, I've discovered a succession of swirls that don't rise much, which may be why I haven't seen them earlier, but that angle away from the shore in a line that suggests a bar. I'll have to stretch for the extra distance, however, and when I feel my way a few steps further into the surf, the bottom slopes off sharply, pressure plasters my waders against my legs, and I'm displacing enough water to make my footing disconcertingly light.

"You're supposed to cast for them, not go get them," Les says, deigning to shout now as he sees me edging out.

"Yeah," I shout back. "I know."

I mean this to be reassuring, but I don't much like such light footing myself given the way I'll be leaning on my casts. If I should slip or stumble, I might just snag my line around the tip and lose a rig. But I could also go down. If I did that and filled my waders, Les would probably feel compelled to come in to help me. Before we left the house,

Dolly had taken pains to remind me in private of how physically faulty Les was. She'd said specifically that she didn't even want him to get excited. But I've now pressed my way into a depth of water that could easily cause excitement, and the odd thing is that even if I did hook a fish and kept on my feet, I wouldn't give myself more than a fifty-fifty chance that the worn gears of the Ru would let me bring it in. I seem to want even that long chance though pretty badly.

Les's lure splashes down a short way out to my left again and I wait for it to pop back past me before I make my own cast both because it's easier to avoid if I don't have a lure in the water myself and because I think I can count on him then to wait in turn and not cast across me. He's talking as he retrieves, about how outside—framing, boarding, or shingling—he can at least see what he's done at the end of a day, but inside where he'll be most of the time soon doing finish, a day's work will just disappear, and I shout that I guess that's right.

As his lure sideslips by me, opening the water in a soft white line, my own lure glints blue and silver over my right shoulder at the end of eighteen inches of steel leader and the same length again of green translucent monofilament. I bring my right hand back, hinging with my left, then flip the rod forward and feel the extended instant that cocks the tip when rod and lure are moving in opposite directions. The sustained sibilance of the nylon loops coming off the spool then when the tip snaps forward means a long cast, and cheered by this sound I pitch forward, stumble, but keep the rod steady, and jam my front foot between two large stones. I've managed to straighten again in time to see the lure splash down a few feet to the right of the swirl line and fifteen or twenty feet out along it.

I reel fast at first to get the lure popping, then more slowly when I can see it, and at more or less the same instant that I do, what might be another lure a hundred times the size of the two-ounce Atom surfaces behind it in a furl of white water. My pulse catches to the feel of weight on the line, a drag that isn't yet opposition, but I only continue to reel slowly while I might count ten but don't. Then as weight becomes pull, I lift the tip, and my right hand, arm, and shoulder take a pumping shock. The fish plunges for deep water and is turned, plunges and is turned again, then holds straight off arcing the rod. Each plunge forces drag, and as line peels off with a coarse whine, my pulse begins to knock an echo that stretches the lining of my trachea.

"By Christ, that's where they are!" Les says. Reinforced by determination, his voice is alarmingly audible now, and I shout back to him not to dare cast over me with only the briefest twinge of shame.

I hold the arc, waiting for the fish to use its first strength and not even trying to move it. Braced against the pull, my waders sink in soft sand and shifting stones knock against my ankle bones, and when I lift my feet carefully to feel for solider bottom, they dig in again as soon as I've placed them. "You can't just tie him up out there and leave him," Les shouts, and when I say I know I don't even shout now, but am talking mostly to myself.

Tentatively, knowing the chances, I raise the tip of the rod, and the vital weight at the end of the line peels off drag at once. I wait another ten or fifteen seconds then try again, and I actually move the fish this time—but slowly and not much and always on the edge of the drag, and when I lower the tip and turn the handle to take up the small gain, the gears slip and pay out line without resistance before they catch again.

"Whatever it is you're doing," Les shouts, "you're going to lose him that way for sure."

"That's right," I say, again more or less to myself, and begin backing toward the beach with the rod at sixty degrees, and have taken only three careful steps and am unbalanced for a fourth when the fish plunges again and I stumble forward and just manage not to fall. Holding once more then, hoping for the fish to tire, I notice that the world around me appears to be swaying slightly, as though on gimbals, and meanwhile, no doubt in relation to this, that my pulse is knocking and fluttering in very disorderly fashion and my breathing isn't functioning as it's supposed to either. The only encouraging thing, I see over my shoulder, is that Les has gotten the idea that something's amiss, that I'm not just being stupid. His line is in, and he's leaning on his rod and watching me with squint-eyed attention.

When I begin to back toward the shore again, there's a slight easing on the line as the fish, responding, makes its first jump. It rockets straight up out of the water almost clearing its tail—and at its apogee it shakes its oversized head and rattles the lure.

"Tip down," Les shouts, which I've done already, and backing again then to take advantage of the interval when the fish will be weakened by its gymnastics, I make it two-thirds of the way to the beach and am a lot more solidly on my feet before a surge peels off drag again.

"What's the trouble?" Les asks from this more conversational distance.

"Worn gears, I guess. They slip as soon as I turn the handle. It's going to be some trick to back him all the way in without taking up line."

"You could try turning the bail with a finger. The anti-reverse seems okay."

This is something I hadn't thought of, and ten minutes later the sun has dropped behind the earth, the bluefish is drying on the beach after I'd backed almost to the dunes to get it there, and the index finger of my left hand with which I've been turning the bail when I could is raw and angry from running against the line. The fish should have died from exhaustion given the time this has taken, but even its final jump, in the shallows where I was sure I was going to lose it, had been spectacular against the last half round of the sinking sun. On the beach though, pulsing, patchy where scales have rubbed off over the stones and with a layer of sand on its exposed eye, it begins to lose color at once though it still doesn't relax the clamp of its jaw over the lure. It had taken the forward treble hook, and two of the three barbs are fast in the cartilaginous hinge of the jaw.

Even as the torpedo body slid up on the sand out of the surf, flopping over and over powerfully but irregularly as though on an eccentric shaft, I'd felt exhilaration draining away and by now it's hard to imagine how or why it could have seemed so crucial just moments before not to lose this fish; had felt as though landing it would settle something. "Take my rod if you think he's got a friend," Les says when I've reeled up the slack line and cut the leader free. "I'm not getting out there anyway."

"That's okay," I say. "I'm finished."

Carrying the fish by its tail, I can feel intimations of its uncontainable opposition, strong discrete throbs to which my own heightened and irregular pulse seems direct response. I lay it in the back of the jeep, glad to break this connection, and when we've mounted our rods in the carrier and Les has lighted a cigarette, we stand together alongside the jeep facing west over the water. The sunset is remarkably pale, the metallic orange of a fall rather than a summer sunset, and the air too has definite edge. Gulls mew in the dunes behind us and small mixed bands—mature and immature—fly out to the west, circle, and return, the deliberateness of their flight emphasized by the single scoter flying low over the water from the north pursuing the line of its neck with frantic wing beats. I'm no longer giddy, but my pulse is still bumping hard in my throat.

"I've lost the touch," Les says elegiacally. "I've only hooked into two blues all summer and one of those got away. But this is the part of fishing I always liked best anyway."

His tanned, leathery face, with only a flat band of forehead between his wide-spaced eyes and the bill of his swordfishing cap, glows in the orange light. Fingering the cigarette, turning it under his nose, he spaces drags and watches the smoke, inhaling only fragrance. When he turns toward me then, taking his cap off as he does this in order not to bump me with the long bill, I have additional measure of his shrinkage. His eyes are not only farther below mine than I'd expected them to be, but they seem to have recessed farther too, all but hidden under the over-arching span of forehead that's continuous with but considerably more weathered than the flat bald baby-pink scalp he's uncovered. His waders, which hang from his shoulders on red firemen's suspenders, hoop clear of his body and sag over his legs, and the material shrinkage of which this could be still another evidence, seems also to intensify his concentration. When he tilts his head back and thrusts his chin up and at me like Popeye, I feel in hazard of exposure, as though the disorder inside my throat and chest that had subsided considerably in the past few minutes but acts up again abruptly under this inspection, might turn out to be visible. "When I used to catch fish," Les says, "I sure got a bigger kick out of it than you do."

He says this though I see at once with the familiar sardonic pride that is as much the guise of his vestigial but persistent glamour as a somewhat cooler detachment is of Dolly's. It's no more inquiring than it is accusatory. Instead, and essentially, it's self-regarding, and his next statement makes this entirely evident. "What I can still do though is knock nails," he says, "and one way or another I'm going to get the house fit to live in this fall even if I have to bust my hump doing it. The downstairs anyway. The second floor's all extra and it can wait."

Disabused of the threat of discovery, my pulse slows and softens once more. But curiously, though I am relieved when it does, this subsidence also feels like an unwanted departure.

11

WHEN WE'VE RETURNED to the house—after we put away our gear and I've dressed my fish—I pick up again where I'd left off on the beach that afternoon. First I tell Les and Dolly enough about Gretta not to sound too offhand, and then I ask whether they'd be willing to rent the cabin to her for a week or so, and the arrangement I'd been stalling over all day is made quite simply. Nothing new has occurred to me to resolve my earlier hesitations, but the knocking inside my rib cage—at the very least a declaration of functions I'm used to having performed in a more orderly and less clamorous fashion—seems a call for resolution by fiat. This commotion had quieted considerably before Les and I left the beach, but it remains with me as a residual presence. Something in my chest there sends out a signal that it could erupt again at any moment and perhaps will. I also find disquieting a notion that I can't quite be rid of no matter how nonsensical it seems, that this disturbance was transmitted to me from my fish by way of a hundred feet or so of monofilament first, and then directly by the harsh spasmodic movement of the base of its tail inside my hand—an emanation of vital will that my organs can't quite accommodate.

Once I've asked for the cabin though, this threatening interior presence becomes more residual still, and I call Gretta then to report what I've done and ask when she wants her vacation to begin. Her initial response is that I'm great and that the cabin sounds wonderful. Then she checks herself or is checked, I can't tell which. She'll need another day or possibly two before she can actually make plans though, she says. She certainly wants to bring Michael to the isthmus and thinks she should be able to, but she can't be certain about it yet. She's afraid she'd been a little hasty when she pressed this office on me "out of wishful enthusiasm." This is all the explanation she offers, and we leave it that we'll see each other and talk further after my return tomorrow evening.

It had worried me, phoning, that Gretta might have left the motel or even simply gone out for a while and that I wouldn't be able to reach her, but it hadn't even occurred to me that she might suggest some hitherto unmentioned impediment to a plan I'd lent myself to in the first place only at her request but to which my relationship has now changed. I seem now almost to be its originator. This declaration of a necessary delay—and the possibility that delay could become cancellation—feels like interference now with my own forward motion which I sustain as best I can by taking a bus the next morning so early that I get to Boston, go home, clean up and change my clothes, and am still at my desk at Municipal Systems before eleven. Around noon it occurs to me that Gretta and I had neglected even to set a time and place to meet later in the day, but when I call the motel she isn't in, and I can only leave a message for her to call me back when she returns.

I stay working at my desk through the lunch hour not to miss her, and though she doesn't call me back, I gain something by this nonetheless. Leaning over my desk so that the tunafish salad sandwich I'd sent out for won't shed onto my lap, with my head and neck stretched forward like a duck in flight, I become aware that Hans Scherman who is eating at his desk too as he does though habitually unless he has a business lunch, is regarding me from his glass box with manifest favor. Benevolence and approbation gleam from his eyes and cheekbones over his own sandwich, and this uncharacteristic notice is then expressed when I'm still at my desk in the otherwise empty office at the end of the day, and Scherman, who is generally the last person to leave the office as well as the first to arrive, passes me on his way out.

"Don't overdo it," he says, with something like surprise now as well as approbation. "You've more than made up your lost time, I'm sure."

I assure him almost vehemently that I'll be leaving soon, aware as he can't be that I'm at my desk still, as I'd been too during the lunch hour, only because I'm waiting for Gretta to return my call. But I really have done a lot of work in one day by the time she does call, around six thirty. She hadn't called earlier because things were still up in the air she says using the same evasive locution for evasion that she'd used the night before. This time though she adds some explanation. "Did I ever tell you," she asks, which means at once that she hasn't, "that Michael was scheduled to go off with his father later this week to Nantucket? Probably I didn't. In my own mind I'd vetoed the plan a long time back. Only somehow I'd neglected to communicate my veto even to his father until this morning, by which time I also had to tell him that I wanted to take Michael to the isthmus. Tricky, no?"

"Very," I say. "You're a rather uncertain communicator."

"I talk mostly to myself," she says. "But anyway this second piece of news took a lot of the cogency out of what I had to say about the risks of going to Nantucket. Though even if I'd stated my objections to the first plan promptly, I don't think Henry would have believed now that I hadn't had the isthmus in mind the whole time. He's a lawyer after all, which means he lives in a world of calculation. But anyway it was heavy going, and not made any lighter by my having to work Michael's hospital visit into my reasoning also—as well, God help me, as my skipping out on Alf without notice. When I think about it, I admire the nerve I had for trying."

"For sure," I say. "What happened?"

"I don't know exactly. Henry was disquietingly jolly, reminding me of what a very nice man he really is. But he's also, as I've said, a lawyer. He wouldn't commit himself. He

said he had to think about it a while. That was this morning, and then just a few minutes ago, when I was about to
call you, there was a call from Alf who said he was calling
for Henry. Wow, was he chilly! But anyway, Michael and
I are now going off to the Ritz Grill so that the three of us
can talk the situation out face to face over an expensive
dinner that will go I guess on Henry's account. He's em-
powered, he says, to act for Henry. But in fairness to Alf,
I'd have to say that he thinks of the Ritz Grill as a kind of
sanctum. He even finds it intimate."

She talks on rapidly a little longer, assuring me that she
still has her heart set on going to the isthmus with Michael.
She'd rather be dealing with Henry directly over this, she
says, because Henry has certain human susceptibilities that
Alf has been spared. But that's also undoubtedly why
Henry has asked Alf to represent him. Dealing with Alf is
going to be hard, and made no easier by eating and drinking. She counts on the fact that it can only go on so long,
however, she says, and asks me to meet her at the motel
around nine-thirty. By that time the "negotiation" as she's
called it several times should have been concluded. She's
sure Alf will be tough, but she's pretty sure too that if she
sticks to her guns as she intends to, she'll have her way.

Despite her confidence, it seems to me that I've been
hearing a kind of geological fault just under the surface of
her account which I'm inclined to attribute not so much to
her impending meeting with Alf, to whom she has always
seemed to me to be all but invulnerable, as to this renewed
communication with her ex-husband. I can't know though
how much this may be projection. After some number of
weeks of complete silence, Janet had called me a few days
before to let me know that she and Staines were flying to
Boston, he to attend a conference at Arthur D. Little
and she to put in some time at Widener Library. Three
thousand miles away in California, Janet still carries a
torch for Widener which she doesn't carry for me, but
I'm pretty sure that I'm also drawing her East this time, and

the prospect of having dinner with her and Staines Friday evening, as we'd then planned, has been giving me the willies whenever I don't have anything more compelling on my mind. And Janet and I, unlike Gretta and Henry, have nothing to negotiate any longer. That really means though only that we have nothing limited to negotiate any longer. Janet does want me to witness how well her life is going and how much better also it's going than my own is, and though I'm sure she has also, as she'd said when she called, continued to be disturbed by my crack-up and wants to see how I'm doing, these two sets of wants are not exclusive.

Whatever the ultimate cause of Gretta's uneasiness really is however, her stated concern about dealing with Alf seems justified when I arrive at the motel on schedule and find that he has returned from dinner with her and Michael. The three of them are waiting together for my arrival in a bright, clean, double room on the third floor. He has some further questions, Alf says, that Gretta couldn't be expected to answer but that he imagines I can—and he indicates further who's planned this unscheduled meeting by offering me the one chair in the room.

The physical arrangements of the motel room are uncannily reminiscent of those in the hospital room up the block where I'd visited, also for a meeting, on Saturday. There are two beds this time though with an aisle between them, and the chair has been placed at the open end of the aisle. Gretta and Michael are sitting side by side on the far bed facing the aisle, and Alf, once he's let me in and seated me, reseats himself opposite them on the near bed, and they dodge knees in the constrained space between them. "You're doubtless surprised to find me here," Alf says. "Be assured that if I could choose freely I wouldn't be. Gretta may have told you that I'm acting on Henry Pines' behalf. As his surrogate, you might say. Since Henry was my friend long before he became Gretta's husband or Michael's father, it's appropriate for me to act for him in this way. There are two related matters he's asked me to inquire into for him. Two concerns. You'll only, I'd think, be able to shed direct light on one of them, but will be interested in the other as well."

He looks rigidly uncomfortable and somewhat precarious on the soft, dipping edge of the bed as he says this, but when he leans forward from the waist, presumably to ease himself, his head seems to intrude between Michael and Gretta and he retracts it and straightens up again at once. It's in part this combination of manner and discomfort governing his posture I think that suggests to me that he may be making an indictment in the guise of explanation and inquiry, and that caution is therefore in order. "The first matter," he says, "has to do with whether it's more prudent for Michael to vacation with his mother on what is I gather called the isthmus?"

"That is, so far as I know, its only designation," I say.

"Okay," he says, "whether it makes more sense for him to go there than it would for him to go to Nantucket as planned with Henry and his wife and infant daughter—Michael's half-sister, that is."

Having made this identification more or less parenthetically, he pauses before proceeding to let it sink in. "That's the question on which I will look for some help from you," he says then, "and the second, related question is whether it's prudent for him to leave the Boston area at all right now. On this I wouldn't expect you to have much to offer, except that it may be affected by what you have to say on the first. If major hospital facilities are significantly more accessible from the isthmus than from Nantucket, that could influence Henry's instinct, which I share, that with Michael's condition as uncertain and hard to predict right now from day to day as Gretta has reported, Boston is the best place for him until things either take a turn or steady out. Henry is altogether ready to concede the disadvantages of Nantucket. A storm or heavy fog limits medical aid there to the facilities of the island itself and they're not all one could ask. Though in summer at least, he says, they're not as limited as one might assume either. Among the many distinguished people who choose to vacation on Nantucket, there are always some eminent doctors. He knows of three who'll be vacationing on the island in the next several weeks but who'll have their black bags with them and to whom he'd have no hesitation about turning for help if it was required, and he's sure there'd be others as well whom it would be an interesting project to discover. As he understands it though, Michael's medical needs are not likely to be complicated. What could be important is the speed with which treatment is begun. He'd like me to find out therefore how quickly Gretta could count on getting medical care for Michael if he required it from the isthmus."

"She could get him back here by car in under two hours," I say, "door to door."

"That's not bad," he says. "Even by airplane, when the planes are flying, it can't take much less than that altogether from Nantucket, and fog can make air travel from the islands very undependable in summer. How about help right there though, in the event of an unforeseen emergency?"

When I look at Gretta now more or less for the first time, I detect an expression of amusement around her lips that looks fixed rather than active, as though left over from some earlier conversation or occasion. "It wouldn't take more than forty minutes or an hour at most to drive to County General," I say, " and I'm told that's not a bad hospital. But right on the spot, the isthmus isn't much like Nantucket. If there are any doctors who vacation there I don't know who they are and I suspect they wouldn't be very eminent. It's a different kind of place. My friends who own the cabin Gretta would be renting though are dependable people."

"Henry will be glad to hear that," Alf says, "and he assumes of course that you'll be there yourself."

"I have no plans," I say, and with only that impermanent answer to fall behind, I'm relieved to hear Gretta break her silence.

"Come on, Alf," she says. "That's twice now you've had the same answer to a question, if it is a question, that you have no real excuse for asking since it shouldn't affect your client's interest in any way."

"Perhaps," Alf says. "But it apparently does affect his natural curiosity."

He sustains a kind of affability even when he's pressed, and since affability isn't in my experience his natural demeanor, I find it somewhat alarming. This willingness not to press his friend's case as hard as he might—Gretta's position even on this last question after all is not invulnerable—again suggests the possibility that what he's really doing is laying the ground for a later weightier case, and I watch him shift deliberately a few degrees around to his left on the bed now, away from me and past Gretta, toward Michael. So far Michael has been utterly silent. Sitting close enough beside Gretta though that his left arm can touch her right from time to time as if by chance, he's followed the conversation, this time largely between Alf and myself, with the same absolute and impassive attention he'd displayed at the hospital, shifting his eyes from speaker to speaker as though following a Ping-Pong match. Now though, Alf asks him directly whether he still thinks the isthmus is where he wants to be. Apparently he's declared his preference earlier, and Alf is recognizing this but making certain he hasn't changed his mind. Verifying the evidence. And Michael reaffirms a considered decision. He says that of course he'd like to see Nantucket some time but that he's equally curious about the isthmus which he's never seen either, and that he thinks Gretta probably knows what's best for him. She knows him better than anyone else does, and in addition, she's the one who's just talked to the doctors.

Alf allows this analysis to be decisive. It's a reasonable

view of the situation, he says, and he's proud of Michael for being so reasonable. He only hopes that Gretta is being equally reasonable. He knows that Henry accepts her judgment that Nantucket is probably not a great place for Michael right now and is even made happy by the thought that this judgment is based on appropriate caution. But he'd be happier still if, on this same basis, Michael remained in the Boston area, went nowhere. Deprived of his son's companionship, it would be nice for him to have maximum ease of mind at least in exchange while he was on vacation, and he won't have that with Michael on the isthmus even if he accepts the idea that the risks in his being there are small.

Alf rises as he's speaking, so that he's standing above Gretta and Michael talking down to them and they, in almost perfect parallel, are looking up at him. "I'm sure Henry will honor your judgment that the risks are low," he says toward rather than to Gretta's upturned exposed face. "That he'll accept it as a responsible judgment. He has little choice of course but to count on this, given the arrangements agreed on between you. But you also know those arrangements are subject to rearrangement for cause, and Henry gave me a message for you if I concurred on his behalf in your plans. I was to say, 'Don't blow it, old girl.' "

"For sure," Gretta says.

Alf has been moving as he talked, slowly at first but with purposeful acceleration, and he's cleared the narrow aisle and turned toward the door before Gretta has made this brief reply. She's talking therefore to his back when she does make it. I've come to my feet, both to be out of his way and from some uncertain sense of appropriateness, but she, and Michael with her, remain seated. She seems not just seated but inert, deprived for the moment of the possibility of rising by the assault of Alf's message. Expecting him to be gone without further exchange—his departure palpable to me as a consequence before it has quite occurred—I watch him suddenly falter instead as he approaches the door, and then break from this arrest and turn toward

Gretta again with his hand still on the knob. "I assume you will have to come back to the house at some time before you go to the isthmus, long enough to unpack and repack at any event," he says. His face, which has been consistently composed before, is now curiously discomposed, jarred out of control though it does not reveal what emotion or combination of emotions has caused this, as he waits for Gretta to answer.

When she only nods, he says, "I'd appreciate it if you'd let me know when you were coming. I'll make no point of being either at home or not at home for that occasion, but I'd like to know nonetheless. I've known all along of course that there was something odd at least about the terms under which we shared a house, but it's only in the past week that I've felt demeaned by them, and I find it hard to tolerate that feeling."

He turns again, opens the door, and is out of the room before Gretta can say anything this time even if she wishes to, as though propelled out by the reactive force of his words behind him in the enclosed room.

12

"THAT'S MUCH BETTER," Gretta says. "I was feeling like shit by the time Alf left. Not without reason. But now I'm remarkably better."

"I'm glad," I say.

"Oh?" Gretta says, hearing the quality of this gladness, as though after running hard for a train while expecting to miss it, I'd caught it at the last possible instant. "I suppose I might have known, but I wasn't really in any condition to pay attention."

"Naturally," I say.

"Don't begrudge it to me, Fish," she says. "It's probably only hoarding that's really wasteful."

I tell her I believe that may be true too, but welded hip to hip on the daybed in Christine's study, I don't tell her that it was sheer possibility and not any question of balance of trade that had made me gloomy, that the combination of her unrecognizing exigency and the mortuary chill of the air conditioning had all but neutralized me. The narrowness of the daybed hadn't helped either, but that had been my choice. My "peculiar preference," Gretta had called it. She herself had favored the queen-size bed in the bedroom which she was sure that Christine, who was spending the night in her lab, would have been happy to have us use. Gretta's exigency also made her undependable though I thought about the borders of Christine's generosity, and I'd agreed to come here at all only because Gretta had insisted we didn't have time to go to my apartment.

Alf's request to talk to me too had thrown off her plans, she said. That, and then the last-minute declaration by the student nurse who was to stay with Michael that her boyfriend didn't like her to stay out after midnight. It was a plot against happiness, Gretta said. Against what she'd planned as a celebration. It wasn't clear to me though that limitation of time really had much to do with her hurry, and she seems utterly unpressed now at least when she knees her way over me to go to the kitchen, and returns gnawing a soda cracker and carrying a glass of milk. Washing the dry cracker down with the milk in front of the window, looking out over the river, her skin looks nacreous and unsubstantial in the pale light even though I retain the feel of its actual ruddy thickness still in my own skin. Her throat shimmers as she swallows and even the rise and fall of her breasts is confusingly indefinite. But when she's left the emptied glass on Christine's desk and climbed back over me into bed again, and is shifting for place between me and the wall, her body proves its substantiality once more.

"It occurs to me that I haven't shared again," she says, "but I really figured you weren't starved the way I was. I didn't seem to want to eat much of that fine dinner at the Ritz."

"I'm not hungry," I say, "but a token might have been nice anyway."

"You think?" she says.

I let this go as a statement in the form of a question, knowing that she might well have picked up some sense of how unreceptive to simple pleasure my body is right now while she was climbing over me. She's arrived at that knock-about state in which even unfocused sensation is agreeable, but having performed by needs not my own—and it had been little more than performance, and just barely that— I'm not ready for these next-stage gratifications. Lost opportunity isn't all that's dragging me, however. The cardiac tricks that had erupted when I was fishing with Les the night before and have erupted several times again then in the past twenty-four hours have put me in uncertain relationship with my body anyway. By now this phenomenon that had surprised me last night has become a routine. First a run of irregular beats, some hard and some mere butterfly flutters, and then a line of what feel like minute bubbles that originate deep in my throat, rise, and break sharply in my mouth. As though I'd gulped a mouthful of ginger ale. Not much finally happens, and what does seems to have insufficient dignity to be granted importance. Unless that is these are only truncated instances and the full phenomenon is still to occur. Some apprehension that this may be so adds to my difficulty in receiving the jolting of Gretta's hipbone against my own as the hearty acts of indiscriminate affection they feel like to her.

Impact is actually above my hipbone into the lower, less stable ribs when she turns from her back onto her right side to face me and simultaneously moves up on the couch, a complex feat that can't be accomplished without violence in such limited space. Her head is free then above me when she settles again, and believing her maneuver has been in the interest of speech, I'm unprepared to respond to the passage of a relaxed nipple across my lips. "What's wrong now?" she asks.

"Still the slow boat, I guess," I say, sounding gloomier than I'd known or intended.

I feel her watching me as she can in the dark. "Okay," she says, "let's be more verbal then. What did you think of that for a team performance? The way Alf acted for his old buddy, I mean?"

"I'd never seen Alf acting for a client before, but he didn't exactly surprise me—not until the end anyway, when he wasn't, and wasn't performing either. The person I wondered about though was his client."

"Henry?" she said. "He's very unlike Alf even if they are both lawyers and have been remarkably constant friends. He's very, very rich to begin with, whereas Alf just has a certain amount of money. He's rich enough, for example, to hire another character for himself when he needs it. That's simplifying, and Henry's essentially a kindly and even jolly man. His jollity was considerably reduced when he had me dragging him, but now when I talk to him he sounds like he was when I first met him again, which I'm finding a little confusing. He's also though a very shrewd number."

"I doubt that you dragged him," I say. "He sounds, I don't know, a little dopey. Or maybe too jolly to be believed."

"He's a lot shrewder than you may want to understand," Gretta says, "and you're plain wrong about whether I was dragging him."

A light clicks on brutally above the bed now, and my eyes are still shrinking from the glare when she places her left hand under my nose, palm up. "*Regarde ça,*" she says, mock-imperious.

"That's what I'm doing," I say, "as well as I can with that light in my eyes. What am I supposed to see?"

"On the wrist," she says. "It may not be obvious, but it's not invisible either. The badge."

When I do see it now, I know too by its familiarity that I've seen it there before—a thin glossy interruption of the skin's texture about three-eighths of an inch long that intersects the fine blue lines where they branch below the heel of the hand. "When did it happen?" I ask.

"It didn't exactly happen, dummy."

"Okay."

The hand withdraws, and the light blears away instead of going all at once. My eyes untense gradually to let the dark soothe them. "You never noticed it before?" Gretta asks.

"I must have."

"Oh? It's not so blatant. I only used the point. Pushing seemed easier than slicing, less deliberate, but I wasn't even then taking any chances with my precious beauty either."

Her body holds off now too in the narrow space of which my own is the outer limit. A hand is braced against my thigh, and I lie legs together and arms folded over my chest like a figure on a stone sarcophagus, a rigid and invulnerable similitude of the true vulnerable flesh. "When?" I ask.

I feel her hand cup against my thigh so that only the fingertips are touching me, and her nails are not really painful but vivid. "When did I do it?"

"Yes."

"A little more than four years ago."

She hesitates, taking time I think to remember it right. "A surprising amount of blood came out of that little incision," she says, registering that surprise once more as she says it, "but not exactly in a rush. It was particularly slow at first, as if it took time for this alternate avenue to be discovered. Even after the discovery had been made, the blood only welled. It never came in a real flow. But it came wonderfully steadily, looking as if it might go on that way forever. A bemusing notion. My arm was lying over the sink wrist up, I'd turned on the taps as I knew you were supposed to, and I watched the regular replacement of the blood that fell off my skin and washed away with fascination. I remember thinking how extraordinary it was, and that I hadn't surprised myself this much in a long time. Only there was a further less pleasing surprise then as I realized I was about to pass out and that what I'd caused to happen so trivially was now entirely uncontrollable and probably decisive.

"This was at about three o'clock in the morning, and when I did pass out and collapsed, the fall was noisy enough to wake Henry even though I'd closed the door between the bathroom and the bedroom. Henry's very competent. That's another of his positive characteristics that I neglected to mention. He tourniqueted me, called an ambulance, and had me hustled to the emergency room at New York Hospital where they reversed my route. An efficient and entirely routine procedure. Then after a certain number of days when I had my full quota of blood again, a lot of which really belonged by rights of manufacture to various other people, I was transferred to Payne Whitney and spent most of a month there which I didn't altogether hate. The company convinced me that I wasn't really crazy, and since I hadn't been sure before, this was gratifying."

Thinking about this, she moves her nails distractedly against my thigh, which does cause pain finally. It's still not simple pain though, and its rousing aspects seem grotesquely inappropriate both to what she's telling me and to the commotion occurring elsewhere in my body, the cardiac clatter which can scarcely remain a secret very long even if Gretta's only to be aware of it as I was of the scar on her wrist before she directed me to look at it. More or less subliminally. The bubbles travelling up my throat feel like the flow from an aquarium aerator, and the aired roof of my mouth where they burst is as dry as a blotter.

"Henry agreed to a divorce before I left the bin, but he agreed to my having custody of Michael only on condition that I live with Alf. I was to have custody of Michael, that is, only if Alf had custody of us both. He and Alf cooked that one up together. They're oldest buddies, not just from college and law school but all the way back to the third grade at Fieldston. They both had to know of course that it was a condition that might not hold up in court if it was challenged, but they must also have calculated that I wouldn't be in a challenging mood. And I wasn't. My lawyer had pointed out to me that given my history, Henry could probably have custody if he asked for it. All he'd have to do was show he could provide Michael with a reasonable home and that was easy. He has more than enough money to hire help and I knew anyway that he'd be remarried within a year. He's not only the marrying kind, as Alf isn't, but he's also the kind of man any reasonable woman would want to marry. Jolly, undemanding, shrewd, competent—a good provider in almost all ways."

When she shifts again now—or flexes really which is all there's room for, ending up pretty much where she'd begun —the rake of her nails is more extensive and I really have to count on the self-absorption that had given me trouble earlier, to aid me now. That she will notice nothing. For I'm afflicted by appetite while she tells me a terrible story, and simultaneously—and, so far as I can tell, entirely separately —I also feel my vital signs going truly haywire.

"I was looking for a long chance," Gretta says, "but I also had sense enough not to give up Michael. If Alf's scrutiny was the price I had to pay for having both, I was prepared to pay it. The arrangement didn't even seem uniquely humiliating at first, maybe because of recent experiences. It's not exactly pride-supporting either, after all, to discover that you can't kill yourself when you thought that was the only thing for which you still had any real appetite. And if Alf who was my brother wanted the social semblance of a married life without being married because he couldn't like any woman long enough to marry her, I could understand that, and why shouldn't I therefore make it possible? Help him to entertain the way he wanted to— I'm not bad at that you know if I can put my mind to it— and also make it possible for him to buy the kind of house in which he thought entertaining of this sort should take place but which he couldn't afford on his own. I'd pay rent which would help him some, and for the rest Henry would give him a mortgage at a more favorable rate than any bank in exchange for his good offices. It all worked out for a while too, maybe because it wasn't obvious to me at first quite what Henry's stake in the arrangement was. It took me time to realize that he was really paying Alf to keep an eye on Michael until I went bananas again, when he could have Michael whether I did myself in or not without feeling like a heel. He really would like to have Michael even if he's too nice to force the issue. But he's also too smart to believe that a divorce alone would make my attachment to life that much more dependable."

Though this sounds conclusive, it's also her teasing way of sounding conclusive that's meant to smoke me out, and as is frequently the case when she affects this, I don't know how to come out very far. "It didn't do that?" I say.

"Not exactly," she says, extending the phrase by stretching its long sounds, "but I also found out about Michael right about then. Everyone thinks I got more mileage than I did out of being free of Henry. The truth is that if I'd known about Michael a little sooner I might not even have left him. Once I didn't really want Henry anymore, living with him seemed intolerable because there wasn't anything else I wanted very much either. Then suddenly there was. I wanted Michael not to lose any more than he had to any sooner than he had to, and that's been something I could want ever since. Even those days when it isn't quite enough, it's a lot more than I'd expected for a long time. And sometimes I can even want it enough to want some other things too, as you can testify."

"A modus vivendi," I say.

"Not quite," she says. "As a system it really takes no looking into. That may be why I'm so greedy when I do manage to want something else as well. I'm never sure how long I'll want it or whether I'll ever want it again. So now you know the whole sordid story. What time is it getting to be?"

This time she really is being conclusive. She heaves up and across me for the watch she'd left on the low table next to the bed, and I turn away from her quickly but not quickly enough. "Oh, Lord," she says, "I really do go on once I've had my portion, don't I? And now there's no time left for reciprocity. I have to get back to the motel before that twitchy little nurse leaves to get hers."

She climbs over me, cautiously now, to get her clothes, and I get up and begin to dress too. "It's okay," I say. "I guess I'm just getting too old for quickies."

"Me too, as a general thing," she says. "You'll be coming out there to visit though, won't you? I'd feel better in various ways if you were. I know I shouldn't really be doing this. Not if I want to play it safest. But I keep thinking that it may be Michael's last chance ever to take a vacation without taking along a portable drug store and I want him to have it. Only I could easily blow it, and smart, old, jolly Henry knows that and is doing his own calculating."

I promise that I will come to the isthmus over the weekend. Then, remembering that I'm having dinner with Janet and Staines Friday evening, add that I won't be able to get there though until Saturday morning. I don't say why I can't come earlier and Gretta is in too much of a hurry to ask. We're both shy of touch now too, and walk around each other with care as we dress and make up the daybed again. Then we go down in the elevator and out to her car which is parked legally this time, and she drives me to Charles Street Station. When she pulls over to the curb on Cambridge Street to let me out, she keeps her hands on the wheel and her eyes straight ahead as though she can hardly bear to stop. Not quite ready to get out though, I reach across her to touch the underside of her left wrist where I imagine the white hyphen to be. "It's not a bad story," I say.

"It's not the end of the story either," she says. "As long as Michael is only threatened, I can figure I'm trying to hang onto it all for him, and that's very energizing. Once he's actually sick though, the best I can do is help him cut his losses. He'll have no more than a specifiable run then, give or take a few years."

"That's not so distinctive," I say.

"I told you I know I have no system," she says. "I'm an easy gambler but a bad loser, which makes for something less than a system."

She says this with dismissive impatience, and I get out of the car then and close the door, and over the tinny crash of its closure, I can just hear her say she'll be looking for me Saturday morning.

13

THE CITY IS RANK as an old shoe this evening, but this corrupt air off the river at its late summer low that blows through my apartment in fluctuating densities is not at all unpleasant. I find it an alerting medium, in which I am for the moment way over toward plus on the present-absent scale. A rare and not necessarily dependable state. Instead of having to hustle to the Square, I am my own diversion. Nothing makes more for presence than auguries of change, and in the past day or so Gretta and Michael have been installed on the isthmus, I've had the unsolicited offer of a permanent job at Municipal Systems at a large though still unspecified salary, and I've also had the regular companionship of my new mechanism. This inner entity turns out to be an unrivalled reminder of the possibility of change. It could scarcely be either more immediate or more dependable. Its runs vary considerably in both duration and intensity, but the sequence is always the same and always commanding. Something goes palpably haywire at vital center, spasm replaces the regular imperceptible alternations, and small sharp bubbles dry a startling path up my throat into the chamber of my mouth. A peremptory sequence. But in fact my attention is solicited more or less equally even when nothing is actually happening and the mechanism is only potential, a pregnant quiescence that's held now save for some minor tremors since sometime before Gretta called me yesterday afternoon to announce that she and Michael had arrived on the isthmus in good order. Easy now, uncharged, she told me that Dolly had been on hand to settle them and that the place was "heaven"—and this clinker, one of several vestiges of a style to which she'd been educated in her youth that seem more anomalous to me still I think despite their familiarity than they do to her, had stirred something without quite rousing it, a minimal response appropriate to the occasion, a recognition that didn't exaggerate. By then my simple feelings of apprehension had given way to something more like awe at a phenomenon so sentient that its responses to my experience might be more accurate than my own. I still however don't know what to make of the mechanism, not even whether to think of it as a caution or an incentive.

What puzzles me also though this evening in this generative air in which even puzzles seem to prosper, is my persistent memory of the phrase "scraping along" that punctuated the end of my conversation with Hans Scherman and changed its flavor. This was to be my last week at Municipal Systems, and Scherman had taken extravagant cognizance of this. When he called me into his office not long after Gretta had called to announce her arrival on the isthmus, I saw his summons being delivered as I listened to it—saw him talking into his phone but looking at me purposefully through the glass partition between us in effect as though he were conducting two complementary conversations simultaneously.

I walked through the partition door, and was mildly surprised right off the bat to hear him ask me to sit down. On all previous occasions when I'd been in this cubicle the exchange had been too efficiently rapid for such amenities to make much sense. This time though we were evidently to have a genuine conversation.

Scherman began by telling me that he thought he could take best advantage of the few days I still had at Municipal Systems by having me rewrite a report on the first year's operation of an extensive system of services for senior citizens in Redford, Massachusetts. Redford was a manufacturing town of about twenty thousand on the South Shore, he explained, and his assumption that I'd never heard of it had been entirely accurate. "Small town, small program," he

said, but offset this belittling quip by adding that the program was a federally funded pilot that could be expected
to have an effect disproportionate to its size. Thanks to the
advances of medicine, he said, our national geriatric population was increasing rapidly, and half the towns and small
cities in the country could be expected to take an interest in
the Redford plan. Dissemination was critical, therefore, and
though the evaluation team's report was thorough, it made
pretty rough reading, and could really profit from my
attention.

These were actually heady words coming from a man
who expects people to do their work with the same dedi-
cation with which he does his, and isn't consequently
much given to praise. Headier still though was the gulf that
opened as I listened to him between the way I knew I'd
perceive the Redford report and the way he was talking
about it. For me, there'd be words on a page that I'd try to
improve. I'd do my best, that is, to make the bright clarity
I was ready to ascribe to the writers' intentions emerge
from the thickets they'd created. But no matter what a
kick I got out of this, far too little of the substantial world
would adhere to the report in my reading of it to make me
believe that anything in that world stood to be changed by
how well I did my work. As he talked now though, I could
both see and hear that Scherman was actually picturing the
halt, the senile, the dropsical, and the blind—men and
women variously and particularly worn and damaged—
being mini-bused to lunch, or shopping, or to their doctors
or bridge clubs in an actual city. And beyond them, in full
color, ranks of senior citizens all across the country waiting
for appropriate dissemination of the Redford report to
bring them equally concrete and needed services. A clear
and benevolent vision that seemed about as dependable to
me nonetheless as a wingless airplane. My stomach yawed
in misery.

When he said then that this would have to be my last
assignment for Municipal Systems, Scherman's regret car-

ried some of this same high flavor. But he'd also said this already, and sitting with him in his tight glass box was bringing back the unease I'd felt when I first came to work for Municipal Systems in June and thought I'd overcome or transformed. The back of my head was beginning to prickle as I imagined it to be under the sustained and uncharitable gaze of Mrs. Phillips, the receptionist in the outer room, who must by now have been wondering what we were talking about so long. And Scherman was still not finished. He wanted to make sure I realized how much I'd done for the quality of the company's work in the short time I'd been here. He'd been astonished, and didn't see how he could replace me. He'd hire another editor of course, but whoever he hired was going to have a hard time trying to step into my shoes.

At that point I recognized a distinct impulse to say something gracious and get out. What I said though was that I'd found my summer's work congenial and gratifying. I sounded as though I'd assumed Scherman's stiff version of discomfort by contagion, but this didn't stop him. Looking at me from under the energized oatmeal brush of his crew-cut with a directness that was both determined and confusingly intimate, he told me now that I'd made him aware for the first time of how much responsibility he'd gotten used to carrying alone, and of how little sense that made any longer. The business had grown too large, and he really needed someone with my qualifications now not just to manage the final clearing of reports but to help him keep the entire operation in view. Given any encouragement, he said, he was prepared to go a long way to encourage me to take on that job and watch with him as Municipal Systems doubled in size again in the next three or four years.

This growth too, I thought, was pictured concretely, as a kind of time-lapse film. I said that I was already under contract to teach at Hillside that year, and however true, it was an entirely inadequate response to the offer of something more like an alliance than a job. But it was once more all I could find to say, and Scherman took it absolutely in stride. It would be immodest for him to suggest, he said, that working with him would be more interesting in the long run than teaching at Hillside, but he could assure me that it would be more remunerative. He was prepared to see to it that if I came to work at Municipal Systems I'd no longer have to scrape along. He couldn't hold his offer open indefinitely he said, becoming suddenly more brisk and more businesslike, but he would give me until Thanksgiving to consider it seriously. He thought I'd certainly want to do that.

It might have been the equanimity with which he took my flat responses that kept me from speaking the still flatter but more decisive response that was now crowding my mouth—the sense conveyed by the steady, clear, ineluctably innocent eyes regarding me out of that dun, weathered, coherent face, that he judged my existence and my needs more fairly than I could myself. Thanksgiving was three months in the future still, and if Scherman believed I could use three months to think about his offer, perhaps I could. Or should rather, since the truth is that lacking his kind of concrete imagination just about completely, I don't really see how I'm going to think any more about his offer in three months than I have already. Not turning it down, I've committed myself to little more therefore than living with it for a while and seeing how or whether it lives with me. That would be an even more absurd test though if the idea of teaching again at Hillside were living with me now with much vividness. In fact, my picture of the Hillside students I'm scheduled to meet again in a couple of weeks is little less blurry or more convincing than my picture of the senior citizens of Redford. I've had to remind myself assiduously for days that teaching has never seemed a very substantial possibility to me in the summer when I wasn't doing it, but has somehow recovered substance each time I've begun doing it once more. If this resubstantiation shouldn't again take place though, working at Municipal Systems would be no airier and I might then want to think about the difference in pay. It might behoove me to think about that difference. Though money may seem no more material to me than the senior citizens of Redford and beyond, it translates itself readily into material objects, and even if these objects can then immaterialize themselves again with devastating speed, my failure to ask just how much money I was being offered must have seemed ultimately queer to Scherman.

Except that what seems queerest to me in turn then, twenty-four hours later, is his confident assertion that I've been scraping along. I'd brought the Redford report home with me this evening in order to be sure of finishing it by Friday, but after working on it for a couple of hours I can see that finishing it is going to be no problem, and I put it aside. I pick up a volume of Chekov stories and begin to reread "The Peasants," but it's pretty quickly apparent that I don't require the dark squalor of Melikovo this evening any more than I do the civil enlightenment of Redford. I'm sufficiently present even doing nothing, and when I turn out the lights in emblematic recognition of this, it becomes even more true. I am optimally here. The breeze off the river ripens in the dark, and what had been only a low level of dim general noise becomes significant sounds. Cars start and stop, buses grind, voices speak words, an ambulance winds its alarm, and out over Brattle Square the crescendo that brings the jugglers' act to its disintegrative climax is followed by a rattle of applause.

Close below me, this spring's new neighbor who strikes me as an elongated version of Giulietta Masina, a radiant but not quite intact survivor, is making ready to nurse her baby. Though we still exchange no more than formal "hellos" when we meet on the street or the stairs, I've come to know more about her in these past weeks through our adjoining open windows than she may understand since my life is so much quieter than hers. The sequence I hear now is entirely familiar—the way the infant's initiating anxious whimpers are answered by her reiterated "well, well!," a kind of litany of encouragement that she sustains until the moment the taut lips have sealed themselves to her compliant breast and anxiety ceases. Then a complex sound of breathing and swallowing is accompanied by the equally regular but simpler sound of a rocking chair in its motion, and after two or three minutes she apostrophises the infant as her "sweet little bastard." This is almost equally ritual and familiar, a recognition of unexpected good fortune meant I think to ward off bad luck. She isn't I don't think actually married to the older, white-haired, elegantly stoop-shouldered man with whom she lives, and she's fully old enough herself to regard her infant daughter with a mixture of wonder and something less than ease.

This familiar overheard act of nurture rounds out my proximate life. Three or four paces from my chair, the pots and dishes I'd used at dinner are stacked next to the sink, and when I've washed them—which I will do soon—I'll proceed a similar distance to bed. Sink and bed both loom solidly but indeterminately in the dark, as do the shelves holding half the books I own and haven't cared to read this evening. The black-and-white rectangle on the wall opposite the books, a Piranesi, is even more obscure. Little of its detail is distinguishable at all, and I can distinguish black and white too on the Oaxaca serape covering my bed, but virtually none of its precise geometry. Obscurity casts no doubt though on these dependable portions of the generally elusive world.

If I am scraping along, I'm doing it by a plan of sorts, and tonight this admittedly insufficient plan is working as I'd like it to always but it rarely does. Observation has none of the sadness of possession, and less feels right. I'd certainly done no better when I had more. Ultimately, which hadn't even been very long, I'd done very badly. Only Hans Scherman can't be expected to know that I actually went to work for him this summer not so much to pay for a new car—which I could as well have done by dipping into some of the AT&T stock my father had given me as a kind of dowry when Janet and I were married and of which I'm to get another bundle when his estate is settled—as to avoid running any more cars off the road. And yet neither the job at Municipal Systems nor my wilfully compressed and detached existence has always given me the gravity I required to keep from vagueing my head off. My aim has been a limited palpable focus. When that works, as it's working this evening, I'm fine. Even now though, when I think about it, I feel rather like the blind Clym Yeobright living in reprieve, and when it doesn't work I have the thin corrosive taste to myself of brass.

How does Hans Scherman imagine the senior citizens of Redford to dependable existence when my own imagination requires the regular nurture of sensation to function at all? Even the life I'm in the midst of this evening as it requires imagining Gretta and Michael on the isthmus—asleep by now I assume in the cabin, Gretta in the sagging double bed and Michael in my bed in the loft—is in hazard no matter how much better I know them and the place in which I imagine them than I do my audible neighbor and her child in the unknown apartment below me. All day Thursday, I keep anticipating a report from Gretta on how things are going and find it hard to resist the idea that the absence of this call which she hasn't after all promised is itself a message. Along with these background perturbations, I can feel the mechanism becoming restive, and when by the end of the afternoon the Redford report is finished and I have only odds and ends left on my desk to clear up, it occurs to me with nagging force that if it weren't for my dinner date with Janet and Staines, I could probably finish everything I have to do by noon the next day and take off for the isthmus. That dinner is a must though, and I deal with my unease as I can instead by deciding to telephone Dolly to tell her I'm coming down Saturday morning which she may not know, and ask whether I can bring a sleeping bag and camp in one of the upstairs bedrooms.

I wait to call until mid-evening when all I'll interrupt will be the evening run of tv which I know Dolly watches only faute de mieux. When she answers the phone it's obvious that she's tickled to talk to me. All seems to be going well in the cabin, she says, and I can certainly have one of the spare bedrooms. Empty bedrooms are what they have in God's plenty she says. Then, because she doesn't really want to talk business but wants to gossip, she volunteers that though she really does like Gretta a lot she doesn't think much of her taste in friends.

"Friends?" I ask.

"Friend really," she says. "Just one, and I figured you knew about her. A lady named Christine. She arrived around lunch time today in a white Mercedes convertible and I haven't the foggiest notion where she plans to stay. She could just cozy in with Gretta and Michael in the cabin, but that doesn't seem to be her style."

"Not exactly," I say, and a preliminary stirring under my ribs—more decisive than the restiveness I'd been feeling earlier in the day—indicates I suppose that things are not only not as I imagined them on the isthmus, but that they're not as I'd wished them either.

Enough of this makes itself known to Dolly to kill her conversational initiative, and she winds things up by saying that she'll meet the early bus Saturday morning. Meanwhile the mechanism has shifted emphatically from potential to actual, and when I leave my apartment now before its run has even subsided, it's to head not for one of my customary evening walks into the Square but the other way, out Brattle Street to visit Yoshalem whom I've thought about visiting for several days but haven't called. I know how little he favors impromptu visits, but my curiosity about the phenomenon declaring itself under my ribs is strong enough to overcome this knowledge. I want to know whether it's a symptom or a sign. A second longer and more dramatic run overtakes me on the empty stretch between the two hulking intrusions of the Mormon tabernacle and the Armenian church and by the time I'm finally climbing the steps of the carriage house with my throat dried half raw, I really want to walk into the long, narrow library saying nothing but holding out my wrist, asking my question without recourse to those inefficiencies of speech that are never more apparent to me than when I speak to Yoshalem.

I do nothing of the kind however. I have to deal first before saying anything in any way with Yoshalem's predictable dismay at my unbidden appearance, and I sense then that he has something to ask me that must also take precedence over anything I wish to ask him. "Hmm," he says, too intentionally for true surprise, "I've been thinking of calling you."

This isn't belated graciousness. With the slow flop of a hand, he grants me the freedom of the room as he returns to his desk and inserts a three-by-five file card to mark his place into the large book propped open on another book that he must have been reading before I arrived. He does this with more care than it requires, and meanwhile his left eyebrow climbs his forehead a couple of times. Finally he says, "You haven't seen my landlord recently, have you?"

"Not since Monday evening."

"No more recently than that?"

"No."

His surprise is genuine this time, and I think it's frequently true that people do not behave as Yoshalem expects them to. I say nothing, and wait for him to get where he wishes to be by his own route. It's also true that when he isn't speaking strictly medically what he says frequently constitutes a kind of tribal knowledge that I don't quite possess myself and should. After another laboring pause and a momentary falling away altogether, he says, "He's very upset about his sister. He thinks she's behaving badly. But he also attributes part of the blame to your influence on her."

"I don't think she's done anything that wasn't her own idea," I say, with what must sound like the easy energy of evasion.

"Perhaps. But London believes she wouldn't have had the stamina to do what she's done even if it were her idea if you weren't helping her."

"He doesn't think she'd have been over there in the house now in any case, does he?" I say.

"Not there exactly. But he says that if you hadn't made her present arrangements for her she'd probably have gone off as she has before with a woman friend of hers whom he doesn't much like but would trust to keep an eye on her and be sensible. He thinks someone should be keeping a sensible eye on her, and on the boy too, and he's probably right."

"I gather her friend's keeping an eye on her right now," I say.

"Why didn't he tell me?" Yoshalem's voice breaks with accumulated annoyance as he asks this.

"Probably he didn't know," I say, not so much to keep London in the clear, as to keep myself there—to be as creditable as I can manage to be. "I don't know how long she means to be doing that, but I'm going down to the isthmus myself Saturday morning."

"Isn't that something new?" he asks, with the same irritated surprise.

"Only relatively."

"Hmm." The resolution of several questions at once is suggested by this apparently non-committal but this time actually quite explicit noise. "That's not so bad then. You won't mind if I tell him?"

I shake my head, and again feel the impulse to avoid the confusions of speech by sticking my wrist directly under his nose. I've begun to clatter once more in earnest, and as Yoshalem fingers his desk top in what appears to be another preparatory gesture, his slow regular taps measure the extent of my disorder. "You know what limits anything I can say to you," he begins. "All three of them are my patients now—London, his sister, and the boy. But some of the instabilities of the situation must be apparent to you without my specifying them, and I assume therefore that you understand what kind of trouble you could be getting into."

"I'm not sure I do," I say.

Yoshalem can't quite suppress a smile that even in its truncated appearance shows disbelief, but this escape doesn't tell me much more than I know already—that as a man rather than more simply as a patient he finds me puzzling in the extreme. It also suggests though that I've at last become the primary subject of our exchange which is a good thing. My clatter has just about peaked I think, and I move purposefully from the chair on which I've been sitting to one immediately in front of Yoshalem's desk and place my wrist on the surface between us. "Can you check out my pulse," I ask, "and tell me what's going on?"

A look of inquiry informs his face now. The smile is gone, though a slight tension of disbelief still hovers around his eyelids. "What do you think's going on?" he demands, ignoring my proffered wrist.

"A case of the staggers?"

I intend this as a disavowal of authority, but he says, "Okay, when did it begin?"

"Sunday evening," I say reluctantly. "Out of the blue so far as I could tell, while I was fishing. Since then it's been on and off. Off altogether for a couple of days—except that I knew it wasn't really gone. It started up again with a bang a little while ago."

"Fishing?" he says in momentary bewilderment while he continues not to touch me. "Okay. And do you have any idea what caused the resumption?"

"Not much." Wanting to have his fingers on that confluence of veins where I'd seen Gretta's faint erasure, I say it abruptly, but when he nods encouragingly I hazard a minimal specification. "Unexpected news?"

"Sure. Why not?"

Now he does finally pick up my wrist, but he holds it only a few seconds. Replacing it on the desk, he takes care to put it back just where he'd picked it up and in the same position, as though to disavow it. Then he touches my throat more inquiringly, and disorder ebbs under his fingers. "You're right," he says.

"Right?"

"Yes," he says. "I could of course call it tachycardia, but that would be no more correct than calling it a case of the staggers and no more useful. Neither one of us would really know any more. And even if we were in the office and I ran a cardiogram, it's still very unlikely that we'd know any more. Something not ordinary is going on in there, but what it means isn't at all clear."

What is clear I think is that this will be Yoshalem's final statement. It's a lot less explicit than I'd expected and seems as much an expression of his disapproval as a bona fide diagnosis, but I can also see that it answers my needs. The message is that I knew whatever there was to know already and, incidentally, that I had no need therefore to intrude on him so precipitously. I can also feel his impatience with the code —that same system of constraints that governs what he can say to me about his patients—that inhibits his desire to reprimand me for what he probably judges to be my several evasions. "If you were ten or fifteen years older and had high blood pressure, I'd hustle you over to Mt. Auburn and maybe even into the cardiac ICU," he says. "But you're not, and your blood pressure's beautiful. Maybe you're doing something unfriendly to yourself."

If he's not breaking the code now, he's certainly getting around it, and the impatience with which he vents what had been giving him trouble when it was contained, suggests too I think how avid he is to reopen the big book on his desk and continue his rationed respite from the human disorders to which he ministers by vocation but from some large part of which he's long since removed himself. And to which he ministers therefore with the advantages and disadvantages of an extraordinary distance. "When was it you planned to go away?" he asks.

"Saturday. The day after tomorrow."

"I know I can't fit you in tomorrow. When you get back to town though I will run some tests. For the record. In case this keeps up or comes back, which I don't expect."

I tell him that's fine, thank him, bid him farewell, and by the time I've concluded this hasty ceremony I surmise, not without a certain anxiety of deprivation, that my mechanism has not only abated but probably been exorcised as well.

14

THERE'S A MOMENT early Friday evening when I'm certain that my notion that having dinner with Janet and Staines was an irrevocable commitment had been utter nonsense, and that I could certainly have used the fact that I was going down to the isthmus tonight after all and not waiting until the next day as an excuse for deferring this ceremony to some future visit. For now it seems less an obligatory test as it had seemed to me in advance than an inevitable disaster exacerbated but not essentially influenced by my bad judgment in the choice of a place for it to take place. The exacerbation though is considerable. La Becasse is neither grand enough for Staines—it was he who had asked me at our first meeting to call him by his surname after calling me at once by mine—nor sufficiently grubby to allow him to think he's slumming. Its real character I see, though I haven't seen this before, is to be modestly pretentious. The wine list in an embossed leather loose-leaf binder with each category of wine typed on its own plastic-enveloped page lists only seventeen wines numbered for convenience in ordering with all of which even I am moderately familiar. I feel myself gripped in ultimate bleakness as I watch Staines turn his way deliberately and attentively through its stiff heavy pages and then look up at the waitress and ask whether the Tavel is a dry Tavel.

His lips as they shape this question are set in an ironic smile that takes full cognizance of both her uneasiness and the unlikelihood that she will know the answer to his question, but indicates nonetheless an unabandonable will to know. They are expressively pliant lips, but their extreme pallor also makes it difficult to know where they leave off

and the rest of the expanse of broad, pale, faintly freckled
face begins. Staines' complexion is more nearly platinum-
pink than the deprived pink of the ordinary albino however, a rich glistening monochrome that radiates the cheer
of employed energy. The unusual tone actually seems an
energy by-product, like heat, and even his pale lank hair
that falls from his neck over his shirt collar in a carefully
feathered line, falls forward energetically in its principal
growth across his forehead and eyes from which, from time
to time, he pushes it straight back with a soft, strong, manicured hand. For a while then until it's agitated by conversation and the directional thrust of its growth it lies where
it's placed in fingered segments, and the horizontal sweep of
hair across his temples is similarly channeled but more static.
His casually rumpled silk suit, dove gray with flecks of
black and bronze, seems quintessential California to me. My
notion of essence here, however, except for the brief visit
I'd made to L.A. just after Christmas last winter on Janet's
pressing invitation, comes chiefly from the movies.

When the soft-spoken student or recent ex-student waitress confesses that all she knows about the Tavel is that it's
a popular selection among their clients, Staines hands the
wine list back to her and orders a bottle of Beaujolais Vil-
lages. "Number 6," he adds, and despite the intended reassurance of his smile, the waitress writes the order on her
pad, thanks him, and bolts for the kitchen on long, tan,
naked legs that graze at the knees as they pass each other.
She is temporarily overwhelmed I think by intimations of
the breadth of a subject she had previously underestimated.

I though might have known if I'd thought about it, that
wine would be one of Staines' areas of non-vocational ex-
pertise. Comparable to the botanical knowledge he'd shared
with me in the course of that California visit in December.
The house in which he and Janet live and which he had
owned for years before they were married perches on
one of the residential canyon sides of Los Angeles' outer
reaches. I say "perch" advisedly. All the houses at La

Trema do that, and on a horizontal plane—which as an actual perspective doesn't exist—they're built wall to wall. They're effectively isolated from each other though by dramatic vertical space, and these escarpments are intensely cultivated both for appearance and to encourage the continued existence of the houses. The limited flat or nearly flat land that Staines owns is just about covered by his house, a good third of which is actually cantilevered over the next drop, and by a pool shaped to the space between the house and the next rise. A narrow strip has been left though between the pool and the rise to facilitate care of the fruit trees and other planting on this near-vertical terrain. All of these trees are exotics, not market fruit, and Staines had told me their Latin names and specified the particular characteristics for which they'd been selected, and done the same then for the ground covers and squat lizard-leafed shrubs that hold the soil in its unnatural position, restrain its urge toward the heated, sky-blue tiled pool. He'd also, with related panache, shown me how the aquatic vacuum cleaner sucked leaves and bugs from the water and erased the algae from the tiles. Removing faint green blurs from these celestial surfaces with a brush on the end of a telescoping aluminum tube, he let me know that though this was a task he didn't generally perform himself, he could do it demonstrably better than the gardener whose work it was. In conclusion he gave me an explanation of the pool's filtering and recirculating system that was so clear and orderly I really thought I'd understood it until I tried to tell Percy how it worked one icy morning the following week, after I'd returned home.

Staines' suave style, bits of which have rubbed off now on Janet, does something disqualifying to this French restaurant. It seems not only different but significantly lesser than I remembered. In the thin, late summer light paled by net curtains behind the storefront windows and then paled further by the frosted glass partition that separates the panelled back dining room where we're seated from a smaller front room, the candles in wax-dripped bottles, the plastic nosegays, and the posters of Vézelay and Carcassonne look like stage props. Why are we here, I ask myself? Why didn't I beg off this morning either on the basis of my bad night, or because I was leaving town? Why should this event take place anyway? For if it was concern that had brought Janet across the continent to ascertain my state of being, it was something else too that I had no responsibility to assist. Her explanation on the telephone when she'd called me last week though had been simple enough. Staines was flying to Boston for a conference, and so when Richard had announced that morning that he was going camping in the Sierras for a few days with some friends, it suddenly made every kind of sense for her to fly to Boston too. She'd put in some time in Widener and see what I'd actually done to myself when I totalled my car.

Richard is Staines' son, a nineteen-year-old surfer with white hair and sun-bleached eyes who also seems quintessential California to me I suppose, and Janet is not only taking parenthood predictably seriously, but prospering on it too, which might have been less predictable. Her prosperity is even more manifest now than it had been in December. Her poised head even with her hair arranged in the loose, glossy chignon that has replaced the far skimpier bun of her graduate student and junior faculty days is still a little small for her top- and center-heavy body which reduces then below the hips to long legs and trim ankles, but even these now somewhat exaggerated disproportions suggest attractive force.

I'd known Janet for three years before we were married, and lived with her for most of that time though only intermittently since for the last two years of the three I was a draftee. We were married the week after I was discharged from the army, in August, and I joined her then in graduate school where she'd been for a couple of years already but in a different department. I was studying English and she was studying history, and it really seemed part of the bond of our marriage at first to have strong daily discontents in common—that too much of the time we were not doing what we thought we should be doing, and doing a lot of things instead that we saw no reason to be doing at all. Only that bond became also a line of strain as we not only discovered that we responded to these discontents in radically different ways, but could see too that these differences were fundamental. For the preceding two years while I'd been in the army we hadn't learned much more about each other I don't think than our tastes and opinions, which were encouragingly similar. Now though we were encountering disposition, and at this level it turned out we were remarkably dissimilar.

I dropped out of graduate school at the end of the year and knew midway through the year that I was going to drop out. What I was doing made no sense to me, and once I'd made up my mind it didn't I could feel my energy leaking away. But though Janet too said that she saw little immediate sense in what she was doing, this was different. She prospered on managing and took energy right where I lost it, from the cross-grained friction of unsatisfactory daily tasks undertaken to get somewhere. This was the way the world worked, she said. The implicit assertion then and through all the dozen years of our disagreements, that the workings of the world were better known to her than to me, was something I soon felt disinclined to deny. She had no confidence in my talk of other futures, she said. I was getting better grades than she'd gotten in her first year in graduate schol, and my decision not to continue for my degree was folly. She never quite called it cowardice, but I knew she thought this too when she said I had an unreal sense of possibility. This claim was an alternate way to talk about the world as known or unknown. If I retreated from anything I didn't like or couldn't make sense of, I was unlikely ever to do very much.

The job I took at the end of the year then at Hillside, a private school in one of the western suburbs, fitted readily into her notion of retreat I think though she didn't quite say that either. And she might well have been right. Being a school teacher has been a sensible enough activity, but it hasn't been very much, and Janet meanwhile has become a professor of American history at U.C.L.A. and is the author of a well-received book on the secret diplomacy of Colonel House, which she didn't much enjoy writing but judged to be essential if she was to get where she required to be.

I made one more try at getting somewhere. A year before Janet left me and her job at B.U. at once to go to U.C.L.A., I entered law school. It was primarily I think a try to offset the attrition of our marriage, but I soon found it impossible to feel that sitting through lectures on torts and contracts could really have anything to do with what was and was not happening between me and Janet. In itself what I was studying meant nothing to me, though I could sometimes, for a short time, become interested in a specific case or theoretical point. Again I stuck it out for the year but had decided to quit at midyears even though, once more, my grades suggested that I was doing very well. The following year I returned to Hillside.

That settled things for Janet, and when she got an offer from U.C.L.A., she bolted. It was me she was leaving more than B.U., for B.U. would have met the U.C.L.A. offer. Her book had been better than well received. It had made ripples both in the history journals and at the A.H.A. meetings that year. But she said she felt that I'd given up on her when I gave up law school, and in a way that was true though I had no inclination either to leave her or be left by her and would even have looked for a job in L.A. if I'd thought she wanted me to do that. If I hadn't known, that is, that it was just what she didn't want. Marriage was significantly unlike graduate school or writing a book. When it no longer made sense to her for itself—when it was not what she wanted and had expected and we had had for a while—she decided it was cowardly not to quit and try to do better for herself, to seek another future.

We really are fundamentally different, and I take it that here too she's shown her better understanding of the world's workings and averages. Her marriage to Staines seems very sure, and whatever concern for me had caused her to wish to see me now, she had come also I was confident because she wanted me to witness this. To put it another way, I think she wanted me to witness the vindication of the claim she'd made many times that she intended not only to be a historian but to have a life in history. Sometimes she even called this a real life, a notion about which I'm skeptical but to which I'm by no means immune. Being a compliant witness therefore has to be trying, and when things take an unexpected but decided turn for the better after we've gotten by the ordering of the wine it's because I make a move to take things in hand instead. This turns out to be remarkably easy to do. Janet his been watching me and Staines alternately though very differently. She looks at Staines with pride but looks at me with curiosity that centers on my new scar. The time is near I think when she will wish to point out the truth or lesson of what I'm witnessing to me. It's to thwart this that I encourage Staines to talk about himself, though I have another less devious reason for encouraging him too. If her marriage to Staines has brought Janet to a life in history, then presumably he lives a life in history too. I really would like to know something about his life, and when I ask him how well he knows the Boston area, the dumb question works a lot better than I could possibly have imagined. He says he's been here many times before, and this is an introduction to the story of his life from a certain point of view.

"Boston and its environs were entirely beyond my horizon when I was growing up in New York," Staines says. "I knew about Boston. I was a voracious reader and vicarious traveller. But I was too poor to travel any farther than I could go on the Staten Island ferry. Or, for a big treat, on the Circle Line."

He allows himself a rubbery-lipped grin when he makes

this joke about the Circle Line, and allows me time to indicate by a reciprocating grin that I know that it is a joke
and that a tour on the Circle Line is a way to end up going
nowhere. Then he goes on to tell me that he was only six-
teen when he graduated from high school and entered the
city college still having gone nowhere and convinced that
he was disadvantaging himself permanently by having to go
to college at home. He was plagued at that time by anguish-
ing fantasies—the expressive lips turn down slightly at one
corner when he says this to indicate the disproportion of
his pain—of what it would be like to go away to school,
with students who had money, whose families were educated, and for whom, already arrived, college didn't have
to be a tooth-and-claw contest to get a start up in the
world. He thought, he said, that no one moved up without
bringing someone else down. He saw this ascent as a version
of getting a seat on the subway during rush hours. There
were never enough seats, and if he got one it meant that
someone else didn't and that probably along the way he
hadn't extended too much courtesy even to the aged and
infirm.

Staines has a strong feeling for narrative—for telling
things in their order. By the time he'd sped through college
in three years and was doing graduate work in chemistry
at Columbia, he says, his view of his deprivation hadn't
changed essentially but it had modulated. He was beginning
to experience the heady spirits of the successful competitor
but still competing without mercy for anyone, least of all
himself, and he found time to wonder about the worldly
and more attractive, better rounded as well as more kindly
man he might have been if he'd gone to Harvard or Yale or
Princeton or Amherst or Williams, and perhaps even become a violinist as he'd once thought of doing instead of a
chemist. It's important to the flavor of his story that he give
the whole catalogue of alternate colleges and not just let
one or two stand for them all. He'd known by then he says
that he was going to get a seat all right, but he thought of

himself as a less than realized person, someone whose poten-
tialities had been truncated. He thought specifically that he
was destined to be successful but not lovable.

"Some worry," Janet says.

This doesn't sound merely like either reassurance or a
boast. It's also testimony, and there's an edge of impatience
as well, as though as much as she enjoys hearing him talk
about himself and having me hear him, she doesn't want him
to go on too long. I'm prepared to have him go on indefinitely, however, both for the intrinsic interest of his account and for what it could be preventing, and I don't
think it seems in the spirit of his storytelling to wind up
quickly. The melancholy facts of his early life don't really
seem melancholy to him at all in recollection. They are the
basis of earned, expansive self-satisfaction. Expansive presumably because earned. "It took me a surprisingly long
time to discover," he says now, giving each word its full
due and whistling his *s*'s with lingering affection, "that
those fantasies of the better man I might have become were
only fantasies."

The tempo of his speech is intended to convey, I suppose,
something of the duration of this process of discovery—that
his worries had been ignorant or innocent, that he'd missed
nothing of real value, that in the long run not only was most
of what was gainable in the world going to come to him
anyway but that if much of it had come earlier and more
easily he might have mistaken those rewards for the whole
process and received less rather than more ultimately. His
vocal indolence, the bright bubble of saliva in the left
corner of his mouth that pulses with those whistled *s*'s,
the amused gravity of his pale, dimpled, nearly beardless
cheeks, the soft gestures of his amber-freckled groomed
hands—all of these strike me as signs of resolved self-satisfaction. He'd begun his narrative just after we were served,
and proceeding slowly and with evident pleasure and not
neglecting his food as he talks—because though a little
earnest the food is really quite good and even the Number 6

wine isn't bad—he brings us all the way to coffee before he finishes. "The Boston area," he says, holding his demitasse poised an inch above its saucer, "seemed as desirable and mysterious to me when I was a kid and had never been here as Mecca, a holy place, but my opinion of it in recent years, when I've had frequent occasion to be here, has become more moderate."

"Moderate," a considered adjective, is savored like the last of the sugared coffee in the cup he raises to his lips now when he's said it, and at this moment too, perhaps in response to his gesture, the waitress brings the check and he looses his hold on the occasion sufficiently to let me take it. When Janet asks whether I can come back to their motel with them to have a drink, I tell her I've arranged to meet a friend in half an hour or so in the Common and be driven by him to the isthmus. "Tonight?" Janet says. "That's nice. But be careful, and be sure to give my love to Les and Dolly."

"Of course," I say, but hear too that this exchange is not conclusive, and that Janet is not quite letting me go yet. She's as resolved a person in her way though as Staines is in his, and she isn't inclined to rush. Not until after we've come out on the street again, walked a couple of blocks, and come to a halt near a take-out shop for fried chicken, clam, and shrimp directly across from their motel to say goodbye does she finally front me. To make certain I'll hear what she's had it well-fixed in her mind to tell me I'd bet since well before she'd boarded the plane in L.A. In the shop window, a portly neon man in a sombrero and cowboy boots is riding a neon hen, and the electric aura of these figures discolors the twilight. Whether at some signal from Janet or with natural tact, Staines has drawn off a few feet, his face set in a smile that drops his prominent dimples into his jaw, and the combined light does weird things to his pallor. The mixed odors of lard, corn meal, and some indeterminate fried flesh in the air are as unnatural as the light, but Janet shows no awareness of these atmospheric discouragements. On the way from the restaurant, I'd been acutely aware once more of the long-waisted bob with which she walked. A stork's motion, but more energetic than any stork I'd ever seen, and at rest now but not quite at ease her body is charged with a gravitational potential as she leans abruptly toward me and then, momentarily startled or bewildered, makes as if to pick something from the shoulder of my jacket. There's nothing there to pick though, and as she looks at the damaged side of my face for the first time from close-up, the hollow inside my chest, conspicuously empty since the mechanism had departed last night at Yoshalem's house, floods with liquid pain. Inert, not interesting, but awful. "It's actually rather attractive, your seasoned look," Janet says, "only that's a dangerously rapid way to season."

"I agree about the speed," I say, "but I have no opinion as to the cosmetic value."

"You can take my word for it," she says. "And you know, I really would have flown East when I got the telephone call from the Connecticut State Police if they hadn't assured me when I called the hospital that you were okay. Cut-up and bunged-up, they said, but okay. I talked to the resident who had you in charge. Caron his name was, which wasn't encouraging, but he not only told me in no uncertain terms that you were going to be okay but took a testy view of anxious questions."

"I'm still embarrassed about all of that," I say. "I'd apparently left my old emergency card tucked back behind a lot of other cards and papers in my wallet where I never noticed it, and when the police found it and couldn't reach you at the address listed they somehow managed to trace you to Los Angeles. God knows how."

"A good thing too. There ought to be someone delegated to pick up the pieces if you take it in mind to smash yourself up."

She rocks back on her heels as she says this and raises her chin so that she's looking not quite down but along her nose at me, issuing a challenge I'd be willing to ignore but don't think I can. "I should have had someone else's name in my wallet by then to notify in case of emergency," I say.

"Someone like who?"

"Maurice," I say tentatively. "Remember him? The nice dependable assistant headmaster at Hillside who you said made you feel so comfortable at a party once that you fell asleep talking to him."

"Great!" she says, and laughs, but not I think entirely willingly.

Even thwarted though she looks so prospering, so buoyantly chesty when she issues that unwilled laugh, that she seems to have the right to tell me how poor my record is. "Okay," I say therefore. "What?"

"Okay!" she says, the repetition an outlet for relief. "Don't you see that you're never going to make it this way? You're carrying so little ballast it's no wonder you can't hold the road. After the description the cops gave me of the condition of the car, I really expected the D.O.A. report when I called the hospital and was bracing myself for it."

"I didn't take it in mind to crack up," I say. "You might like to know that."

"I do like to know it," she says. "Thanks. But what are you doing to yourself?"

The foot or so that separates her face from mine now is exactly the wrong distance, but we're locked into it. "Let's say I've thought I was conducting an experiment," I say, "in which I was my own human subject. It hasn't felt as strange as it sounds when I say it that way, but I think I've more or less come to the conclusion that it's a failure. It's in the nature of experiments I guess that some of them don't work out. Most, probably, only they're not the ones you hear about."

"I gather that it's the character of successful experiments," she says, "that they start from a knowledge of the known facts, and in this case what are known as the facts of life would have suggested that the outlook for yours was poor."

This is her old familiar battle cry, but having granted her right to it actually makes it sound somewhat different. "I've been considering that possibility," I say, "though I also continue to be skeptical that that body of knowledge exists."

Though she is in a sense thwarted again, this time it seems all right. "Oh, Lord!" she says, and when she rocks forward again she does buss me this time, her lips hard and refreshing against my cheek though they don't linger there.

As she rocks away again, I turn my face quickly to make return, and her cheek moves across my lips. Then I wave to Staines, and because it's evening and cool now, and because having said my different goodbyes to each of them I don't want to stand then and wait for a bus, and because I expect Percy is waiting for me by now in the Common, I begin to walk rapidly toward the Square. After about a block, released and antic though my chest is still burdened and I feel as though I might easily cry, which I haven't done without literary provocation for years, I break into a jog and collide at once with a tiny figure I recognize as the Bengali girl with the berry stain in the middle of her forehead and the diamond chip in the left crease of her nose whom I'd seen in the Circulation Room in Widener this summer, sitting on a high stool behind the desk like a presiding deity—and seen once too in the Yard between Widener and Boylston approaching the mouth of the Yenching dragon with a finger that recoiled involuntarily several times before it could confirm the feel of the stone tongue inside the tensed stone lips and rest there a moment. She was gliding out of a grocery store now, a bag of groceries almost half her height and the arm holding the bag on her hip both enclosed in a fold of electric blue sari, and she seems far less startled when I grasp her shoulders to keep from upsetting her than I am to find myself doing this and to find that her shoulders are hard and round through the thin silk and a lot solider altogether than I could have anticipated. I apologize for running into her and she dips her head but says nothing, and when I set off at a more restrained pace then I immediately encounter the Scotsman with the monumental calves who's also been a familiar figure this summer in his gabardine kilt with sporran, knee socks, and brogues with three-quarter-inch soles. Though this I've been told is his summer costume, as such it must be a lot more suited to the highlands than it is to this sub-tropical city, and I've assumed that the fixed, weak smile on his long prognathous face is prescribed too. As distant in his own way as the Bengali girl and not much closer to home, he probably also occupies as she does some place or slot in the university system in which there seem to be places for something of everything.

Staines had brought the story of his life to a climax by explaining that he regularly received offers now from the colleges and universities he'd had anguished fantasies about when he was a boy, and that he regularly and without regret turned them down and stuck with industrial research. The great universities, he'd begun—and paused then, sucking bubbles of saliva in through the corners of his lips instead of continuing, and inclined his head toward Janet so that his hair leaped down over his eyes and had to be pushed back with both hands. The gesture was intended I suppose to show that he knew and respected her alternate opinion. The great universities he continued then seemed to him to be giant containers in which a lot of people, many but by no means all of them talented, were comfortably cared for and allowed extensive license in exchange for not heaving their weight around too much in the rest of the world. It was a trade-off of sorts he said, and with this construction of the situation still fresh in my mind, on this reach of Mass. Avenue north of the Square where a lot of minor university exotics like the Bengali girl and the knuckly-kneed Scotsman live with something of the appearance of specimens, the steep slate roof and stained, salmon brick walls of Holmes Hall where I'd spent so many hours not so much bored as more and more deeply sad the year before Janet left me isn't really very easily distinguishable in this light from the old university museums around on Oxford Street—the Peabody say, or Gray's Herbarium. I don't, however, dwell on this, but pick up my pace again as I approach the Common, quickened by the sound of a rock band that grows louder as I get closer, and that surprises me for only a moment before I remember that it was because there was to be music on the Common this evening that Percy had set this as our meeting place. He'd keep an eye out for me between nine and ten he specified, on the Garden Street side just across from Appian Way.

15

BY THE TIME I've reached the Common, I'm too charged once more for mere walking. After traversing the north edge at a dog trot that's a compromise between impulse and decorum, I turn down the far side on Garden Street and discover that the irregularly shaped plain of scruffy grass and bare beaten earth has been appropriated for the evening and maybe for the night too by an encampment. Hippies, I think, and am embarrassed even as I think it, not knowing what the term can mean now or even, for sure, what it ever meant. Whatever they're to be collectively called though, several hundred casually dressed men, women, and children are sitting or lying on blankets and ponchos or directly on the sorry baked and compacted earth being diverted by a succession of musicians. The rock band I'd heard first from a distance has given way to a blue grass ensemble of fiddle, guitar, and banjo, and there are also four black bongo drummers in reserve still scratching or patting their taut skins and sometimes lowering an ear to them but otherwise waiting their turn with seeming patience. The scene is above all one of patience, which is precisely what I don't feel myself. A few dogs and children are chasing or being chased, and here and there single figures or small groups are dancing, but mostly the crowd seems to be listening with relaxed attention to the musicians clustered around the monument under the benign elevated figure of the Emancipator. It is almost but still not entirely night, a sweet mist hangs more redolently than visibly in the warm air but not a cop is in evidence, and the guitar player has begun to sing in a plaintive pleasant country mush tenor a song about moving on alone.

Checked now, waiting for Percy, I watch and hear through a screen of cars and vans parked on both sides of Garden Street. An extraordinary number and range of vans—Volkswagen buses, campers, retired hearses, modified trucks, even the obligatory ex-school bus all but covered with legends and messages in glo-coat, and all these vehicles fitted out for greater or lesser housekeeping. Nothing about the scene is threatening or subversive. The hippies, if that's what they are, seem rather the latest purest incarnation of the American way. Detroit houses the nation and the nation rolls—comfortable, cosy, independent. Some of the vans are lighted, cooking odors are more conspicuous than the fumes of gasoline, and once I even hear the unmistakeable cascade of a flush toilet issue confidently from a giant Winnebago. On the Common, the musicians pause briefly and then start up again joined now by a woman vocalist. Her diction is a lot clearer than the tenor's, so that I hear all the words of her hymn or invocation:

> *Down in the valley*
> *Runs a little stream;*
> *It seems to whisper*
> *Don't give up the dream.*

I've both heard and not heard this one before, even as I've both seen and not seen this woman herself in her black tank top and white buttock-hugging shorts.

She favors the sweet homiletic style rather than the alternate Appalachian rasp, and in its quiet way, the crowd quite obviously likes her a lot. I do too, off on the edge watching and listening in a space between a Dodge van and a retired delivery truck on whose high sides the legend PEPPERIDGE FARM still shows through an earthy coat of Rust-Oleum. The truck's rear door is open, and behind the rattling strings of metal and glass beads hung in the doorway to deter flies, in glaring gaslight, a man wearing a blue workshirt and jeans and sitting in a Windsor chair, is holding a three- or four-year-old boy on his lap with whom he's

conducting an earnest conversation. Beyond them, behind the driver's compartment, a woman wearing a dirndl
and embroidered blouse washes dishes in a small stainless
steel sink. A refrigerator to one side of the sink and a stove
to the other side are supplied by a tank of propane mounted
on the roof, and the counterpane and stuffed rabbit lying
on the child's bunk fastened to the right inner wall of the
truck are both covered in the same flowered chintz. Is there
or is there not some disparity between this interior and the
radically disconsolate appearance of the man who when he
isn't talking draws the ragged ends of a Pancho Villa mustache between his teeth with practiced movements of his
lips and tongue and chews them reflectively? Dark and
aquiline-featured, he is a manifestly Jewish hippie, a sub-
category so anomalous that it completes the blowing-up of
whatever remnants the category itself still possesses. The
boy and the woman who is presumably his mother however are fair and northern.

"I just don't," the boy says emphatically, and at this log-
ical impasse the man gazes out through the beaded strings.
Though I know how unlikely it is that he can see out into
the dark from that glaring interior, I step back anyway
onto the sidewalk and find myself abruptly face to face
with Percy.

"I got off a little earlier than I expected to and figured
you'd still be over in the thick, so I was rubbernecking,"
I say, moved to explain myself by the amused displacement
of Percy's mobile features to the left side of his face.

I've never been able to determine the difference of meaning when they go left or right, but my hunch is that there
is one, and the displacement is so far left now that it takes
Percy time to speak. Time enough for me to wonder
whether it had been as brilliant an idea as it had seemed at
eight o'clock this morning, some six hours after Gretta had
called, to ask Percy who'd checked in again this morning
on his way home, whether he'd like to drive me to the isthmus this evening. Then it had even seemed a chance to kill

two birds with one stone—to give Percy who had the next two nights off a couple of days in the sun and get myself down to the isthmus a night sooner than I'd otherwise be able to.

From that early morning perspective, twelve hours appeared a large and potentially significant difference, though not precisely time worth saving so much as time that shouldn't be lost. Optimism of any sort is entirely foreign to the dawn view of the world that attaches itself to a waking state but belongs to sleep or some unstable condition between sleep and waking. Gretta hadn't asked me to try to get to the isthmus sooner. She hadn't really, this time, particularly asked me to get there at all. But her night calls never created a clear relationship between what was said and what might be intended, and the mere fact of her call favored the urgency generated by my visit to Yoshalem the previous evening and the related demise of my mechanism. It would be hard to exaggerate the emptiness left by the departure of that regular concatenation of dramatic symptoms, and by morning Gretta's call seemed to have lodged itself directly in that space.

Though the ring of the phone a little before two had broken my first sleep of the night which I hadn't achieved easily or quickly after my return from Yoshalem's, I'd instantly known Gretta's night-call voice with its special mixture of suppression and blur. The suppression is a recognition of the hour, but I'm not sure whether the blur is an effect of alcohol that then also impels her to call or whether she requires the pretext of alcohol in order to be able to call which she wishes to do for essentially non-alcoholic reasons. Recognizably too she didn't identify herself, but plunged directly into what was on her mind—or what she had it in mind to say at least, which is generally not exactly the same. "It's a truly rare place, Fish," she said. "I can see why you might not want to share it with too many of us urban types. Why I had to sort of twist your arm."

"Where are you calling from?" I asked, knowing that a more direct response was neither expected nor useful.

"In the house," she said. "Where else? Dolly told me to use this phone at any time and just make a note on the phone pad. And I've done that already. 'August 28,' it says, '2:10 a.m. Called Harry in Cambridge.' It's a nice private time to call. Les and Dolly are snoring away together down the hall like an old married couple. But of course you may have been snoring too. The funny thing is that I don't know whether you do snore. That says something about us, doesn't it?"

"Something," I said.

"Ah," she said, "talkative."

"Give me a break," I said. "I'm barely conscious."

"I know, I know. I'm teasing again. Which reminds me, am I really a tease? In a fundamental way, I mean? I called expressly to ask you that but might have forgotten anyway if you hadn't reminded me. Don't I say what I mean—in my own way, of course?"

"In your own way, for sure," I said.

"Come on, Fish. You're not sore at me too, are you? Don't be! You're not just my friend any longer. You may well now be my only friend."

"I'm not sore at you," I said. "But what's up?"

"I've had a fight with Christine. Did you know she was here?"

"Dolly reported she was when I called last night."

"Tonight, you mean. Dolly told me you'd called, but she couldn't have told you that Christine had also gone off then in a huff, because she hadn't gone yet when you called. But she sure went, and gave me quite a rundown on my character before she left. She told me among other things that I like to send out distress signals and then pretend I haven't if anyone takes them seriously. That I bite the Good Samaritan's hand, so to speak—among other things of course equally reprehensible."

Evidently Christine had gone on fluently for some time,

though Gretta didn't care to report most of what she'd said. But she did want me to know that she had most specifically and consciously not asked Christine to come to the isthmus. Her visit had been unsolicited as well as unwanted. And though she remembered that she had asked me to come, she wanted it clear that she thought of my visit chiefly as a way to make up for her recent greedy behavior with me—and also, relatedly, to recognize that the isthmus was after all my place. She hadn't for a moment wished to suggest that she was up for adoption, as Christine had at one point quaintly put it. "I wouldn't say I was exactly autonomous," she said, "whatever that is, but neither am I inclined to be a wholly owned subsidiary. The problem is that though I know well enough some of the things I'm not, I'm a lot less clear about just what I am."

That might have been the end of our conversation if I hadn't then asked about Michael. "He's fine, I think," she said. "Anyway, he really likes it here. But I'm scared blue about him all the time just the same."

"Do you want to bring him back?" I asked.

"The problem is, I'm scared both ways," she said. "Scared that I'll cut it too close, and scared that I'll cheat him of something he likes and ought to have by being chicken. It's the combination that gives me the exquisite shakes— live shakes, if you wish. The truth is that I'm only happy scared. Have you caught on to that yet?"

This description of her situation which I'd elicited, elicited in turn a recognition that may cause me to look as impelled now as I feel. Or look that way to Percy at least who also finds it funny. "I spotted you right away making the turn from Waterhouse Street," he says, "because you were still in as much of a hurry as you'd been in this morning. That made you remarkably unlike any other man, woman, child, or animal on the scene."

"I guess," I say. "But I also know another hour isn't going to make any difference, and I don't want to drag you off before you're ready to go."

"Truthfully, I'd be happy to clear off before those bongos get going," he says. "My own musical tastes are simple-minded enough, but these birds are going to be a little too purely simple-minded for me. I like mine hokier."

"He must not be here then?" I say, hazarding an explanation for Percy's mood.

He only shakes his head, negatively. He's dredged a glossy small-bowled pipe and a packet of tobacco from his pocket and is pouring the tobacco slowly into the bowl with one hand and packing it tight as it pours with the thumb of the hand holding it. Lighting it then takes a number of tries with the short, brown-headed wax matches that he favors but that ignite only uncertainly and infuse the air even when they do with a strong smell of rotten egg. The tobacco too sizzles and sputters and requires a lot of heavy drawing, but when it's finally burning dependably, Percy says, "I've been circling around out there for more than an hour. If he had shown, I'd have seen him by now or he'd have seen me. There's no way we could have missed entirely."

"We might as well go then," I say. "Where's the car?"

"Down near the river, on the access street parallel to the Drive—though come to think of it, I don't seem to remember exactly where."

His amusement at this putative failure of memory increases my apprehension about the journey we're about to embark on together. The weather is suddenly not very promising either. As dusk settles to night, clouds herd together ominously overhead, making the dark darker. But we set out nonetheless, down Garden Street into the Square, across it to follow Mass. Avenue around its corner, and then right, toward the river. "Two of the great things about the heap though," Percy says when we've crossed Mt. Auburn Street, "are that no one's going to steal it, and that you're not likely to confuse it with any other car still on the road."

"I imagine," I say. "It must be getting on for unique."

"It is that," he says.

Talking about his beloved car, he at least sounds spirited, and his memory is also a lot less faulty than he'd suggested. We find our way to the blunt-nosed, chromeless, faded blue car without any wandering and on a corner where it can't be blocked. "You remembered to park it in a tactical position," I say.

Percy removes his pipe from his mouth and laughs boisterously. "I don't claim to be stupid," he says. "Only a little demented."

Strategic parking is necessary, because the car hasn't had a dependable starter for over a year. Nor is this its only deficiency. Percy doesn't have the money to keep it in condition, yet loves it too much to give it up. But he also, I suspect, loves it even more dilapidated than he would if it were in better shape. When the starter makes no sound at all now when he tentatively foots it, we simply get out and push from either side, then jump in again at the crest of a shallow drop. Percy shifts into second and releases the clutch, the engine coughs, and the car stops dead. It has sufficient inertia to freewheel again, however, and on the second try it catches with a feeble chatter that he's able to nurse to a roar. "She really is a brave old girl," he says, sounding almost cheerful.

As we proceed across the river and onto Storrow though his features take a slow displacement again, to the right now, and the unreadable play of twitches across them indicates at least that though he's silent, he's engaged in active inner discourse. When we bend around the Esplanade and approach the apartment complex in which Christine lives, I appreciate his silence. Then around the next bend on the ramp, the headlights blaze a bulky man with a red backpack standing alongside the road holding a thumb into the lane. The brakes grasp unevenly, I exclaim "no" without even thinking about it, we careen slightly as Percy releases the brakes again, and I register a vulcanized face with gold-rimmed glasses and a clipped mustache as we go by.

"You really are feeling pressed," Percy says.

That seems an accurate description, as though Gretta's call and Janet's admonitions were actual physical forces, to which Christine then had added impetus. With or without volition, I seem to have to be in motion. Christine had called me at Municipal Systems at nine-thirty exactly this morning. I'd heard the Westminster Chimes from St. Paul's sounding as I heard the phone ring, and knowing something of Christine's orderly habits of mind, I imagine she'd picked this as the time she'd be likely to get me at my desk when I wouldn't yet be very involved with anything. She must have counted on my being undistracted, for she began in a very low key. "Harry?" she said. "It's Christine Kaplan. Do you have a minute?"

Her voice was more mellifluous even than usual over the phone, and laconic enough to sound vague if I hadn't known that she never was vague. "Of course," I said.

The edge of apprehension that made this assurance not quite in the tone of her question didn't seem to bother her. "Good," she said. "I visited Gretta for a few hours yesterday and wanted to talk with you about my impressions."

"I heard you'd been there," I said cautiously.

"Ah," she said. "I didn't realize you were in such regular touch, but I'm glad you are. I would be too."

"Would be if what?"

"If I was the one who'd arranged this vacation for Gretta and Michael."

"I see," I said.

I meant I saw or thought I saw where we were going, but her voice was mild still as she continued. It might even have been called caressive, though as with a caress, I'd have had to believe in its good faith for it to give me pleasure. The tingle her voice caused in my nerves was only abrasive. "I assume you think that's a desirable place for the two of them to be right now," she said.

"I hope it is," I said, "but I didn't exactly recommend it. Gretta said she was looking for a place to get away to with

Michael for a week or so, and it was the first possibility that came into my head. There's no place of the sort I know that I like better."

"It's nice that you feel that way about it," Christine said, "and having been there now, I even think I may understand you a little better than I did before. But your circumstances and theirs are not very similar."

"Obviously," I said, hedging as I heard her closing in.

She was doing this somewhat inefficiently, probably because what she had to say couldn't be accommodated easily to her style and that style was unalterable. But once she'd gathered enough momentum, she'd given me and Gretta jointly an ultimate dressing down. She'd accused us of what she called "principled irresponsibility" and invoked a kind of excommunication for us, except that much of her point was not that the community should or would cut us off, but that we'd chosen to cut ourselves off. Once she was started—once she found I guess that she could say what she wished to say in her own voice—she didn't leave much unscathed. That the cabin itself was a mess without even a proper bathroom was the least of the place's disqualifications, she said, though if Michael became incontinent it would scarcely be a miracle since at night he had to climb down the ladder from the loft first of all and then find his way out to the privy in the dark. Worse than that though was the swimming, which didn't strike her as being the least bit safe. In spite of the strong lateral current that had made it hard even for her to keep her feet, Michael was being encouraged not only to swim by himself but to snorkel. Gretta watched him, but from too great a distance sometimes to do any good if he did get into trouble, and she herself went swimming entirely alone and even at night. Essentially of course they were both alone all the time. My friends might be fine in their own way, but I surely must find them more interesting to talk about than to talk to. Les was surly and hard of hearing—whatever else, effectively out of touch—and Dolly, however good-hearted or well-disposed, was a slob. She wouldn't knock my friends gratuitously, but I'd cited them among the resources of the place and she hated to think that if Michael "were suddenly a sick boy" and Gretta needed help, they were all she'd have to fall back on. They certainly couldn't be looked to for more than "primitive help," and meanwhile the nearest hospital was too far away for comfort, and perhaps not good enough for comfort either.

What made her "furious" though—and once she got going Christine could convincingly declare her fury too in the same controlled, caressive voice—was that all these disqualifications had to be fully as evident to me, and by now also to Gretta, as they were to her, and yet that we both continued to assert that we were acting reasonably. She was shocked by this, and had to recognize once more that there were finally two classes of people. There were those who demonstrated that they were responsible members of society, who won this status as it were, and those who claimed it on the basis of not much more than age and democratic right. The division constituted a class system, and perhaps the only true class system, she said. She knew to which class she belonged herself—or to which at least she wished to belong and gave her allegiance—and had to recognize finally if reluctantly that Gretta and I were not of this class. But Alf, whatever she thought of him otherwise, was, and she owed it to him therefore to let him know at once that she thought Gretta and Michael's situation on the isthmus a lot more hazardous than I'd led him to believe. She was certain he'd feel compelled to communicate this in turn to Michael's father on whose behalf he'd accepted my assurance that the risk was limited. Once he'd done that the fat might well be in the fire, she said, and this vulgar metaphor was remarkably vivid, coming as it did at the end of an otherwise entirely denotative statement of what she thought and proposed to do.

" 'Pressed' is the right word," I say to Percy now. "But also, at the moment, plain tired."

"Cork off for a while," he says. "I know the way as far as the bridge. That should give you an hour anyway."

I accept this as a good idea, and drop off so quickly then that when I come to again with the smell of salt marsh in the air I have no memory of having left the city—of, for example, passing the big gaily painted Boston Gas storage tanks that guard its limits. Nor though, seeing Percy's stiff distant hold on the steering wheel and the abstracted glare he has fixed on the road, do I understand how I allowed myself to do this. Now it strikes me that even if I stayed awake it wasn't sensible, having totalled a car myself so recently that my scars hadn't yet had time to subside fully to their natural color, to be taking passage whatever its seeming advantages in this defective buggy with this highly distractable driver.

"I guess my conscience must be good," I say to announce my return.

"Because you fell asleep so easily?" Percy says.

"That is what I was thinking about."

"Not an altogether trustworthy sign," he says vigorously, even I think antagonistically, but glad too I can see to be talking again after the silence I'd imposed on him by napping. In the headlights of the oncoming cars, his face is concentrated, skin flushed, eyes brilliant.

"I had a Latin teacher in high school," he says, "Pop Wagner—a kraut with a head as bald as a darning egg and much the same shape. He used to say that some of the students in the class must have been good sleepers because they lied so easy. He was no fool, Pop Wagner. During recitations, he'd walk around the classroom swinging a wooden mallet in one hand as a general threat, and a tiny ball-peen hammer in the other hand that he said he reserved for pinheads."

Grooving on memory, Percy chuckles, the only person I know who still manages this antiquated expression of feeling. He's still back there in some number of other ways too, absent rather than present, and out of company most of the time as a consequence. It's only because I'm in intermittent transit between there and here myself that we are sometimes company for each other. "My dear brother Richard was one of the people he said he was reserving that ball-peen hammer for. To try to knock his lightweight parts together. Needless to say he never succeeded, but I can't hold him to blame for that. I've been working to the same end for a much longer time with no better results."

"To get him together?" I say.

"To get him to put it together," he says, "or at least to make a real try. The hallmark of the kid and all his friends —like those potential friends I was looking for him among this evening—is that none of them makes heroic efforts to put it together. They all go, as they'll tell you, with the flow. The flow never quite gets Richard to where he says he expects to be, but it does get him to some odd places. Last winter he had a job working for the Tactical Police in Portland, passing the day in an asbestos suit taking runs across a cyclone-fenced field with a couple of K-9 Corps hounds-in-training running after him and trying to pull him down. An undignified job, and kind of smelly too he said for a meaty fellow to be living in that tooth-proof suit. But it was okay, nonetheless. He quit when he got ahead and did nothing for a few months. Then this spring he took up worming which is apparently Maine's one growth industry, and that's okay too, maybe because he can quit if or when it isn't, and will anyway as soon as he gets ahead again. The thing about going with the flow is that it keeps you from being in any one place long enough to work up any complicating attachments, and it also lets you off being held to where you say you might be next."

Though he'd apparently waited for me to wake up to start talking, I don't feel that he's exactly talking to me. Rather, talk is the simple, external manifestation of a more complicated interior process. His outer consciousness seems very limited in fact in respect either to me or to the circumstances of the road. Traffic is thin now, but the visibility is poor, and observing his fixed but not necessarily comprehending glare through the misted windshield, it occurs to me that the intermittence of the traffic could make the driving more rather than less hazardous, easier for him to forget entirely what he's ostensibly doing. "The Kid never writes of course," he says. "Writing's not spontaneous. But he telephones when or if the mood takes him, and he phoned last week to say that if things worked out he might be in town this evening to catch the concert on the Common. And on the basis of that and not another word since, I've just spent an hour wandering around in the zoo really thinking I might find him. I'm a genuine ineducable idiot not to know that when he said he'd be on the Common if things worked out he wasn't going to be there. Things don't work out. You work them out if you can and if you're lucky."

Somehow this concluding generalization brings him back to greater local consciousness. "Actually, we'll be lucky to get where we're trying to get tonight if this wet in the air turns serious," he says. "The heap's not much of a wet weather machine."

Glad to hear him come back to where we are, I'm less glad to hear him not only make a prediction of failure but make it with a savoring of pleasure. It's more important to me than I can quite account for to get to the isthmus tonight, and however much Percy might have seemed my best bet for doing that this morning, I can see now there'd been better bets. I could have rented a car despite my reluctance to start driving again. I might well even have bought one, since the daily drive to Hillside and back is almost on me whether I can believe in it or not. "Encourage it to do its utmost," I say, and sound grimmer and less witty than I'd intended.

"Driving this baby is a constant process of encouragement," Percy says with an edge of happy antagonism, and just then the high arch of the bridge looms out of the thick air ahead of us without advance notice, indicating both how thick the air really is and that we've come about two-thirds of the way. I direct Percy to the turn, and as we come off the circle, drops of what is now rain rather than mere mist begin to stipple the windshield.

Soon it's raining in earnest, and Percy grins as he reaches for the wiper control, his teeth white between his thin lips with the pipe, dead now, clenched between them. The wiper blades clack and seem to move over rather than against the glass, spreading the drops but not removing them. "If you're eager for some reason to feel lucky," Percy says, "think that the world looks just about like that all the time to someone with cataracts. My grandmother, who's worn flashlight-lens glasses for as long as I can remember, used to tell us kids to stand still and stop wavering."

The world shimmers viscously as we climb a long hill, and when we crest it, five miles or more by now from the bridge, we're looking directly into the oily lights of a big semi that had been writhing over our heads while we were still climbing. The light first and then the sound seem a condition of hazard we have to pass through, and still clutching the edge of the seat with both hands, I'm momentarily relieved when the growing silence that is the other end of this condition is broken by a sound like a large, limp shoe slapping the pavement immediately behind us. Percy brakes, and we skid onto the shoulder spraying mud and gravel. "Should be the left rear," he says, "and the mischief is I don't have a spare. I've been meaning to get one as soon as I got a few dollars ahead. So what we have to do is get the flat off, then see if we can get it somewhere to be fixed and bring it back."

He outlines this procedure with exhilarated skepticism, and we step out of the car into the rain which is coming down hard enough now to soak through our light clothes at once. After a certain amount of rummaging in the trunk, Percy finds the lug wrench and jack under an empty rim. "It may comfort you somewhat to know that this is work

I'm familiar with," he says. "I'd even suggest you sat the whole thing out inside the car and out of the rain if this jack were a likelier piece of equipment. But bumper jacks, except for the heavy duty ones they have in garages, are sorry articles at best, and this one is sorry even of its kind."

"It doesn't matter," I say. "I've gotten as wet already as I'm going to get."

"I guess that's true," Percy says.

Even this brief statement is too energized though to be simple agreement. It has the propulsion instead of profound affirmation, as though the flat were not an accident but a proof, and after he's pried off the hub cap and broken the lugs free, he places the flange of the jack under the lip of the bumper and begins pumping. The body of the car rises slowly away from the wheel without sufficient connection with it to compel it to follow, and when the flange has climbed to within three or four inches of the top of the ratchet, which has assumed a shallow bow by then, the car creeps forward and descends in tantalizing slow motion, allowing Percy time to heave himself out of the way before the jack spins out and thonks against the soft, muffling ground. "When I think of the number of times my daddy warned me to always block one of the good wheels!" he exclaims.

Cheerful still, even bemused, he unjams the jack while I find a couple of suitable stones alongside the road and wedge them under the front wheels. On the second try, the flange goes to the very top of the bowed ratchet before the wheel clears the ground and jiggles loosely then in the hold of the spent springs. The car doesn't move this time and the jack keeps its footing. Working from behind the car, Percy removes the lugs and places them in the hub cap, then comes alongside the wheel to lift it off. He's hunkering so close that it looks for a moment as though he were assisting the jack in holding the car off the ground. "My daddy also warned me about changing an outside wheel," he says, looking up at me over his shoulder. "That it could be the fastest way he knew to reduce."

His white shirt, plastered to his chest, is luminous in the dark except where the grease marks where he'd embraced the wheel simulate shadows. "Now it's our thumbs or shank's mare," he says. "How many cars passed while I was too occupied to count?"

"Not one," I say.

"That's what I thought. And when I look at us, more-over, I see that we look like what everyone is always warned not to pick up."

I agree that this is also true. Together, one to each side of it, we roll the wheel ahead a little distance, so that if a car does come by we'll be more likely to be seen before it's on us. "He had some disparaging things to say about hitchhiking too," Percy says, presumably still talking about his father. "But on any one occasion of course, he could turn out to be wrong no matter how right he was on average."

"Of course," I say.

We wait so long then for a first car, standing each with a hand on the virtually treadless tire between us, that when lights do finally appear they themselves seem what we've been waiting for, and I'm dismayed and unbelieving when the car booms by without slowing and not much less dismayed when a second car hard behind the first does the same thing. "Maybe we ought to lock the wheel for what little it's worth inside the car and mush back to the bridge," Percy says. "We could probably hitch a ride from there to Boston, and I'd come out here again in the morning by bus when the circumstances would be somewhat friendlier, and you could probably take the same bus to the isthmus."

"Let's mush the other way a bit first and see if anything turns up," I say, not just on speculation but because I've just seen a Getty sign brighten into the lights of the second car as it receded into the distance and then fade.

"You're nothing if not persistent," Percy says. "You must really think your getting there tonight instead of tomorrow is going to make some difference. It's funny. I also thought it would make a difference if I showed on the Common this evening before heading out of town."

He's skeptical but unresistant, so that I don't have to tell him that the way I feel seems to have nothing to do with what I think. We turn the wheel together to the right and head down the far side of the hill we'd just climbed when the tire went flat. Braking and guiding the wheel but not having to push it, we have pretty easy going. When we reach the bottom though where another road crosses this one at right angles, the Getty station, in the near left angle of the cross, is closed. "If we'd gotten here a few hours earlier," Percy says, "or if we had the gumption to stay here until morning, this place would certainly be the answer to our problem."

"Yes," I say.

"We might also chance just leaving the tire against the office door, and when I got back in the a.m., it would almost certainly be repaired."

"Okay, hold on," I say, and feel Percy stiffen across the wheel at my sudden heat.

The single naked bulb in the station office creates light in the adjacent garage as well, and through the glass of the big closed overhead doors, I can see the tire-changing apparatus in the left rear corner next to a rack of tires on a dolly. "Would you be able to fix it yourself?" I ask.

"I've done it before," Percy says.

I walk around the station leaving him to wheel the tire after me alone, and find the frosted-glass double-hung window with its lower sash raised six inches off the sill as I'd pictured it would be. I push the sash up as high as it will go then, which is just about enough to let me slide through head first, over the toilet onto the damp tile floor. Then, on my feet, I reach back through the window for the wheel which Percy hands me on the diagonal. "That's breaking and entering if I'm not mistaken," he says, still amused but also somewhat uncertain.

"I'd fix it myself if I knew how," I say, "only unfortunately I'm a city boy."

"That's okay," Percy says, and after straddling the window, he lets himself through with a grace I hadn't even tried for.

The garage, when we emerge into it, is actually a lot brighter even than it had looked from the outside, more like an illuminated aquarium. "I'll watch up front while you're fixing it," I say, "and if I see a car coming we can wait in the john until it's gone by."

"Right," Percy says briskly.

He's no longer waiting for instructions now, but has the wheel on the changing rack and is threading down the clamp that holds the hub. A couple of minutes later, when I spot the revolving roof beacon of a cruiser, we crowd into the john with the door almost closed and watch it go by. "Makes you feel better or worse about the law, depending on how you look at it," Percy says.

The alternating red-and-green flashes disappear rapidly over the crest of the hill, and when we've emerged from the lavatory, Percy—who's had the inner tube in his hands —spreads a section of the black rubber to show me a long slit running between two patches, and three other patches spotting the tube in other places. "This particular piece of rubber isn't likely to hold air again," he says happily. "Not for very long at least."

"Take a new one," I say. "That will give us a chance to patronize the station."

"I see what you mean," he says.

He finds the right tube quickly and takes it out of its box. When he flips the switch of the compressor then, hollow iterations bounce off into the night. The harsh strokes beat on my eardrums, felt as well as heard, but no one, I decide, is likely to be out walking in the rain at this hour. I pick up the empty box Percy had dropped on the floor, walk into the office with it, and place it conspicuously in the middle of the desk. "Five bucks should cover it, shouldn't it?" I call.

"And overhead," Percy answers. "I'll see what I have in a sec."

"Forget it, this one's on me," I say, as cheerful now suddenly as he's been for some time.

16

USING WINDOWS for doors must be an easy habit to acquire, for having climbed in and out of the Getty station rest room that way Friday evening, the next evening I find myself climbing out of my second-story bedroom window in Les and Dolly's house onto the stage and down a ladder then to the ground. An urgent exit, though between the time the airplane buzzed the house in the early morning and the conversation I'd had with Percy a little while before I make this exit, only a moment watching him playing chess with Michael in the late afternoon had done anything either to justify or to dissolve the apprehension that had brought me so uncomfortably to the isthmus the previous night. Even the airplane had been only exacerbating rather than confirming. It had told me no more than I knew already that is, but told it aggressively.

Percy though, in a clean but unironed white shirt and white hospital pants that declared how little he meant to bask in the sun, had been the surprise of the day. Contention lifted from him overnight, he was in his element as I'd never seen him before and, perhaps consequently, a lot more outreaching. Meeting each on his own highly peculiar ground, he'd won the confidence of both Les and Michael neither of whom gave confidence readily. He'd run heating ducts with Les all morning and into the afternoon—another skill he owed he said to his daddy—and it couldn't have been more than half an hour after Les was called out to another septic tank emergency in the middle of the afternoon before he and Michael were sitting on the bank over the beach together, each focused intently on the chessboard lying on top of the bank between them. From my limited view from the stage on the east side of the house where I was shingling with Dolly, I'd seen Michael come out of the cabin without Gretta and at obvious loose ends, and then seen Percy emerge from the cellar equally unoccupied, but their actual meeting, which I can't quite imagine, had taken place unfortunately out of my view.

The airplane though had gotten the day off to a bad start by rekindling my instinct of trouble without nourishing it. My arrival on the isthmus with Percy only a few hours earlier in a true summer squall had after all been a triumph of unfounded urgency over comic obstacles, and when we'd then managed to let ourselves into the house without rousing anyone, and into the two unfinished and unoccupied bedrooms upstairs nakedly empty except for the bed-sized slab of foam rubber Les and Dolly had placed on the floor in each of them, I was suddenly no longer being goaded by apprehension. Here I was, and nothing could be radically amiss after all if no one had even stayed up to meet us. It had even been somehow reassuring too to see Gretta's Beetle drawn up alongside the jeep and the back-hoe in the yard. I took off my clothes, unrolled my sleeping bag on the foam pad, and crawled in, and as the squall blew through and the wind and rain receded, the sound of the roused water turning tons of worn stones in its wake as it alternately assaulted and retreated from the beach was also heartening. I slipped off too, and knew nothing after that until the early sun through the two east windows had begun to cook me inside my feathers. In my condition of semi-conscious stupidity, it took me a while then to realize that I wanted to unzip the bag and a while still after that to do it, and one way and another I never quite fell away again. But I must have dozed for several hours in the warm air nonetheless, holding off thought, before the plane brought me altogether awake. It passed close enough over the roof to rattle the rafters, and my first awareness when I opened my eyes was of the shadow of its wings on the windows.

By the time it had circled and made a second pass, I was up and dressing and saw the airplane body mounted unconvincingly on the high spider frame of the pontoons which almost touched the crests of the waves as it levelled low over them for a moment and then gunned up over the house again. I was dressed and out in the yard then with all the rest of our unlikely household—Les, Dolly, Stevie, Percy, Gretta, and even Michael whom I wouldn't necessarily have expected to turn out so quickly even for an airplane—when it disappeared behind the house on its third descent, then flashed its belly over the roof and banked in a tight semi-circle fifty or seventy-five feet off the ground that kept the window on the passenger's side of the plane turned to us. The face behind that window was broad, confident, even affable as it moved in axis with the pilot's thinner face in dark glasses beyond it, but both faces were inclined toward the ground with chins retracted to survey us. Lords of the earth, I thought, and heard Gretta say, "Golly, Michael, it's your father."

"I know that," Michael said.

The lower half of the window flapped in to open, and a thick hand tossed a pellet of brightness into the air, then pulled back again and waved casually alongside the glass as the plane climbed up over the house a last time and out over the water.

The terms of my own binary division of the world are very unlike Christine's even if they range some of the same people together. I'd have the lords of the earth on one side and the provisionals on the other, and no virtue attaching to either side. My division wouldn't be as comprehensive as hers, however, since there are too many people I can't assign to either class. Les and Dolly, for example. Or even Stevie, who was off after that pellet while it was still descending. Having found and recovered it swiftly and confidently though from a patch of bayberry to the north and west of the house just beyond the line of parked vehicles, he then stood with the protective aluminum canister of a roll of thirty-five millimeter film lying on his open right palm looking leggy and uncertain in his red swimming briefs until Dolly pointed a finger toward Gretta.

Holding the canister in her own open palm then, Gretta had regarded it with a kind of puzzlement that could have been genuine or demonstrative or some combination of the two before she opened it, took out the note that we all I suppose assumed she'd discover, and read it aloud. "Hoped to visit," it said. "Sea too heavy to land. Will try again tomorrow."

A seignorial message, and I might even have found the casualness of its telegraphese more convincing if I hadn't been so certain that this attempted visit was the first consequence of Christine's telephone call to Alf. This was obviously the way lords of the earth would conduct their business—promptly, splendidly, and inexorably as hawks, I thought, remembering the chins retracted between the two pairs of elevated shoulders and the two faces fixed on us as though projecting the radius on which the plane turned. Gretta, after reading the note aloud, had said only that it was a pity they hadn't been able to land after coming across from Nantucket in such an original and foresighted fashion, and I had a conviction that my arrival on the isthmus had after all been late.

We'd broken up then and gone our separate ways, and I only saw Gretta once again, relatively briefly, before I began shingling with Dolly. I sought her out on the beach after breakfast, mostly it turned out to watch her and Michael bob about on the agitated surface of the ocean in what was also, in significant part at least, a demonstrative exercise. The water was too rough to really swim after the storm, and much too rough for Michael to demonstrate his new proficiency with a snorkel, but they both, she said, preferred rough swimming to not swimming at all. They'd gone into the water and come out of the water then together, in inseparable cahoots, and they also, I saw, showed equal exposure to the sun. Even soaking wet though

Michael's tan lacked Gretta's sanguine flush.

This inseparability had made it impossible for me to question Gretta. I could only listen to what she said, wonder as I did so often when her conversation was at its most assertive and supposedly therefore transparent what I was to understand, and feel how this limited my chances of taking any advantage of the twenty-four-hour respite afforded by the rough sea that had kept the hydroplane in the air. But though I couldn't really talk to Gretta, Dolly had been more than ready to talk to me about her.

One of the most attractive things for me about Dolly is the way her operative understanding of the world, whatever its limits, meets her needs. Her curiosity about other people's behavior is more or less disinterested, and reflects chiefly good will and a wish to be amused. But it's keen nonetheless once it's roused, and I could imagine how Gretta's stay here this week might have roused it. Her actual opportunities to talk to me most of the day though were about as constrained as mine were to talk to Gretta though for simpler reasons. Sunday, shingling the west wall of the el, we'd never been more than fifteen feet apart. But today, on the east side of the house, we were shingling separate halves of the main wall to either side of the big central bay window. We started each course therefore almost forty feet apart and finished still eight feet apart. Only public conversation could be managed over this distance, and it was late afternoon when we finally got up over the top of the bay. Percy and Michael were playing chess on the bank a little beyond and below us by that time. Dolly suggested we take a break the first time we actually closed the gap between us, and while she told me how Christine had followed Gretta up to the cabin from the beach Thursday evening just before she took off—Christine in a good summer suit and heels and Gretta in a nightgown and with a towel draped over her shoulders but nothing under the nightgown but her wet flesh—I watched Michael get up suddenly and hurry behind the nearest moderately high clump of bayberry. He stood there for thirty or forty seconds with his forehead and eyes visible over the top of the clump staring into space and I realized that I'd seen him in that same posture behind the same bayberry bushes at least once before since they'd begun playing. I looked at my watch, saw that it read seven minutes to four, then watched him come out from behind the bayberry still adjusting his shorts, moving at a duck-footed rush that looked neither comfortable nor controlled. Seated again though, he waited to restudy the board before making a move he must have been considering and ultimately even picturing while he was gone, and Percy touched one of his own men, hesitated, removed his hand, then reached to another man and did move this time. Percy seemed to signal every thought he had with his hand whereas Michael didn't move until he'd made up his mind. He moved only deliberately even then, but as I watched then I could see that they both played finally at about the same rate of speed.

Dolly, to my right on the stage, was closer to the game than I was but had her back to it, and I was watching them over her head and shoulders as she leaned over the cupped cigarette that would determine the length of the break we were taking. This inclination of the head and shoulders was toward me as well though and also in the interest of confidence. "I wasn't spying on them," she said. "I'd just gotten out of the shower, getting ready to go to bed, but even the bathrooms in this house have views and I wasn't hustling. I don't unfortunately have much reason to hustle to bed any longer. I was brushing my teeth comfortably without thinking much about what I was doing and enjoying the view without paying too much attention to it either when they came across it and suddenly I was paying attention. You couldn't not. I told you earlier that evening that my heart hadn't warmed much to Christine, but I would never have pictured her this way either. Putting herself out this much, I mean. She was trotting along the path next to Gretta, working hard to keep up in her tight skirt and heels while Gretta, who's longer-legged anyway, was also enjoying a lot freer motion. She was also talking as hard as she could and not too happy I thought about what she was saying while Gretta just seemed to be walking away from her. Sailing away you might say, except that it wasn't so much away from her as just staying on course and not paying much attention. Which is what I'm beginning to think she does to all of you. It isn't as though Christine's the only one after her for something. There's you too, and her ex-husband as well I guess, and even her brother from what she says though he hasn't been in evidence yet. She's being pursued by foot, car, and airplane. Everything but boat so far, and I won't be surprised if that comes next. I don't think I quite understand what it is you're all after. My usual rather vulgar notions about such matters don't seem quite adequate. But whatever it is, she just keeps on her way as though she didn't quite know you existed."

"Yes," I'd said.

Dolly looked up expecting something more, and when she saw that I was looking past her at Michael and Percy, she turned on the stage and looked at them too, over her right shoulder. It was Michael's move, and he was studying the board and picking distractedly at his shorts with his left hand, at some felt but not quite registered discomfort, his head and torso independent and relatively still while the hand went about its business. "He's the only one she does seem to pay full attention to," Dolly said, "and that's the other part of the picture I don't get. I know he's not quite right, but she's doing more than taking care of him. Sometimes what's going on between them seems pretty queer."

"Yes," I'd said again.

I hoped that might be enough and thought from experience it would be, that all Dolly probably wanted was to have me listen to her though I also knew she was always glad to have me tell her something she didn't know and always hoped I might tell her something spicy. But I'd underestimated her interest this time, or mistaken its full quality, and the smile with which she looked at me as she ground out her cigarette was at once quizzical and unbelieving. There was some other question she'd have asked I thought if she'd trusted my disposition or my ability to answer it, but she settled for an admonition instead. "Be careful, baby," she said. "I really don't know what's going on, but I have enough general confidence in myself to take that as a bad sign."

This required nothing of me but acknowledgment, and we'd gone back to work then and nailed two long courses of shingles over the window before we quit just before five. It was 4:48 exactly, shortly before we quit, when I saw Michael leave the game and go behind the bayberry again at the same toiling gait—a motion of exasperation and distraction I thought this time, as independent of his stretched but unfractured attention to the board on which he and Percy were moving toward the conclusion of a game as the hand easing his shorts had been a little earlier of his central consciousness.

As Michael looked from the bayberry into some uncertain blank distance that didn't interest him though, I thought Percy might be looking some question at me, and though I had something to ask him as well now before I did anything—something I thought I could probably count on him to know more about anyway than I knew—it was midevening before we were alone together, after several hours of uneasy full-group activity. Dolly had invited Gretta and Michael to join us for dinner, and after dinner, still together and partly I think to make conversation entirely unnecessary, we'd all watched *What's My Line*. TV, even though it meant watching three white hunters tell their life stories with unshareable relish, was less arduous, but when Gretta and Michael took off for the cabin again during the half hour of local news from a station in New Bedford that followed the white hunters, I took off too, upstairs to my bare room where the only way I could even read was to lie down on the mat with my sleeping bag

rolled under my head. I wasn't really in much of a mood
to read though anyway. I simply waited with a book in
my hand for Percy to come upstairs too, and it was almost
an hour before that happened. As soon as Gretta and Michael and I had left he'd gone into high gear. I heard his
excited voice repeatedly over the duller, more modulated
voice of the newscaster, and his face when he did appear in
my room finally was dilated and bright. It was also though
I thought beginning to be rueful, to show a certain skepticism about the pleasure he was still experiencing. "You
weren't asleep were you?" he asked.

"No," I said. "Only it's either lying or standing up, and
lying seems preferable. It's a pretty basic room."

"Clean, well-lighted, I like it," he said. "But it's your
friends I like particularly."

I'd have been kind to forget what I wished to ask him
if I could, and leave him as much of his afterglow as he'd
allow himself. With the sea flattened though, the lords of
the earth would descend on it without difficulty early the
next morning and be among us. At dinner, Gretta had continued to ignore me assiduously, and next to Stevie, to
whom he hadn't so far as I could tell said a word, Michael's
suntan had looked even less an evidence of health than it
had earlier in the day. If he was as bad as I suspected, and a
move was to be made, it had to be made before morning.
But I had only notions about how bad he really was, and
depended on Percy to know more. He could hardly not
know more I thought than I'd picked up in an hour of
reading standing in the library stacks on Tuesday when I
was supposed to be having lunch, giving myself a crash
course for beginners for which I had none of the prerequi-
sites. "You sure hit it off with Les," I said. "With Michael
too as a matter of fact, which was even less to be expected."

"That was different," Percy said. "He plays a mean game
of chess, and not just for a kid. That makes nothing else
necessary."

I could see him shift gears then, reluctantly. "I almost

forgot," he said. "What's he so nervous about?"

"I don't think of him as being nervous exactly," I said, "I'd call him stolid."

"By golly, he sure has nervous kidneys anyway. I lost track of the number of times he quit playing and went into the bushes even though the interruption drove him nuts every time."

"Did they ever talk about polyuria in that quicky course you took before you got the job at Mt. Auburn," I asked.

"Jesus," Percy said. "That?"

"I wouldn't be surprised."

"The three furies," Percy said, "polyuria, polydipsia, and polyphagia. We had a lecture about them, and though I've also seen them in action, you might say, since then, I still find it hard to think of them as just terms for aggravated bodily functions—for pissing too much, or even for insatiable thirst and hunger. They sound more like Greek versions of the plagues that afflicted the Egyptians."

"I timed him once," I said. "It was fifty-five minutes between trips, and for the last fifteen or so at least, he looked pretty afflicted."

"And you knew what it was," Percy said.

"Not for sure," I said. "But I know he's probably been in remission for about three years now though I didn't find that out until last week when he was in the hospital for tests. The doctors released him again on Saturday with no decisive finding and without doing anything, but they weren't happy about it. Releasing him was mostly Gretta's idea. They said he was all right still but probably wouldn't be long. That they figured he was on a kind of edge. I wondered whether you thought he'd gone over it now."

"I wouldn't have the foggiest," Percy said, "except that I'm sure his breath isn't fruity or I'd have noticed that for sure. The first time I got a whiff of that fragrance, it kept me off apples for almost three months, and ordinarily I'm a big apple eater. But I doubt very much that he's all right."

Just inside the door still, puffing whenever he wasn't talk-

ing at the same reluctant pipe he'd had hanging out of his
mouth most of the previous evening, from my vantage on
the floor Percy had looked tall and foreshortened but also
familiarly vague in his white shirt and pants against the
raw white Sheetrock. Then, without changing location,
he'd hunkered down with his buttocks just above but not
touching his raised heels and only his toes on the floor. A
weightless float that shouldn't have been stable but seemed
to be. The pipe too floated, with only the very end of the
stem between his teeth. "I'd say you ought to scoop him
up, take him back to that hospital, and let them do whatever they thought they should do next. If you don't you're
liable to have a very sick kid on your hands."

"I imagine," I said, watching him roll the waxy inch of
a spent match between the thumb and forefinger of his left
hand, thinking, and finding thought hard to tolerate.

"Is that why you were so bound and determined to get
out here last night?" he asked.

"That—and some other related considerations."

"Naturally. But you haven't seen that much of him since
you've been here. Or of his mother, so far as I can tell. I
thought she was your friend."

"Odd, isn't it," I said.

"It seems odder than hell to me, to tell you the truth,"
he said, and his vehemence caused him to bob slightly on his
toes. "Les and Dolly are my kind of folks. A kind I don't
see much these days. Stevie too. They make me realize
how little I understand most people. What's your friend
Gretta been up to all day? And why does the kid have to
be so concerned about her when he's the one to be concerned about? He told me that if she came out of the cabin
he figured he'd better quit playing chess and go swimming
with her. Not that he loved swimming so much. He didn't,
and snorkeling made him feel half-drowned all the time
he had his face in the water. But she thought it was good
for him, and he knew it made her feel good to see him doing it. Brother! If he were my kid, I'd have him back up in

that hospital so fast it might make his head swim."

At about that point I'd thanked Percy for telling me what he could, but he'd worked himself up too much talking to be satisfied by gratitude. Maybe he ought to take another look at Michael, he said. Knowing what he now knew, he might see something he hadn't seen before. Or if I just decided I wanted to get him back up to Boston, he and the heap were at my disposal. He wasn't the least bit tired. He'd cork off of course right away now if he lay down, but that was just a habit he'd inherited from his provident ancestors. You didn't waste the chance to sleep when you got it, and he stored sleep the way other fatter people stored calories. He could wake and be ready to go at a moment's notice, bright-eyed and bushy-tailed.

He was in fact so revved up to go, to do something or anything, that I wait almost an hour before I do anything myself, to be pretty sure he's asleep. By then I think I can count on Dolly too to be asleep, for I want her assumptions about what's drawing me to the cabin at this hour of the night as little as I want his assistance. Nonetheless, when I climb out the bedroom window onto the stage and then down the ladder, the image of myself as Dolly would see me plays uncomfortably against my true situation. On the ground, I give the house a wide berth on the odd chance that she may still be awake after all and looking for diversion—but also, I think, because the slightly longer walk is attractive after my last hour of confinement, waiting to get out, the last waker in a sleeping house.

A big piece of moon is still so low in the east that when I do circle back into the yard, I cross through the shadow of the house, a black rectangular blank that ends on a precise line fifteen or twenty feet short of the cabin. Beyond the line, the air is lucid once more and the ground is bright, and the far paler light inside the cabin makes the screen door glow dully and casts no radiance. The peepers' electronic whine seems the audible accompaniment to the moon's brightness, the other portion of a single atmosphere.

I scratch the screen, and Michael instantly says, "Gretta?"

"No," I say. "It's me."

"She's not here right now," he says. "She's gone for a swim. But you can come in and wait for her if you want."

I step in quickly, to thwart the insects and moths clinging to the outside of the screen, and almost trip over a rank of luggage just inside the door—a large aluminum valise, a brown duffle, and a brown canvas bag. Michael, in pale blue pajamas, is sunk in the farther of the two splayed mushroom chairs with a book in his lap. "You're up late," I say, mildly.

"I'm not feeling very well," he says.

"Is it bad?"

"Not very. But I couldn't get to sleep."

"And that's why you're all packed up?"

"We were thinking about driving back to Boston a little while ago, but then Gretta thought maybe it would be just as well to wait for my father to get here in the morning and let him fly me there."

The statement would be relatively affectless if it didn't have the inflection of a question and if it weren't for the hand moving aimlessly against the open page of the book as he makes it. "How long ago did Gretta go swimming?" I ask.

"I'm not sure," he says. "A while. She says she swims the way some people meditate."

"My friend Percy says you play chess the way most kids your age play casino," I say.

"That's more my thing, I guess," he says. "I'd have played a little better though if I'd been feeling better."

"How long have you been feeling bad?"

"I've been having a pretty good time until today," he says, "and Gretta was having a great time. Now I have to go messing it all up."

"You can't help it."

"I don't know," he says. "Maybe we could still wait a couple of days and see what happens."

"Are you scared?"

He's kept his eyes at least half on his book as though not to lose his place while he was talking, but now he looks full at me. "Not very," he says. "Gretta's probably a lot more scared."

He doesn't look frightened at all, and certainly not nervous. The salt water and the sun have curled and matted his hair, and this dense cap low over his eyes and the tops of his ears and the low relief of his broad face make him look like a medallion portrait of some Roman emperor in his youth. Claudius perhaps, or Octavian, I can't remember which though I remember the face perfectly from the engraving in my first Latin reader. "I kind of wish it had happened already," he says. "I don't think I'll be such a drag once it has and they've figured it out. If I can learn to give myself those shots that is. Gretta's not going to be too good at that either."

"That's not going to be any big deal," I say. "Not after the first couple of times anyway."

"I don't know," he says. "Gretta's pretty bothered. I guess that's why she's thinking about having my father fly me up to Boston in the morning. She seems to think it might be better if he took care of me for a while."

"What do you think?" I ask.

"I don't know," he says again, and crossing his legs, sliding one full thigh surreptitiously over the other, he looks distressed though still not really nervous. What makes his tan so unencouraging I see now finally under artificial light, as I watch him scratch his right or upper knee with the nail of his right index finger, is its dry glaze.

"Gretta and I are really a lot more like each other than I am like my father," he says, "so it seems to me I probably ought to stay with her. And anyway, don't you think things could be better once it does happen, even if we have some trouble getting used to it?"

"I'd bet on it," I say. "I'd like to bet on it as a matter of fact."

"You're not just trying to jolly me?" he says.

"Not a bit," I say. "Maybe I'll go down to the beach and see what Gretta's up to."

"Sure," he says. "Christine said she shouldn't be swimming alone like that anyway."

"You might lie down and get some rest," I say. "In case it turns out to be a long night."

"Even if I know I won't go to sleep?"

"Why not?" I say. "Even if it's only to take it a little easier."

"Okay, but I'll lie down on Gretta's bed and not bother to climb up into the loft," he says, and I stall, leaving, and watch him double the pillows one onto the other so that he's half-sitting up when he does get onto the bed, his shoulders, neck, and head on the ramp he's constructed, hands under his neck, and arms winged out stiffly to either side of his head.

Outside then, I make another detour around the house and reach the bank at the south end of the shallow crescent that's a couple of hundred yards across from horn to horn. The sea is virtually flat now under the low moon's blanket of brilliance, a thick dazzle into which it's hard to see, and I have an interval of impending panic before I locate the flat white of Gretta's bathing cap somewhere midway across. When I determine that it's moving toward rather than away from me, I climb down the bank to the beach. The sand, which had been almost too hot to walk on when I was here this morning, chills my feet right through my sneakers.

A little way down the beach, I discover Gretta's nightgown and towel on a rock near the water's edge, and seat myself on the rock to wait for her, and as she comes abreast of me, I can distinguish her arms, first one and then the other, lifting brightness from the water in deliberate alternation. She doesn't turn toward me though as I'd expected, but continues past me to the south. Her arms first and then her bathing cap too disappear into the brilliant surface, and five minutes or more go by before she re-appears, cap first this time, and then her arms moving in inexorable alternation.

When she passes me again now, I realize that I have little idea how long she's been doing this, and no idea how long she'll continue. Anything seems possible. As I watch her I lose all sense of a body of substantial weight moving through a substantial resistant medium, and see only the spectral cap, weightless and frictionless, drawn along the surface by a largely invisible, seemingly inexhaustible, re-ciprocating machine. Only for the short time she's passing in front of me does this become two arms whose fullness and weight are sheathed in immaterial brightness, and whose regular alternation begins to seem an appalling ex-ercise of secrecy.

She passes me three times this way at unchanging speed, twice swimming to the south and once to the north before, going north again, she does finally turn toward me. It's only the rock of course she knows she's turned toward, and her nightgown and towel, and I stand up, therefore, while she's still well out in the water to give her opportunity to see me before she's actually on me. The moment when she does this is visible—when the rhythm of her swimming, which had seemed inexorable, changes. She stops altogether, treads water, then switches from crawl to a breaststroke that's not intended to carry her onto the beach but to allow her to ride in on the light surf. When she's beached herself then on its furthest carriage, she draws her knees under her and rises on them and her hands. Her pendulous breasts sway below her trunk and her head—deprived of hair by the white bathing cap, cruelly reduced—hangs too for a moment, exposing the bent, submissive back of her neck.

The fatigue of what, however contrary to its appearance, has to have been sustained incremental effort, is evident now in the uncertainty with which she negotiates her re-turn to land and full gravity. Balance faulty, she makes two tries and falls back to her knees each time before she's actually able to get to her feet. She still looks uncertain on the shingle bottom when I wade the couple of steps between us, soaking my shoes and my trousers to the knee. I hand her the towel which she holds in front of her while she dries her face first, slowly, blotting rather than rubbing, then wraps around her like a sarong, securing it to herself under her left armpit. "What brings you here?" she asks, moving up past me but not looking at me.

"I went over to the cabin," I say, "and when I discovered you were packed and Michael told me where I could find you, I decided to catch you before you took off. To ask if I could go with you."

She stops walking. A piece of the tightly wrapped towel is clutched in her right hand, and she uses this to mop the water dripping down from under her bathing cap out of her eyes, then removes the bathing cap with her other hand. Her shoulders elevate slightly, tentatively I think, before she says, "For the trip?"

"For some time longer than that, I thought. Just how long would have to be arrived at, but since it's still a little more than a week before I have to start turning up at Hillside, I thought for that long anyway."

"You're crazy, Fish," she says. "Clean out of your cotton-picking mind." She still doesn't turn to look at me, but she drops her shoulders in what I take to be assent before she bends to the rock to pick up her nightgown.

"An old story," I say. "I could go up to the house, pick up my stuff, and meet you at the cabin in fifteen or twenty minutes."

"That soon?" she says, and I hear a premonition of panic.

"It seems like the best plan," I say, "unless you have a better one."

She hangs a moment, feet apart and dug into the sand, before she unweights and begins to walk away. "I guess that is the best plan," she says. "Or it might be anyway."

"Of course," I say. "That's all there is."

17

MICHAEL WAS in the hospital in Boston for almost three weeks. He was never, so far as I could tell, in much worse shape than when Gretta and I drove him there in the middle of the night in convoy, Percy tailing us all the way in the heap as a kind of volunteer medical and mechanical escort and standby transport, but it was a couple of weeks before he began to be stabilized, and several additional days then before he was sent home on a trial regimen that I was to monitor and assist. I could tell just from the way Yoshalem insisted that it was only a matter of time before his condition would be brought entirely under control, that this wasn't so clear, and that as a patient, Michael was being interesting rather than satisfying. Something about the ways he both responded and didn't respond to treatment remained a persistent medical mystery.

Halfway through his stay in the hospital my vacation had ended, and on my way to see him and Gretta in my new diesel Rabbit before driving out to Hillside the morning after his release from the hospital, to give him his daily insulin shot, it occurs to me that I've been teaching for ten days and have not yet had the teacher dream. A record, but not in itself positive evidence that teaching is any longer what I should be doing. It could just as well suggest what I think I know anyway, that teaching has become an uncathected activity for me, and that I'm ready and have even begun to give it up.

It may not, however, be just the absence of the teaching dream that suggests this. It may be the dreams I do have as well, though because they drop away as fast as I have them and I recover them, when I do, only accidentally and faintly, I can't be sure. In the Square a couple of days ago, I watched an old man and woman, an ancient Yankee couple, walking together, but walking not one next to the other but in file. They were probably doing errands, since the man in his neat short-sleeved blue shirt and khaki trousers had a black plastic shopping bag hung over the bare crook of his right elbow and the woman, whose thin legs, dismayingly girlish still, emerged from under a long, pleated, rough cotton skirt and then disappeared again at the ankle into white athletic socks and sneakers, had a piece of paper in her hand that I took to be a shopping list. The man was stiff and upright, but the woman, the frailer of the two though also the leader, walked at a forward inclination as though to convert the energy of an involuntary motion, falling, into voluntary locomotion. The constant five- or six-foot interval between them, and even a physical resemblance that was not I thought genetic but rather the mark of half a century of common habits and mutual influence, established their attachment, but they didn't talk, the woman didn't look behind her to ascertain whether the man was still following her, and the man seemed to keep no more than her white socks and sneakers in his field of vision.

I was equally sure that I'd seen them before and hadn't seen them here. This conviction could have been no more than some residuum of my work on the report on the geriatric program in Redford which had recurred to me more frequently anyway in the intervening weeks than I'd have expected, but my déjà vu seemed too particular for this. I believed I'd seen these two old people or two others remarkably like them in both appearance and circumstances either in the flesh or it seemed to me more probably —since the impression was persistently elusive—in a still largely unrecovered dream. One way and another though, Hans Scherman's offer was rapidly taking on rather than losing substance, and I'd called him the previous afternoon, after I'd finished teaching for the day, which was some hours before he left his desk, and arranged to have lunch with him next Saturday, to get the particulars of his offer that I hadn't bothered to ask about when he'd made it because of a degree of skepticism I no longer felt. On the phone, he sounded neither surprised nor even particularly gratified but entirely businesslike. Lucidly businesslike, I thought, and found this too more alluring than I'd remembered.

Gretta and Michael are back in Alf's house again, but living with him on terms of what might be called systematic avoidance, and in addition I'm distinctly persona non grata to him for having prevented a crisis that he believes might better for the sake of the long run have occurred. I enter the house by the back door therefore, and in the kitchen where she's waiting for me, Gretta gives me a sealed, long, gray paper envelope containing one of the disquietingly light disposable plastic syringes that I've just learned to use, still uneasily, and a small vial of insulin cold from the refrigerator. She's anxious and untalkative, and I tell her that I'd love a cup of coffee when I come down again and go directly up the kitchen stairs to the back hall on the second floor from which both her bedroom and Michael's open. The door at the end of the hall, however, leading to the front hall, is closed, which makes of the two bedrooms and the bathroom across from them not only separate quarters but something very like the servants' quarters they'd once obviously been.

It's just seven-thirty, and Michael, who's supposed to have his insulin half an hour before breakfast, is still in bed. Awake though, and washed, he looks pale and concentrated against the white bed clothes. His unconvincing tan has all but disappeared and he's also lost weight, a combination that makes his true or essential face more visible. "You're right on time," he says, by way of greeting.

"I plan to be," I say.

"I don't know how long you'll have to keep coming," he says. "If you explain what you're doing as you do it, I think I will learn how to do it myself after all, after a while."

"Good," I say.

"Gretta and I both have trouble with this shot business," he says, "but it's not exactly the same trouble for both of us. She wants to know I've had the shot but doesn't want to know anything about it. That way she can almost think there's nothing wrong with me. But I just have trouble sticking myself. I know I'm sick, and anything that can make me less sick seems pretty interesting."

"To me too," I say. "Very."

I've in fact been concealing from Gretta just how interested in Michael's therapy I am ever since she accused me one day in the hospital of having a morbid mind and atrophied feelings after I'd asked Young Groucho enough questions to set him lecturing enthusiastically for almost half an hour. A lecture I'd found useful if also odd. There's a bottle of alcohol and a covered bowl of cotton balls on the table next to Michael's bed, and when I take the cover off the bowl he pushes down the sheet and unbuttons his pajama top. His loss of weight shows on his abdomen too. The skin of his former larger self, unfilled, sags, and its contour—neither flat nor assertively domed now, but indecisively in between—is disconsolate. "The last one was around ten o'clock, wasn't it?" I ask.

"I have to think a minute, that's upside down for me," Michael says, and cranes his neck from the pillow to look.

"Yes, that's right," he says after a moment, and lets his head fall back.

"Eleven o'clock then today?" I say.

"That system sure makes it easy to keep track," he says.

I wipe a small swathe of skin with a ball of cotton moistened slightly with alcohol a couple of inches above and to the left of the convoluted bud of his navel, wiping slowly to ascertain too that there really is still more flesh under the skin than the half-inch needle can possibly go through. Then careful not to touch the needle, I remove the syringe from the gray envelope, push the rubber end of the plunger snug into the bottom of the doubly calibrated tube, then push the needle through the diaphragm of the insulin vial. This is already a vivid process, since the feel of the diaphragm through the syringe is enough like living tissue to give me a buzz. Michael's eyes, fixed on my hands, strain to miss nothing as I retract the plunger and watch the fluid climb the unit calibrations to my left on the tube. "You're scheduled for twenty-six today," I say. "That's the same number you had yesterday and the day before, only today you're supposed to walk a half mile too, otherwise it would be more. You won't forget to take that walk?"

"No," he says.

When the fluid reaches the right line, I withdraw the needle from the vial and hold it straight up to double check, then look down again and see that Michael has tensed his stomach muscles in anticipation. "It makes me nervous too," I say, "so the sooner the better."

"It's funny," Michael says. "The idea of it doesn't bother me at all—until the time comes."

"It's like persuading yourself to lean downhill when you ski," I say, not sure as I say it that the analogy has any exactness at all but remembering that Yoshalem had told me to "javelin" the needle. "You're convinced it's right, but at the last minute, in anticipation, it feels wrong."

"I don't ski," Michael says.

"Ah. Well anyway," I say.

Taking the syringe between my thumb and forefinger close behind the needle, I enjoin my nerves first not to check me when the needle breaks through the skin so that I have to push it the rest of the way. I thrust it more like a dart I think than a javelin, but unlike either, I can't simply after a time let it go. "It didn't really hurt," Michael says, his neck strained again to keep his eyes on my hands.

"It didn't hurt me too much either," I say, "and all that's left now is to pull back the plunger a bit to make sure the needle isn't into a vein which it isn't, and then push it in slowly but steadily without pushing the needle at the same time until it won't go any further."

"That's the easy part," Michael says. "Maybe after a couple of days, once you get the needle in I can do the rest myself for a start."

"Good plan," I say.

Though in his head he's relaxed now, his stomach muscles retain their constriction until I've withdrawn the needle. Then, while pressing the fresh cotton ball I've placed over the puncture with his right index finger, he says, "It doesn't seem quite as simple as I thought it was going to be."

"The shot you mean?" I'm pretty sure it isn't what he means, but reluctant to get into deeper water than I have to.

"Figuring out the right amount," he says. "And then even if they do get it figured out right, having to change it depending on what I eat or what I do."

"It's a complicated business," I say. "It takes real dealing with. Does that bother you?"

"Not much. I told you I think it's interesting."

This statement is somewhat querulous and decidedly inconclusive, so after giving him an opportunity he doesn't take to continue, I say, "But?"

He looks at me querulously too, as though he'd rather not explain, but says, "Well, it may just be too complicated for me to figure it all out alone, until I'm older anyway, and that means I can be a drag for Gretta for quite a while still. That's what I told you I hoped would be all over."

"Since we're the two interested ones, we could do most of the figuring between us," I say.

"You and me?"

"Why not?"

His eyes move slowly from my face to the finger on his abdomen. "You think I can take it off now?" he asks.

"Sure, give it to me."

"I'd probably have to see a lot of you. At least for a while."

"You will," I say, and my hesitation before saying it is only fleeting.

"Maybe it's not going to be a problem then," he says, rebuttoning his pajamas. "That's what I figured before, but I was beginning to think I'd been wrong. I guess I'll just read now for a bit, until it's time for my breakfast."

By the time I've picked up the vial with the remaining insulin, and the hypodermic, its discarded envelope, and the used cotton balls—what is to be the daily trash that Gretta doesn't want to have accumulate in his room—he's folded his pillow over on itself to prop his head higher and has a book standing open on his chest. The narrow back stairs look steep as a ladder going down. Somewhat light-headed, I consolidate the trash in my left hand so that my right is free to hold the banister. Just the feel of the smooth hand-polished wood is steadying, and downstairs in the kitchen Gretta has heard me coming and poured the coffee. "Was that okay?" she asks.

"Fine," I say. "But because we also chatted a bit, I have just about enough time left to drink my coffee and run. When does Alf have his breakfast?"

"He's changed his habits. Either he goes without, or he's having it downtown these days," she says.

This could be jocular but I don't think it is, and though she isn't really dressed yet—she's wearing a zippered housecoat and her hair with its tapered white center line is brushed back and held in a clip—her face is resolved and definite enough to suggest either that she's been awake for some time already, or that she hadn't slept seriously when she was asleep. "Wouldn't you like to be out of this house?" I ask.

"I'd like to be various unlikely things," she says.

Now she is being jocular even if somewhat ponderously, and though that's never been among her tones one of the ones to which I can respond in kind and it frequently as a consequence makes me feel like an ass and could again, for the moment the sound of it is welcome. "I'm considering moving myself," I say. "Maybe we could find a place together."

"Really?" she says, unrelenting. "I wonder whether you have any idea how expensive Michael and I would be as roommates?"

"Only notions," I say, "but I figure on being a lot more prosperous in the near future."

"Your portion from your father?"

"Not just that," I say, "Earned money too. I'm probably going to accept Hans Scherman's offer after all. I've just about decided to come out into the world to see if it exists."

"You really are crazy!" she says.

"That remains to be seen," I say. "But let me tell you more about it when I have more time. This evening maybe."

"Why not?" she says. "I'm sure to be in."

Her lips circle and proffer her last words ironically, but the line of compression across the bridge of her nose that persists even when she stops talking, between her eyes, has to be less intentional, and when I've left the house and climbed into the car, in the bright unhistorical odors of its newness this is what I remember.

MONROE ENGEL

For most of the past twenty-six years, Monroe Engel has lived with his wife and their four growing and then dispersing children in Cambridge, Massachusetts, where he teaches English at Harvard University. Though he enjoys rural respites, he is basically and by strong inclination a city dweller, and has spent varying lengths of time in New York (where he was born in 1921), Chicago, San Francisco, Florence, Rome, and London. He likes reading, conversation, music, carpentry, swimming, and surf-casting, and detests all games.